IN SEARCH OF
HEAVEN

Barrington Family Saga
VOLUME ONE

IN SEARCH OF HEAVEN

ANITA STANSFIELD

Covenant Communications, Inc.

Covenant.

Cover image *Edwardian Interior* by Harold Gilman © Art Resource, NY.

Cover design copyrighted 2007 by Covenant Communications, Inc.

Published by Covenant Communications, Inc.
American Fork, Utah

Printed in Canada
First Printing: February 2007

13 12 11 10 09 08 07   10 9 8 7 6 5 4 3 2 1

ISBN 978-1-59811-309-9

FOREWORD

I have been writing about the human relationship for nearly thirty years, always revolving the relationships in my stories around varying degrees of social and emotional issues. And the journey has been remarkable! My fascination with human behavior and its irrevocable ties to our spiritual nature has taken me vicariously through some of the greatest difficulties and most profound joys of this mortal experience, while I have surely learned far more than I could ever share with my readers. Topics and storylines come to me with no logical explanation, always leading me to avenues of research into the human experience that leave me stunned—and altered—by the struggles and challenges of real life.

Living vicariously through my characters, I have seen the powerful impact of choices made for good or ill, confirming the profound need to live according to the guidance of a loving Father in Heaven so that we may receive His choicest blessings. I've also seen much evidence of Satan's evil designs to stand in the way of allowing us to partake of the greatest joys this life can offer. His ability and determination to counteract the positive with negative grow startlingly more clear as the war for souls intensifies.

While this universal law applies to every aspect of life, I've felt a growing concern to see how cleverly he has distorted the issue of human intimacy. Because it is *the* most sacred and profound element of the human experience, it stands to reason that Satan's efforts in combating it would be his most tireless and skillful. Nowhere is his insidiousness made more evident than in the gray areas of distortion regarding the sexual relationship that rightfully belongs in a marriage between a man and a woman. While we are continually hearing of the evils of pornography and immorality in our world—and for good reason—I wonder how often we stop to consider the reasons for concern in these matters.

I've written about disease, death, abuse, sin, and many aspects of dysfunction and suffering, always with the solutions coming from correct psychology and correct gospel principles, and I have learned that the two are dovetailed perfectly. The teachings of our Savior in the New Testament are the tip of deep icebergs of psychological truth. Each of the topics I've studied and in which I've immersed myself into in order to write about them more accurately have given me cause for deep introspection and a sense of understanding and empathy that can only be called a divine gift. On my own, I could never grasp and portray all I have felt inspired to address.

One of the common elements that I have woven through every story is the coming together, and keeping together, of that most beloved marriage relationship. I've recently gained a new understanding of how thoroughly distorted it has become in our world. In a vigilant effort to protect ourselves and our children, it seems that many people have lost sight of the very purpose for this battle. As we cry out for the eradication of the ripples of evil caused by pornography's disparagement of the human body, do we pause to remember the counterpoint that the body is a temple, a gift from God—His greatest creation? Do we honor its magnificent abilities related to the power of creating life in partnership with God? While we redouble our efforts to push away the gross distortions of the world's view of these things, do we remember—and teach our youth—to revere and treasure how glorious and wondrous God intended that relationship to be when used within its proper boundaries? I believe that many of us, without consciously thinking about it, have become so understandably concerned about fighting the battle against evil, we haven't stopped to realize that Satan has led us to feel uncomfortable about any discussion of human intimacy. While the world mocks it with crudeness and vulgarity, have we become afraid to talk about it at all for fear of putting ourselves into that worldly category?

Throughout my life I've seen much evidence of how Satan destroys what is good by creating unwarranted guilt and misunderstanding. Isaiah said, "Wo unto them that call evil good, and good evil" (2 Ne. 15:20). It would seem that Satan is capable of doing as much damage with one attitude as he is with the other. In these, the last days, the lines between good and evil must be defined more clearly than ever. I believe that Satan is keenly aware of the damage he can do to the human relationship with his ability to "call evil good, and good evil." I've seen marriages crumble and youth become lost over the failure to understand that our war against pornography and immorality is for the sole purpose of preserving and defending that most sacred aspect of the marriage relationship. It is discussed frankly in the temple and by our latter-day prophets, but we hesitate to talk about it enough to thwart Satan's effort to distort and confuse the issue.

I am absolutely certain this story was given to me as one tiny effort to shed some light of understanding on what is right and good in matters of human intimacy. Through these characters' eyes I have gained a new level of understanding on the stages of human emotion that are irrevocably connected to our God-given instincts. I hope you will enjoy the story for what it is—a story. And I hope that perhaps you'll find some new perspective that could possibly make your own life and relationships a little better. Perhaps it will give you a point of reference for discussing a sensitive topic with your spouse or your children. And may God be with us all as we continue to fight the battle.

Anita Stansfield

To all who have need of a Physician.

MATTHEW 9:12

Chapter One
T H E   B O O K

England—1838

Eleanore Layne hurriedly wove her dark auburn hair into a long braid, tied it with a black ribbon, and tossed it over her shoulder. She laced up her shoes and rushed down the back stairs, anxious to get as much of her work done as possible before breakfast. Today was Wednesday, the only day of the week when she could leave early and spend hours doing whatever she pleased—but only after her required tasks were completed. On other days there were only brief breaks from her work and limited opportunities for leisure time. On Sundays she was allowed to attend church with the other servants, even though there was work to be done both before and after the services. But only on Wednesdays could she disappear from the household and not be missed. It was her favorite time in all the world.

Less than two hours past breakfast, Eleanore finished scrubbing the last of the huge pile of pans left from cooking the previous evening's dinner for the Barrington household. When they were all dried and shined and put away properly, she sought out Mrs. Bixby, the housekeeper. The woman was thin and graying, and oversaw the running of the huge home with the efficiency of a military general. But she was kind and appreciative toward those who earned her respect by doing what was expected of them and not causing her any trouble. And Eleanore knew she was high on that list. She'd been working in the Barrington home since the age of seven when her mother had come here searching for work after the unexpected death of her husband. Eleanore had been given simple, menial tasks at first, with the opportunity to earn tidbits of money and also to have playtime with the other children. Throughout the nine years since then, her income had increased in proportion to the tasks she was given. At her mother's death more than a year ago, she had been given the choice to remain employed by the Barringtons. And she was grateful. James Edward Barrington had a reputation for treating his servants fairly. In return, he expected integrity and hard work. But Eleanore knew that all households were not so equitable. She'd heard of many atrocities in the way that girls of her class had been treated by their employers, and she considered it a great blessing to be able to work here. And her mother had always taught her to be mindful of her blessings.

"Might I leave now?" she asked Mrs. Bixby.

"If your work is finished," she said with a little smile. She knew Eleanore wouldn't ask if it weren't. "You be careful now."

"Of course," she said. "I'll be home for supper."

She went to the kitchen where Miss Gibbs, the head cook, always had some lunch wrapped up in a napkin for her to take along. "Thank you," she said, tucking it into the basket hooked over her arm. "You're far too kind to me."

Miss Gibbs, whose plumpness was likely a result of too many years in the kitchen, gave Eleanore a smile. "For *you* it is a pleasure." Eleanore counted another blessing. Her mother's kind demeanor and warm relationship with many servants in the household had left her in good standing with them as well.

The walk into town was long, but Eleanore didn't mind. In fact she relished being in the open air, especially on such a beautiful spring day. She often closed her eyes to more fully absorb the sounds surrounding her: birds chirping and chattering, a wispy breeze teasing the trees, the occasional bleating of sheep. Most of the tenant farms she passed, all owned by Mr. Barrington, were well kept and lovely. Occasionally she stopped to visit with someone who was out working in a garden or feeding animals. More than once she found children playing outside, and she took a few minutes to talk with them or even participate in whatever they might be doing.

Arriving in town, Eleanore found a place at the edge of the high street to sit and eat her lunch of buttered dark bread, cheese, and an apple that didn't taste bad, but it was far too soft to be pleasurable. She ate most of it anyway, longing for autumn, when they would be fresh and crisp again. With her stomach full, she hurried to indulge herself in the greatest passion of her life. Upon entering the bookshop, she always had to close her eyes and take a deep breath, just to inhale the smell of books. Then she stood for a long moment and looked around, pondering all the magic within the pages of the neatly organized books for sale. There were two other customers in the shop, quietly perusing the shelves. Mr. Harvey looked up from behind the counter, peering at her over his glasses, the same pleasant expression on his face that appeared each time she came here.

Eleanore spent nearly two hours in the bookshop, examining the morsels available, and talking candidly with Mr. Harvey in between his helping customers and doing his work. She was grateful for their comfortable friendship that had emerged from their common passion for books. And one of the greatest blessings in her life was his willingness to allow her to borrow books to read, so long as she treated them very carefully, which she always did. On her limited funds, buying a book was a luxury reserved only for her very favorites, those she would want to read over and over. Beyond the money required to meet her personal needs, and a small portion set aside each month for an emergency, every penny she made went into buying books. But it never seemed enough. She felt certain she would shrivel up inside were it not for her arrangement with Mr. Harvey. In return for his exclusive rental policy, she occasionally helped him with some extra cleaning or organizing in his shop, and the deal worked out nicely for both of them.

Today Eleanore left the shop with three books in her basket, one being Jane Austen's last, which she had purchased after reading it twice. She took the long way home, going through the hills and woods that surrounded the Barrington estate. She came out of the trees at a place that perfectly overlooked the place where she lived and worked—a magnificent home surrounded by lovely manicured gardens and stately trees. From this perspective, the size and grandeur always left her stunned. She knew that in truth the Barringtons were titled, but apparently they had some personal aversion to being referred to as lord and lady, and they had requested that they be addressed simply by their names. Eleanore had heard that the Barringtons had been ridiculed by some members of polite society for such a preference, but apparently the opinions of others were not a high priority with them.

Eleanore sat on the ground in a shady spot and read while intermittently pondering the view, then she started reluctantly home, arriving just before supper was served for the staff. She contended with an unusual restlessness that night until she finally left her bed behind, took up a candle, and sneaked quietly down to the library, checking carefully at every turn to be absolutely certain she was alone and that she had remained unseen. Her status in the household would never allow for her to even enter this part of the house, let alone spend time in the library or make use of the books there. She had never removed a single book from the Barrington library, in spite of the frequent burning temptation to do so. She had walked the room and examined the titles and authors, in awe of the wealth of stories and information residing there with no apparent purpose except to adorn the shelves. Occasionally she noticed a book missing, then it would be returned later, which meant that *someone* was doing occasional reading. She'd told herself that if she borrowed a book here and there, it surely wouldn't be missed. But it was against the rules, and if she were discovered it could cost her employment. And she could not take that risk. There was only one book she ever touched in the library, reading from it only in the darkness of night by candlelight when she was least likely to be discovered. Its pages called to her now as she stepped through the door and closed it quietly behind her, pausing for a long moment to close her eyes and take a deep, luxurious breath, just to inhale the fragrance of the books. She held the candle high and bathed her spirit in the presence of bound pages that left her wondering over their contents. A certain reverence overtook her, then deepened as she hurried to find the object of her quest. Setting the candle on the floor, she carefully lifted the huge Barrington Family Bible from its resting place. With the book open on the carpet, Eleanore placed the candle at its head and spread herself out behind one of the long leather couches, leaning on her elbows to read from its pages the most glorious things she'd ever read anywhere. It was a perfectly comfortable spot to read, but she'd long ago examined the design of the room and knew that if someone were to come in, she would be well hidden. She'd been coming here for years, and nothing had ever happened, but she wasn't taking any chances.

Eleanore touched the book as if in greeting, then sighed deeply as she immersed herself in it. Sometimes she reread stories and passages that were her favorites, always finding some new concept she'd never considered before. And sometimes she searched for something she'd never read before. In such little snatches of time, she felt certain she would never be able to read the entire book in her lifetime, but she loved to turn its pages and purposely allow her feelings to guide her to stop at a certain place. Her study of the Bible had become somewhat of a laboratory for testing her instincts and learning to trust them; they always guided her to some tiny measure of peace or understanding of the life she lived and the questions that rattled around in her busy brain. And her very favorite reading was that of the life of Jesus. While there were stories in the Old Testament that she dearly loved, her mother had taught her that the example and teachings of Jesus would always be her greatest source of guidance and happiness in her life. She had long ago discovered on her own that her mother had been right.

Eleanore attended church every Sunday and enjoyed listening to the sermons given there. Her mother had instilled in her a strong belief that God would always hear her prayers and send angels from heaven to watch over and guide her. Sometimes things were said in the sermons that didn't make sense to her, but Eleanore had found that she could read in the Bible and pray for understanding, and some degree of enlightenment would come. Somehow she would be able to grasp concepts that made sense to her, even when she didn't always agree with what was said at church. In some respects she felt that the sermons contradicted the scriptures. But she kept her opinions to herself, not wanting to be thought of as wicked or rebellious.

Eleanore was contentedly lost in the story of Esther when footsteps and voices startled her. Never once had she confronted anyone in this part of the house during the night. As the footsteps came decidedly closer she closed the book and blew out the candle, pressing herself tightly against the back of the couch, praying that whoever it was would not come into the library. And then the door opened, and light spilled into the room along with a man's angry voice. She'd not heard Mr. Barrington speak enough to know if it was him. But who else would it be? There were no guests in the home at the moment.

"Did you follow me here to completely ruin what few minutes might be left of my day, or is there something you need to say that warrants such attention, Mrs. Barrington?" His voice sounded bitter and cold, and she felt tempted not to like him. But the thought caused confusion when it so strongly contradicted everything she'd heard about him.

Eleanore had rarely even seen Mr. or Mrs. Barrington, since her work required no actual interaction with them. But the servants who worked directly with them often spoke of their kindness and fair natures. Mrs. Barrington was known for being somewhat melancholy and guarded, and Mr. Barrington mildly arrogant and brash. But he was still reputed to be a good man.

"You're a heartless man, James," Mrs. Barrington said, equally bitter. Having heard their names, Eleanore knew for certain who was talking, but she felt shocked and utterly horrified to realize that their marriage was not what the servants believed it to be. Were the Barringtons that skilled at keeping their true feelings from showing unless they believed they were completely alone?

"Is such a statement meant to be a revelation to me?" he asked, and she heard a lamp being set down. "Why don't you just say what you need to say and leave me in peace? What is it you need this time that your allowance is not sufficient to cover?"

"I need a governess for the children," she said.

"This again?" His voice was acrid. "They have a nanny, and they have a mother, and that is more than sufficient."

"But they need their lessons every day and—"

"And you are perfectly capable of teaching your children to read and write. When they're older we will—"

"I can't do it with my health, James. I've told you this before." Her plea sounded humble, perhaps timid.

"And I've told *you* before that it requires little energy to be in the same room with the children you brought into this world. You can't sit in your bed and read with them? What activities in your life are being neglected by the need to actually *be* a mother?"

Her voiced tightened defensively. "They wear on my nerves."

"And yet you're having another one," he said, his voice rank with contempt. "If children are such a burden to you, my dear, I wonder you don't figure out what causes them and put a stop to it."

Eleanore put a hand over her mouth to keep from gasping. How could a man say such a horrible thing to his wife? She heard her mother's voice in her memory reminding her not to pass judgment or assume to know what might be at the root of a person's behavior, but she couldn't imagine anything that might justify such a horrid attitude.

"Oh, and you would love that, wouldn't you." Her sarcasm was cutting, her humility completely absent, and Eleanore decided she didn't like either one of them. "It's far too late to believe that such a thing would ever solve the problems between us."

"Well, at least we agree on that."

"I'm done talking to you," she said.

"That's positively the best news I've heard in days. Good night, Mrs. Barrington."

Eleanore heard the woman leave the room and slam the door. Then James Barrington cursed aloud, and she heard him pacing for several minutes while she prayed he wouldn't discover her presence. She couldn't even imagine what he might do—have her immediately dispelled from his service, no doubt. Her heart pounded while the conversation circled around in her mind as he continued to pace. He finally extinguished the lamp, and she could hear him getting comfortable on the couch, but he cursed again before the room became eerily still. Eleanore waited, barely breathing, while she pondered what little she knew about the Barringtons. It was common knowledge among the household that he was in his late thirties and his wife was seven years younger. He'd done extensive traveling abroad before he'd married, and she had apparently been old enough to be considered a spinster before he made her his wife. Eleanore wondered if they had ever cared for each other at all, or if it had only been a marriage of convenience.

It felt like an eternity before Mr. Barrington's breathing became rhythmic with certain sleep. Taking her unlit candle, she crept quietly from the room, leaving the Bible on the floor, not daring to even attempt to put it back. Once free of the room, she ran as fast as she dared through the darkened hallways and up the back stairs, keeping a hand against the walls and banisters to guide her. Alone in her room she heaved for breath and fervently thanked God for letting her escape undetected. But lying in bed, the argument she'd overheard became haunting. And she wept, surprised at her own heartache on behalf of these people who were so thoroughly unhappy.

The following day, Eleanore managed to sneak into the library and found the Bible where she'd left it. She returned it to the shelf and left again, grateful to get out of that part of the house without being seen. She fought to stay busy with her work and push away the words she'd overheard. Lunchtime proved a delightful distraction when she ended up eating with two of her favorite people in the household. Eleanore often went late to lunch, preferring to avoid the majority of the other servants. She often felt annoyed by their senseless prattle and gossip. But she enjoyed Lizzie's company more than anyone else who lived under this roof. Lizzie was average in build with a roundish, freckled face and carrot-colored hair full of tight curls. The woman was old enough to be Eleanore's mother, and in fact had been a good friend of Mariah Layne. Upon Mariah's death, Lizzie and Eleanore had bonded more deeply in order to compensate for the loss. They could talk about anything, and Eleanore knew she could trust her completely. Lizzie wasn't a gossipmonger like many women in the household, who apparently had no hobby beyond speculating over the lives of others. While Lizzie was barely literate and didn't enjoy reading the way Eleanore did, she liked to hear about the adventures Eleanore found in her books, and they never ran out of conversation. Lizzie had never been married and admitted that she likely never would be. Not that she didn't have the desire, but she accepted that it simply wasn't a practical expectation, given her circumstances. But Lizzie had a happy demeanor and found contentment in her simple life. Lizzie's job was specifically in the kitchen as one of the many assistants to the head cook, Miss

Gibbs. While some of Eleanore's work was in the kitchen, she also did other odd jobs throughout the house. But whenever Eleanore got to the kitchen for lunch, Lizzie would usually stop what she was doing, and they would eat together. Today, however, they were fortunate enough to have Mr. Higgins sitting down to eat at exactly the same time.

Beyond Lizzie, Mrs. Bixby, the head housekeeper, and Miss Gibbs, the cook, Higgins was the only other servant in the household that Eleanore had ever enjoyed conversing with. He was more than fifty, tall and thin with graying blond hair, and his status in the Barrington home was as high as a servant could go. He was something between a butler and a valet; most specifically, he was paid to closely attend Mr. Barrington in any way needed. It was rumored that they were almost friends, as far as such a thing was possible between a lord and his manservant.

When Miss Gibbs personally brought Higgins his lunch, she asked, "And how is Mr. Barrington today?" Eleanore knew it was a genuinely polite inquiry, whereas many of the other servants would ask such a question with the hope of gleaning some tidbit of gossip. She too was commonly drawn to conversation with Mr. Higgins, which made the foursome in the room comfortable.

"He's well, I believe," Higgins said. And that was all he said on the matter. He did not speak much about the Barringtons, which made Eleanore respect him more fully. She thought of the conversation she'd overheard and wondered what Higgins's perspective might be of the things she had heard. Did he know the marriage suffered? Or was he as ignorant as the rest of the staff?

Eleanore felt eerily uncomfortable when Miss Gibbs added, "I do believe he's greatly anticipating the birth of this baby."

"I believe he is," Lizzie said. Higgins didn't comment. Did he know what Eleanore had overheard a hint of? That Mr. Barrington's feelings over the birth of this child were not positive at all? Or were his feelings more complicated than that? "He does so adore his children," Lizzie added.

"Yes, the children are certainly most important to him," Higgins stated, and Eleanore felt confused. But she said nothing. She would never speak of what she'd overheard to anyone. Never. It simply wouldn't be right.

Lizzie finished eating before Eleanore and went into another section of the huge kitchens with Miss Gibbs to return to work, leaving Eleanore alone with Higgins. "And how are you, Miss Layne?" he asked.

"I'm well, and you?"

"Very well, thank you. Tell me what you've been reading."

She took a few minutes to tell him about the books she'd gotten yesterday. He teased her about her romantic notions and about spending that much money on a Jane Austen novel. But he winked when he said it, and he had some interesting insights on the story of Esther when she admitted that she'd been reading it the previous night. She'd never actually admitted to sneaking into the family library. But the people close enough to her to know of her love for the Bible would also know she could never afford to have one in her own possession. Where else would she read it?

Higgins finally glanced at his watch and left, stating that Mr. Barrington would be leaving soon for an afternoon at his gentlemen's club in town. Eleanore returned to her work, wishing she could forget about the conversation she'd heard last night and the confusing messages it implied. She was grateful to finally finish her work and find time to immerse herself in a novel. There she could forget about everything.

A week later, Eleanore returned home from a glorious half day off to find the household in an uproar. The moment she walked into the kitchen she knew something wasn't right, and as soon as the majority of the servants were gathered for supper, Mrs. Bixby announced while occasionally dabbing at her tears that Mrs. Barrington had unexpectedly gone into premature labor. The doctor was with her, but it was reported that the situation had become very grave. She pressed a handkerchief briefly over her lips to subdue her emotion, then spoke as if these people were her own family. "I've never seen Mr. Barrington so upset. I simply can't imagine what he'll do if he loses his dear wife. And the children . . . " She sobbed quietly. "Those sweet children . . . they're so attached to their mother. Of course, Lucy is with them now." Eleanore knew that Lucy was the nanny. "We must all pray very hard that Mrs. Barrington comes through safely."

Right then and there they all joined hands, and Higgins offered a verbal prayer on behalf of the situation. They all spoke a firm and unified amen that hovered as a preamble to the morose silence at the supper table.

Before getting into bed, Eleanore spent a long while on her knees, praying for Mr. and Mrs. Barrington and their children, intermittently allowing her thoughts to wander through the personal evidence she had of the relationship between these people. Was it possible that she'd only stumbled upon an angry moment and they truly did love each other? She wanted to think so, and truly hoped that Mrs. Barrington would come through all right. And the baby too. Although it wasn't likely, being this many weeks premature. She hoped that perhaps the problem was not as serious as Mrs. Bixby had made it sound; she could tend to become overly alarmed at times. Perhaps morning would bring news that the ordeal was over and the lady of the house would be fine.

After lying in bed for more than an hour, Eleanore finally gave in to the insatiable urge to creep to the library. She set the candle in its usual place and reached for the Bible, already praying that she could find some lovely verses that might soothe her troubled spirit. She barely had the book in her hands when the door swung open. She clutched the heavy book against her and barely kept it from dropping as she turned to find herself facing James Barrington. It had never happened before. At most she had passed him in a hallway, and he'd politely ignored her. He was still dressed as if he'd never gotten ready for bed, even though it was past two in the morning. Except that his feet were bare, which perhaps explained why she'd not heard footsteps approaching. He was tall and lean with nearly black hair that was normally combed back off his face, but which presently looked disheveled. The sleeves of his shirt were rolled up haphazardly. His waistcoat was unbuttoned. His countenance looked exhausted and troubled, but his eyes were clearly angry. His sharp voice broke the air. "What are you doing?" She felt certain her employment would be terminated and she'd be out on the streets within hours.

"Forgive me, sir," she said and hurried to put the book away as she spoke, her heart pounding with fear. "I just . . . couldn't sleep and . . . I . . . I find peace and understanding in the Bible, sir."

He seemed to contemplate her explanation through a torturous moment of silence while Eleanore's heart threatened to stop. She couldn't leave because he was blocking the door. And what else could she possibly say? Images of losing her position tightened her every nerve.

"Bring it here," he ordered, nodding toward the book she'd just put away. She took the heavy Bible back from the shelf and handed it to him, trying not to think about the fact that she was wearing only a nightgown. Buttoned to the throat and wrists as it was, she was grateful to know that it covered far more than a typical dress. But the very fact of being in her nightclothes added embarrassment to her anxiety.

He turned to leave, apparently unconcerned with her having broken a household rule. She hoped she wouldn't regret asking, "How is Mrs. Barrington, sir?"

He hesitated and barely glanced over his shoulder. "I have no idea. The doctor's not let me anywhere near her for hours." The subtle bitterness in his tone turned mildly sarcastic as he added, "Perhaps some reading will bring me peace and understanding."

As he left the room she added, "I shall remember her in my prayers, sir. And you."

Again he tossed her a quick glance, then hurried away. Eleanore sank onto the couch, heaving to catch her breath, thanking heaven that Mr. Barrington had not reprimanded her for being in his library. He was likely too upset over the present situation to give the matter much thought. Perhaps once he did think about it, he'd be dismissing her anyway. She prayed that wouldn't happen, prayed again for him and his wife, then went back to bed, grateful for the sleep that rescued her from her turbulent thoughts.

Morning brought the announcement that Mrs. Barrington had passed on in the night, taking with her the baby that had precipitated the problem. Mr. Barrington was sleeping with the assistance of the laudanum the doctor had given him, since he'd been inconsolably upset. The children were struggling with the news and were in the care of the nanny. Eleanore was grateful not to have *her* job on such a day. The household had officially gone into mourning, and preparations for the funeral were underway.

Once Eleanore had heard the news, she found a quiet place to be alone, stunned by the amount of tears she shed over a death that held no personal attachment to her. She couldn't rid her mind of the image of Mr. Barrington's weary countenance when she'd seen him in the library, and wondered over his motivation in coming there in search of the Bible. She imagined him grieving deeply for a woman he loved, certain the argument she'd overheard was simply a bad moment on a difficult day, not necessarily an indication of their deeper feelings. And Eleanore cried for the children. She'd not encountered them any more than she had their parents, but they were children who had just lost their mother. She knew that David had recently turned six, and Iris was nearly four. Eleanore knew what it was like to lose a parent; she'd lost both of hers. In fact, she had not been much older than David when her father had died tragically. She'd not been a child at the death of her mother, but it had traumatized her nevertheless. And she ached for the children. She wanted to find them and take them in her arms and cry with them. But she would never be allowed anywhere near them. So she cried in solitude, then dried her tears and got to work, keeping a prayer in her heart for Mr. Barrington and his children.

Eleanore hated the mood that prevailed in the home during the days that led up to the funeral. She longed for it to be over if only for the feeling that life would again move forward once the rituals of death were put behind. She didn't go to the library again until the night after the funeral. She wondered if the Bible would be back in its place. And it was. She opened it to the pages where the family records were kept, noting the freshly scribed information relating to the death of Caroline Barrington. She thought of Mr. Barrington writing it and wept. She pondered the other dates written there, scanning the brief record of generations of Barringtons. She was surprised to realize that Mr. Barrington had two siblings, both of whom were deceased. There was a brother born in 1798, two years before James Barrington had been born in 1800. The brother had died the month before James had been born. There was also a sister born in 1804, who had died at the age of seven. And so he'd been raised as an only child. Eleanore considered how horrid that must have been for his parents, losing two children to death. She couldn't even imagine!

The following Wednesday, Eleanore endured a light drizzling as she huddled beneath the hood of her cloak and walked quickly toward town, longing for a new book to distract herself. With her head down she saw nothing but the road beneath her feet, which grew steadily more muddy as the rain continued. She gasped when she nearly tripped over a book lying directly in her path. She stared at it as the people of Moses surely must have stared at manna the first time they saw it. She turned and looked in every direction, as if she might find the negligent owner. But she saw nothing, no one. This road had to be traversed to get from one town to another. It branched off to more than one estate and many tenant farms, but the majority of people traveling it would have remained on its course to farther destinations. The book had likely fallen from a wagon, or carriage, or saddlebags.

Reverently Eleanore stooped down to pick it up, shaking the water and mud from the cover. She lifted her skirt and used her dry, clean petticoat to dry the book, grateful to note that the rain had been slight enough not to have damaged the cover any more than a little spotting, and the pages hadn't been moistened beyond just a tiny bit around the edges that would dry quickly. She stood there in the rain, huddled over the book, protecting it with her bowed head while the rain soaked into the hood of her cloak. She opened it, noting the strange title, touching it while experiencing an inexplicable awe. She flipped through its pages, catching strange words she'd never heard before. A mystifying warmth accompanied a quickening of her heart as she realized that it read like scripture. Oh, how deeply she loved scripture! And then she hesitated at a certain page and read the first phrase where her eyes were drawn. . . . *And there is none other way nor name given under heaven whereby man can be saved in the kingdom of God. And now, behold, this is the doctrine of Christ, and the only and true doctrine of the Father, and of the Son, and of the Holy Ghost* . . .

Her heart quickened even more, and she scanned down a little farther, reading, . . . *Feast upon the words of Christ; for behold, the words of Christ will tell you all things what ye should do.*

And a little farther. *But behold, I say unto you that ye must pray always, and not faint; that ye must not perform any thing unto the Lord save in the first place ye shall pray unto the Father in the name of Christ, that he will consecrate thy performance unto thee, that thy performance may be for the welfare of thy soul.*

"Heaven be merciful!" she breathed, feeling the words pierce her heart, as if the very way she had strived to live her life had just been summed up before her eyes. And here in her hands, by some miracle beyond her wildest comprehension, were the words of Christ. She clutched the book to her breast and looked frantically around, thinking that it should be returned to its rightful owner, but at the same time fearing that she might ever have to let it go. Again she found herself completely alone. The rain hinted at becoming heavier, and she turned abruptly, walking back toward home. The distance into town would be wasted. She felt certain there was nothing in Mr. Harvey's bookshop that could ever fill her desire to read as this would.

Back at the house she crept quietly to her room, not wanting anyone to know she was here; she wanted complete privacy. Shedding her wet cloak and shoes, she slipped her cold feet beneath her bedcovers and leaned against the headboard. She pressed her fingers over the cover of the book, as if it were spun from gold. She took a deep breath and opened the book, wanting to read it slowly and savor every word, and at the same time devour it if only to have every word etched into her mind. While she wanted to read from beginning to end, she felt momentarily more compelled to flip through its pages and pause where her feelings might lead her, just as she did with the Bible. As phrases here and there caught her attention, she was struck by two prominent thoughts. In some ways it had a feeling very similar to the Bible, which left her deeply comfortable with the book. Some phrases were almost identical, as if this were somehow more teachings of Jesus, or perhaps just a repetition of His teachings. Her other thought was how thoroughly unfamiliar the names and stories and places were, which made the book so different from the Bible.

Once content with her sporadic exploration, she turned to the beginning and read, so deeply intrigued that it almost frightened her. She took no break except to light a lamp when the room became too dark for her to see. Lizzie came in search of her, saying that she and Miss Gibbs had been concerned when she'd not come for supper.

"Forgive me," Eleanore said, feeling no hunger. "I just . . . got reading . . . and lost track of the time."

"Well, you'd do well to come and eat before it's all put away," Lizzie said and left her alone. Eleanore made no effort to leave her bed and this great book.

A short while later Lizzie brought her some food, saying with a chuckle, "That must really be some book. What author would keep you so enthralled as to starve yourself?"

Eleanore just smiled and thanked her for the food, grateful to be left alone again, reading even as she ate. The night deepened, and she felt no desire for sleep, even though her eyes burned. Still, she didn't move through the book nearly fast enough, for she found herself pausing to contemplate what she'd read, and then to think it through. At one point she stopped and stared toward the window where rain slithered over the other side of the glass. Her thoughts raced and whirled until one question stood out strongly. Could any writing beyond the Bible truly be considered scripture? Was she reading truth, or a glorious fiction interspersed with the teachings of Jesus? With the question unanswered she read on, gasping aloud as she came across the words, *Thou fool, that shall say: A Bible, we have got a Bible, and we need no more Bible . . . Know ye not that there are more nations than one? Know ye not that I, the Lord your God, have created all men . . . and that I rule in the heavens above and in the earth beneath; and I bring forth my word unto the children of men, yea, even upon all the nations of the earth?*

"Heaven be merciful," she muttered again as something warm and unmistakably real stirred her heart. The words themselves could have been written by anyone, conjured as part of a fiction. But the feeling that came with the words left her with no doubt whatsoever. This book was true. These *were* the words of Christ. And she could only get down on her knees and thank God for allowing *her* to be the one who had found this lost book, discarded in the mud. In a matter of hours it had become her greatest treasure.

Chapter Two
THE PROMOTION

The following day Eleanore found it more difficult than it had ever been to put herself to work and remain with it during the course of the day. Her mind was fully absorbed with the book, and she longed only to be alone with it, absorbing the words and messages into her spirit. After supper she delightfully found the hair ribbon she had tucked inside the book to mark her place and took herself into its pages, remaining there until exhaustion cut short their time together.

During Sunday service Eleanore barely heard the sermon; her mind was preoccupied with concepts she had learned from her new book. She thought of the many times she had felt mildly uncomfortable with the things taught over the pulpit, as if the teachings of God had somehow been subtly tainted by man over the centuries, whether by ignorance or for some selfish purposes; she didn't know, and it didn't matter. She only knew that in her deepest self she believed that while some of what she heard was true, it wasn't entirely true; or perhaps it wasn't the entire truth. But she kept her thoughts to herself. She was a lowly servant girl, not expected to have a brain beyond the capacity to scrub floors or scour pots. Her opinions would be meaningless to anyone but herself, and that was where she preferred to keep them.

When Wednesday came again she had read the book all the way through and had reread some sections multiple times. She took it with her into town, grateful for a day free of rain, although it was cloudy and gray. At the bookshop she waited for some time alone with Mr. Harvey before she brought the book out and showed it to him. He looked through it with fascination while she told him how she'd found it and had thoroughly enjoyed reading it. She didn't tell him how completely obsessed she'd become with it, or how deeply it had affected her. Such feelings felt too tender and close to her heart. She didn't want them made light of to any degree. When she asked if he knew anything about the origin of the book, he pointed out that it had been printed in New York. Somehow she'd missed that in the information that had been printed prior to the first chapter. He said that he'd heard rumors of a new church that had been founded in America, and that missionaries had come here, telling anyone who would listen about a great book they wanted to share. He felt certain this was that book. He also said he'd heard that while some had embraced these new beliefs, others were strongly opposed to them and were not happy with the missionaries and their new version of the Bible. This left Eleanore mildly disconcerted, but no less firm in what she'd come to know in her heart. He'd also heard of a family joining this church and immediately moving to America.

America? Eleanore could hardly breathe as she listened to him. *A new religion?* The very idea gave her a secret thrill. In the passing of a heartbeat, she felt the purpose of her life change. She had always expected her future to be spent as a servant, hopefully always in a household that treated her as fairly as she was being treated now. She hoped eventually to marry and have children of her own, to find love in her life not unlike that her parents had shared. Beyond that she had never contemplated the course of her future to any degree. But that was no longer the case. She desperately wanted to go to America, to find this new religion and make herself a part of it. Because she knew it was true.

When Mr. Harvey had told her all he knew, he handed the book back to her. "I wonder who lost it," she said. If she had lost such a book, she would have been heartbroken. "There's no name inside or—"

"It would be impossible to ever find its rightful owner, Ellie," he said. "You should consider the book a gift and enjoy it. I suspect if missionaries have been in the area, passing the book to others, it's probably a copy they lost, and they would want you to have it."

Eleanore liked that idea. During her walk home, she wished that she might have been able to meet and talk with such missionaries, to ask them questions. Just to converse with someone who felt as she did about the book would be heavenly. She wondered if there were people in the area who had copies of the book, who might have embraced this religion. Even if there were, she was a servant. She did not go out to socialize with others. And Mr. Harvey had said he'd heard that some who had joined this church had migrated to America so they could band together. It wasn't likely that she would find others who shared her feelings. She considered sharing the book with Lizzie, or Higgins, perhaps even Miss Gibbs or Mrs. Bixby. But instinctively she knew they were content with their religion, and this was too new and strange for such people to accept readily. Her heart told her it was best kept to herself, at least for now.

While she felt right about remaining alone in her beliefs, she also felt deeply lonely. America silently beckoned to her, even though she knew little if anything about this new land. She'd been versed in its history, how it had rebelliously broken away from the British crown. And she'd heard of its beautiful ports and cities, and vast plains and farmland more wide and rich than the people of England had ever seen. Then a thought occurred to her that she recalled from those history lessons. She stopped walking as the memory came to her. After some lengthy studying together, Eleanore's mother had quizzed her knowledge by asking, "And what do you think the main reason was for people from our country to settle in America?"

There had been many reasons that had come up, but in Eleanore's mind the *main* reason had been obvious. "Religious freedom," she'd said. And her mother had smiled.

The answer now chilled her deeply as she started walking again. It was as if God had planted the notion into her mind many years ago, preparing her for this step that she knew she must take. *America!* Thoughts of sailing there and finding a new life filled her with a thrill unlike anything she'd ever known. Then her heart dropped painfully, and again she had to stop for a long moment to absorb the thought. It could take her years on a servant's wages to save enough money to get to America and keep herself fed until she found these people and a means of support. *Years!* She felt almost sick. How could she bear it? She continued walking while she pondered every aspect of her circumstances, her new dreams, and what she knew in her heart. If it took years, so be it. This journey was the quest of a lifetime. She would work hard, and she would save every penny. She would go without wherever possible. She would even stop buying books. She'd simply have to borrow them or reread those she had. Surely this heavenly book she now possessed could be reread hundreds of times and always give her new things to think about. No matter how long it took, or what she had to do, she would find a way to get to America. In her heart she knew that God would guide her. He had guided the book into her hands, and He had let her know unquestionably that it was true. She had only to keep following her heart, and surely her every dream would come to pass.

* * *

The next morning Eleanore was surprised to be approached by Mrs. Bixby, who said, "There is a meeting you are required to attend this afternoon at five."

"Me? Why?"

"Just be there," Mrs. Bixby said and hurried away, apparently busy.

At the meeting, Eleanore found a group of women of varying ages who held various positions in the household. Mrs. Bixby informed the group that Mr. Barrington was seeking out a governess for his children who could help compensate for the loss of their mother. He had been spending his days with the children and attempting to care for them himself, but he had come to feel that they needed more of a woman's influence. The nanny cared for the children's personal needs both morning and evening. The governess would take them from after breakfast until prior to supper, interspersing some lessons and appropriate activities to keep them happy and active and to stimulate their thinking. Occasionally their father would have lunch with the children or spend time with them, which would require the governess to be flexible and readily available during those hours. He had informed Mrs. Bixby, for reasons he did not go into, that he preferred to hire someone who was already established in the household. The women who had been invited to this meeting were chosen due to their literacy skills. Those who could not read and write were not eligible. Because the children were young, he was not concerned about extensive education and lessons, just simple literacy. He was looking more for a woman who could watch over them with some tender care, filling in duties that were not covered by the nanny. Eleanore listened to the job requirements and felt certain this was a waste of her time. She had nothing against children, but she had absolutely no experience with them. And while her tasks were tedious and menial, they were predictable. And then Mrs. Bixby said that the salary of a governess was significantly more than any of the maids were currently earning. This prompted Eleanore's heart to pound. She could get to America all the faster on such an income. But she immediately settled on not getting her hopes up. She simply wasn't qualified for the job and decided that putting any effort into getting it would simply set her up for inevitable disappointment. Then Mrs. Bixby announced that Mr. Barrington would be interviewing each of them individually, and that she had written out a schedule of their appointed times.

When the meeting was over, Eleanore spoke privately with Mrs. Bixby. "I don't want to interview for the position; I'm not qualified."

"We'll let Mr. Barrington be the judge of that. He insisted that *all* the female servants who were literate would be interviewed. Be certain you're not late."

Eleanore kept her exasperation to herself. Her interview time was set for the following afternoon at one o'clock. As the time approached, she could barely eat her lunch, and then she found a private spot to pace the floor and wring her hands while her encounters with Mr. Barrington rumbled through her mind. Both times had been in the library: the first while he'd been arguing with his wife, the second while she had been dying.

When Eleanore was shown into Mr. Barrington's private office, she felt so full of nerves she wanted to scream and run. As the door was closed behind her, she took quick notice of the elaborate decor in dark colors, but the drapes were pulled back to let in the light of a cloudy day. Mr. Barrington was busy writing something, which kept his attention from being focused on her as he said, "Please sit down."

She did so, aware of the imposing desk between them. She wasn't certain if it made her feel protected or intimidated.

"What is your name?" he asked.

"Eleanore Layne, sir."

Without looking up from the paper on his desk where he continued writing, he asked, "And you read and write?"

"Yes, sir."

"Are you well practiced at it?" he asked. While she was considering how to answer, he added with a subtle edge of impatience, "How *much* do you read and write?"

"I keep a detailed journal nearly every day, sir. And I read every minute I get when I'm not working. It's my passion."

He looked up then and seemed to take her in. "You're the girl who reads my Bible in the middle of the night."

"Yes, sir," she admitted, certain he would put an end to the interview. Or worse, dismiss her from her present position altogether now that he'd been reminded of the incident. "I meant no harm or—"

"It's fine," he said. "As long as you don't take it out of the library." Eleanore couldn't believe it. Had he truly just given her permission to read his Bible? Any question on that matter was put to rest when he added, "Although you might find the light better earlier in the day."

"Thank you, sir," was all she could think to say.

Mr. Barrington leaned back in his chair and asked, "What do you feel is most important to teach a child in their growing years?"

"I have no experience with children, Mr. Barrington. I can only say that my mother taught me to be honest and kind no matter what challenges life might bring. And she reminded me daily, by word and by example, the importance of honoring one's feelings and beliefs in order to find true happiness and peace. These things were always coupled with the importance of education. She instilled in me my love of reading and my craving for knowledge."

He looked a little stunned, and she wondered if she had spoken too boldly, or said too much. He simply said, "Your mother must have been an amazing woman."

"She worked here for nearly ten years, sir. She always spoke very highly of you."

"And do you have any other family connections?"

"None of any importance, sir."

Again he was silent a long moment before he said, "May I ask what your goals for the future are, Miss Layne? Do you have any aspirations beyond serving in this household?"

While she wanted to tell him of her desire to go to America, she felt certain it would be regarded as frivolous and irrelevant. She answered the question by saying, "I believe that God has a path for each of us, sir. I will trust the journey that life gives me by choosing what best honors my feelings and beliefs. Beyond that I can only say that I wish to one day be a mother and have children of my own."

He abruptly thanked her for her time and invited her to leave. Eleanore had to find a quiet place and sit for several minutes, wondering why she felt so shaken over the interview. She finally decided that James Barrington was an intimidating man and that she preferred working some distance from him. Caring for his children would likely cause their paths to cross more often, and she wasn't certain she was up to it. She could easily imagine that for all his reputation of being a kind and decent man, he could likely be demanding and difficult to please as well. She felt certain her own strong will would not be suited to the position, and wished she would have told him as much. Recalling the argument she'd heard between him and his wife only added to her desire to never interact with him enough to bring out his angry side. The only intrigue she felt at all for the promotion was the possibility of making more money in order to get to America more quickly. But would it be worth it?

An hour later Mrs. Bixby found her, saying that Mr. Barrington wanted to speak to her immediately. *What on earth for?* she wanted to shout. Her stomach tightened, and her palms turned sweaty. Stepping into his office, Eleanore realized she didn't want this job, and if he had called her back to give it to her, she needed to politely decline. Once seated across from him he quickly said, "I've selected you to be the governess for my children."

"But sir, I—"

"You will move your things tonight to a vacant room in the same wing as the children and—"

"But sir, I—"

"Is there a problem, Miss Layne?"

"Yes sir, there is. I do not wish to be impertinent but—"

"I am offering you a significant promotion that brings prestige and a profound raise in your income. I would think you'd be grateful."

"I *am* grateful, Mr. Barrington. Your confidence in me is very flattering, but truly . . . I know nothing of working with children. I'm not certain I'm the right woman for the job."

"Are you questioning my judgment, Miss Layne?"

"Yes sir, I am," she said, and his eyes widened.

"I see," he said, clearly taken aback.

"Why do you not seek out a woman who has been trained to be a governess?"

"I want someone who is comfortable with the household, and—"

"But I'm far better suited to—"

"Miss Layne!" he nearly shouted. "If you will allow me to finish a sentence, I will explain myself."

"Forgive me, sir. I can be terribly willful at times, which is perhaps the biggest reason I might . . . question your judgment."

"And do you question God's judgment, Miss Layne?"

"No, sir. I do not," she answered without hesitation.

"You told me once that you are a person who prays. Surely you can understand what I mean when I say that I have been praying to find the right woman to help guide my children beyond the death of their mother. I pray, and I follow my instincts. It's the only way I know how to live my life. I knew that the right woman was already in my household, and after speaking with you, I am absolutely certain you are that woman." After a methodical pause, he said with an edge of satire in his voice, "Are you not going to argue with me, Miss Layne?"

"No, sir," she said, feeling sorely humbled and deeply terrified.

"At this stage in my children's lives, I am not so much concerned about their secular knowledge as I am their gaining some understanding of the importance of literacy, and having some confidence in their ability to get beyond their grief. I want my children to learn integrity and compassion. I do not delude myself into believing that I am a warm man, or tender by nature. My children need a sense of security and the tenderness and guidance that a woman like yourself is capable of giving them. I'm certainly not going to demand that you take the position, but I'm telling you that my reasons for giving it to you are not careless. I would ask that you give this a fair chance. If six months pass and you still don't feel suited to it, then we will make other arrangements. Can you accept such an agreement, Miss Layne?"

Eleanore was speechless. How could she possibly turn down such an offer, especially when the sincerity in his eyes was evident? Her respect for him deepened. She could only swallow and say, "Very well, Mr. Barrington. I will do my best and give it a fair chance."

"Thank you, Miss Layne. Mrs. Bixby will let you know their schedule and all that. If you observe any behaviors or attitudes in my children that cause you concern, I wish for you to bring them directly to me. I'm not a harsh disciplinarian, but I do intend to be actively involved in my children's lives and to be the one who corrects them when necessary."

"I understand," she said. "And I would certainly appreciate any guidance or opinion you might offer."

He nodded. "You will start the day after tomorrow, but as of this moment you will no longer be seeing to any duties you have done previously. You will spend the time becoming acquainted with your responsibilities, and tomorrow you will be taken into town to be fitted for a new wardrobe."

"A new wardrobe?" she echoed. His eyes widened at her sharp tone.

"You will dress like a governess, Miss Layne, not a kitchen maid. I will cover all the costs. See that you order ample of everything you need." She wanted to thank him but felt too stunned. "That will be all then," he added. "Thank you, Miss Layne."

Eleanore rushed from the room, wanting only to be alone and come to terms with such dramatic, unexpected changes in her life. But she found Mrs. Bixby in the hall, waiting for her.

"Congratulations," she said with a little smile. "Most young women only dream of such an opportunity." Eleanore said nothing. She felt too afraid of the changes that lay before her to see this as an opportunity. She knew nothing about children. What if she handled them poorly or proved completely inadequate?

Mrs. Bixby asked Eleanore to walk with her while she discussed her specific duties with the children and familiarized her with their established schedule. She was grateful to be given a notebook where Mrs. Bixby had written everything down for her. They went upstairs and into the wing where the children's rooms were located. Since they were presently elsewhere with the nanny, Mrs. Bixby was able to give her a thorough tour without disturbing them. From the items in David's room, Eleanore was able to surmise that he liked horses and dragons and playing cricket. Iris owned more dolls than Eleanore had ever dreamed existed, and she also liked castles. Her closet was filled with beautiful dresses, and her dressing table was covered with hair ribbons that she clearly played with as much as she wore. Each bedroom had a framed pencil sketch of their mother on the wall. Between the children's bedrooms was a sitting room, equipped with table and chairs. Mrs. Bixby explained that the room was used for the children's studying and for playing games and other activities. The children also had most of their meals there.

"Don't they eat with their father?" she asked.

"Rarely," Mrs. Bixby said. "It's not customary."

Eleanore was taken aback, both by the ridiculousness of such a custom, and also her ignorance of such a ritual when she'd lived in the household for so long.

The nursery was across the hall—a huge room filled with a variety and abundance of toys that stunned Eleanore. The nanny's room was to one side of the nursery, and Eleanore's new room was on the other. She resisted the urge to gasp as they entered her new bedroom. It was more than double the size of where she stayed now, near the back of the house on the third floor. This room wasn't drab and practical. It had fine decor, a lovely, four-poster bed, and an elegant dressing table with a large mirror. The draperies and bedspread were coordinated in deep shades of blue. Such lovely surroundings took some of the edge off her concerns over taking this position.

As they stepped back into the hall, Eleanore was told that Mr. Barrington's room was at the end of the wing, should he ever be needed in the event of an emergency. A maid named Jennifer, a young woman with whom Eleanore was barely acquainted, had helped some with the children when Lucy, the nanny, hadn't been available. Jennifer would also be on hand to fill in if it ever became necessary. Eleanore would be allowed to leave early on one afternoon a week in order to see to any personal needs or errands.

After supper, Lizzie helped Eleanore move her things to her new room. It didn't take long, because she didn't have much. Lizzie chattered with excitement over this opportunity, as if Eleanore had just been promoted to royalty. She joked about her hopes that Eleanore wouldn't treat her old friends any differently now that she'd risen to new heights, but Eleanore didn't find that amusing in the least. She wasn't at all fond of the social ladder that existed, even within a household. She simply made it clear to Lizzie that this changed nothing except that Eleanore would have to walk farther to come to Lizzie's room to visit.

While Lizzie helped put Eleanore's things away, she rambled comfortably of how she'd twice worked as a lady's maid, and had been trained in her youth regarding all the related duties. Such work paid better and had more prestige than the kitchen work

Lizzie was doing. But both the ladies she'd worked for had been so snobbish and difficult to please that Lizzie had chosen work that kept some distance between herself and the aristocracy who provided her income.

"But you'll not have that problem with Mr. Barrington," she said. "I understand he's a very kind man." Eleanore made no comment. She couldn't be completely certain on that account.

Eleanore purposely avoided seeing Lucy or the children that evening. She could hear them in the nursery once she'd settled into her room, but she didn't feel prepared to meet them yet and longed instead for solitude in order to come to terms with this unexpected change. She sat at the dressing table studying her reflection while she unwound her long braid and brushed it out. She didn't look like a governess, and she certainly didn't feel like one. But looking around the room, she couldn't help but feel a serenity that calmed her spirit. It wasn't just the pleasant atmosphere of the room, but more a sense of belonging. In her heart she knew this was where she needed to be. And spending some time on her knees only brought this feeling of peace home to her more deeply. She didn't feel unafraid, but she did feel more prepared, knowing it was the course God would have her take. Climbing into bed, she noticed her miracle book on the bedside table and reminded herself that this new occupation would get her to America that much quicker. Perhaps this was God's way of answering her prayers.

The following morning, Eleanore left her room to go downstairs before the children were even up. Mrs. Bixby informed her at the breakfast table that a carriage would be taking her into town for a fitting at the dress shop. She handed Eleanore a list that included separate stops to order shoes, gloves, and hats as well. And at the bottom of the list it read, *Books. Supplies.*

"What is this?"

"Mr. Barrington wants you to purchase whatever you might want in order to give the children a wide range of learning activities.

He has accounts at each establishment. They know you're coming. You can get anything you like; just tell them you're Mr. Barrington's new governess."

Eleanore tried to let that soak in during the ride into town. She'd never even been inside a carriage before, and never imagined that it was so fine. The time it took to arrive seemed like nothing when she was accustomed to such a long walk. At the dress shop she felt mildly uncomfortable with how the women there fussed over her, but she was grateful that they apparently knew the type of clothing she should order, and exactly what she would need. It was the same with her other stops. She wasn't certain what to purchase under the heading of *supplies,* but recalled things her mother had done with her in her childhood. She even had some memories of doing things with her father before his death. She picked up only a few things, not certain what might already be available. It was startling to see how easily the purchases were charged to Mr. Barrington's account, and a little unnerving to consider this evidence of the trust he'd put in her to be spending his money.

Eleanore's final errand was at Mr. Harvey's bookshop. Only one other customer was there when she walked in. He looked surprised to see her. She wondered why until he said, "It's not Wednesday." She offered a faint smile, not certain how to explain. He added, "I was informed that Mr. Barrington has a new governess and she would be coming in to . . ." He stopped, and enlightenment came to his eyes.

"That's right," she said. "*I* am the new governess."

"That's wonderful, Ellie," he said with a generous grin.

"Perhaps," was all she said. "I could use your help finding some books suitable to share with the children. I really have no idea what I'm doing."

Eleanore was grateful for the time Mr. Harvey took to guide her in finding some children's literature, also offering her some simple advice, having raised children of his own. He assured her that if any of the books were duplicates of those already owned, they could be exchanged.

Eleanore arrived home exhausted and overwhelmed. Mrs. Bixby told her the children had gone for a walk with Jennifer, and right after supper Mr. Barrington wanted to see her. And she should look her best; she would be meeting the children. Before supper she barely had time to sort her purchases and change into her best dress, which had previously been saved for Sundays. Then she remembered that Mrs. Bixby had mentioned that she should wear her hair up, and had provided her with some hairpins. Eleanore had never done anything more than braid her unruly hair in order to keep it out of the way. It took several tries to wind the braid at the back of her head and pin it so that it might actually stay in place.

At supper, the other servants teased her lightheartedly over her promotion, but Eleanore found difficulty seeing the humor in the situation. She felt nervous and disoriented, both of which intensified as she knocked at the door of Mr. Barrington's office. He opened the door, saying, "Good, you're here," before he walked past her and toward the stairs. "Come along."

Eleanore had never used the front stairs before, which made ascending at the side of her employer feel all the more dreamlike.

"Did your errands go well?" he asked, but she sensed that he was simply trying to make conversation rather than having any real interest in her shopping.

"Yes, thank you," she said. "You're very generous."

He made no further comment.

At the nursery door, Eleanore hesitated, saying, "Forgive me . . . I need a moment . . . please."

She stepped back. He turned, surprised. "What is it, Miss Layne? Are you not well?"

"I'm fine, thank you. I just need to . . . catch my breath; I'm a bit nervous, I confess."

He chuckled kindly. "No need for that. They're just children. And they're not difficult by nature. They're actually rather well behaved, as far as children go."

"That's good to hear," she admitted, "considering that you've hired a woman to care for them who knows absolutely nothing about children." She was hoping to imply that her nerves were his fault, but he only smiled and opened the door.

Eleanore hovered at the door, grateful to feel invisible while the children greeted their father. They both jumped up from the floor where they were playing and rushed toward him. He laughed and picked them both up at once, even though David looked too big to be picked up at all. They kissed his cheeks, then he groaned facetiously and commented on how big they were getting before he set them down and said, "I've brought Miss Layne to meet you. She is to be your new governess."

The children turned toward her, and she got her first good look at them. Their coloring was similar, although much more fair than their father. In fact, they were as blond as he was dark. Iris was a head shorter than her brother, so beautiful she almost looked like a doll. Her eyes held a sparkle of intrigue; David's were subtly skeptical. He was a handsome boy with a generous hint of his father's firm features. They both gave her perfectly proper greetings, just as one might expect from children raised in an aristocratic home. Eleanore told them how pleased she was to meet them and that she was looking forward to all the things they would do together. She tried to make it sound sincere.

She was relieved when their attention turned back to their father and she was able to discreetly observe them. She wondered why she felt surprised to see how comfortably he interacted with them, and their obvious affection for him. Had she assumed that his being harsh with his wife might also make him harsh with his children? A few minutes later she was dismissed, and she left the room once she told the children she would see them in the morning.

Eleanore had trouble sleeping that night, but she put effort into replacing her anxiety with prayer, hoping God might consider her effort toward some degree of faith, and that He would be with her as she took on this new assignment.

The first hour that Eleanore was alone with the children had to be the most awkward hour of her life. She asked them frivolous questions about themselves and the things they enjoyed, and she received equally ridiculous answers. She asked what they would like to do before lunch, thinking she would save studies for the afternoon; however, since it was raining, the possibilities for recreation were limited. The morning was saved when Iris asked if she would read a story to them. Eleanore wondered how she, of all people, could have overlooked such a possibility, especially with the new books she'd brought home specifically for that purpose. Impulsively she decided to save those and said, "Why don't each of you bring me your favorite storybook, and after we read them you can tell me why you like them."

This idea proved to Eleanore that she had a common interest with the children, and gave her hope that they could form some kind of bond. The children's love for reading was quickly evidenced by their enthusiasm as they sat on either side of her and eagerly listened while she read with animation and expression. She was pleasantly surprised after a while when Iris climbed onto her lap and David eased closer to her side. She felt near tears at such simple acceptance. Surely winning them over had to be more difficult than this. Between stories she found a clue to their warmth when Iris said, "Mama didn't wike to wead stowies."

Eleanore didn't want to speak ill of their mother, and simply commented, "I'm certain your mother loved the both of you very much."

"Mama died," Iris said with matter-of-fact maturity.

"I know she did," Eleanore said gently. "It's very sad to have your mother die. My mother died too."

"Do you miss her?" David asked.

"I do, but whenever I wish she was here, I think about the happy things we did together, and my memories make me feel better. What are some happy things you did with your mother?"

Silence was their only response.

"Don't you want to talk about your mother?" she asked, deciding frank honesty would be best.

"We can if you want to," David said, and she saw an undeniable glimpse of his father in his face.

"It's up to you," she said. "Why don't you tell me what your mother liked to do?"

"She was too sweepy to do things with us," Iris said, and Eleanore recalled that their mother had been pregnant for several months prior to her death. She'd heard mention of Mrs. Barrington's poor health in the argument she'd been privy to.

Then David added, "She liked to go visit her friends and go shopping. Sometimes she would be gone for a few days, and she'd come home with lots of new things, and she'd always have something new for us, but then she'd be tired and sleep."

Eleanore felt increasingly uneasy even before she had a perfect recollection of overhearing James Barrington say to his wife, *It requires little energy to be in the same room with the children you brought into this world. You can't sit in your bed and read with them? What activities in your life are being neglected by the need to actually be a mother?*

Eleanore put an arm around each of the children and held them close for just a moment, suddenly grateful to be where she was as the idea occurred to her that being a part of their lives might actually give her an opportunity to make something valuable of her own life, as opposed to scrubbing pots and floors and waxing furniture. She silently uttered a prayer of thanks for this opportunity and its attendant blessings, then she distracted them with another story. Some time later she was surprised to look up and see Mr. Barrington leaning against the doorjamb, his arms folded, watching them. She wondered how long he had been there, but at least he seemed pleased. The children ran to greet him as they had the previous evening, then he said, "I thought we could eat lunch together. Eating in the nursery is much more delightful than that dreadful dining room."

The children were obviously pleased, but Eleanore wasn't quite sure how to make a gracious exit. She'd been told she needed to be flexible and allow their father time with them when he wanted, which was fine, but she wondered where he might expect to find her once he needed to leave. He proved himself insightful and effective at communication when he turned to her and said, "You're welcome to join us, Miss Layne, or you're free to go for a while; whichever you prefer."

"Thank you, sir," she said. Certain it would be best for the children to be alone with their father, which aided her own wish to have some time to gather her thoughts, she added, "I'll get some lunch in the kitchen and then be in my room when you need me."

"Very good," he said, distracted by something Iris was trying to tell him. Eleanore hurried from the room, breathing a deep sigh of relief to realize she'd made it through the first morning. If David and Iris were normally so agreeable and easy to please, then this job would surely be heaven-sent.

Chapter Three

KEEPING CONFIDENCE

Following lunch, the children were put back in her care. Eleanore felt blessed to note that the typical gray sky had given way to unusual, high floaty clouds. So she took the children out to the gardens and announced with great aplomb that they would now become seriously engaged in finding cloud pictures. The three of them lay on their backs for more than an hour looking for images in the sky. Iris began to giggle each time she saw something, and after a while David joined in her laughter. When they became bored with that they explored the gardens, as Eleanore had never had the privilege of doing before, then they went inside to draw what they had seen in the sky. They used pieces of charcoal taken from where Eleanore knew the household ashes were dumped. There were certainly other drawing materials available, but the adventure of dong it this way intrigued the children. They thoroughly enjoyed drawing black clouds on white paper, and Eleanore was glad for the opportunity to get them all cleaned up long before they were turned over to Lucy for the evening.

The following day Eleanore did not dread her work; in fact she could hardly wait to be with the children. She had them work on some writing and reading before lunch, interspersed with some learning games she'd remembered doing with her mother. Mr. Barrington didn't show himself so Eleanore had lunch in the nursery with the children and enjoyed that as well, even though a little tiff broke out between the children over who had eaten their vegetables most quickly. After lunch they had another stroll through the gardens and played hide-and-seek in the maze of hedges. Back in the house she made a game of sneaking into the kitchen to steal some biscuits, while Miss Gibbs pretended not to see them, which made the children giggle.

The next day it rained, and Eleanore brought out the journals she had purchased for them with their father's money. She showed them her own current journal and told them how the book had become like a secret friend who would listen to anything she wanted to say. She told them she would be happy to help them write in their journals, and if they wanted to share what they wrote with her or each other they could, but they didn't have to. David's eyes showed deep intrigue as she spoke, and he was apparently most taken with the *secret* aspect of this project. He asked to be excused to his room; he agreed to keep the door open, however, so that she could know he was all right. She'd seen his writing enough to know that he did very well, even though he occasionally misspelled words, writing them phonetically as he attempted to sound out what he wanted to write. Iris was just learning her letters and not putting words together yet, but Eleanore remembered how her own first journal entries had been dictated to her mother. So she asked Iris what she wanted to write. The child looked perplexed, and Eleanore suggested, "Perhaps you could write down something fun you did that you want to remember, and when you get older you can come back and read it and remember."

"Wike when I am six?" she asked eagerly.

"Of course." Eleanore smiled.

"I want to wite down that we wooked at cwouds and made pictures."

Eleanore said the words out loud as she wrote them, and Iris patiently kept at it for quite some time.

Mr. Barrington came to the sitting room, and Eleanore tried not to feel uneasy. It was difficult to know if he was simply making an appearance with his children, or checking up on her as their governess. Once Iris had given him the usual greeting, he glanced around and asked Eleanore, "Where is David?"

"He's in his room," she nodded to where she could see him through the partially open door, "writing in his new journal. He wanted some privacy."

"I see," Mr. Barrington said and didn't seem displeased.

Iris then informed him that she had a journal as well, and she sat on his lap to show him what Miss Layne had helped her write, although she adorably called Eleanore 'Miss Wayne.' He glanced at Eleanore and said, "You're welcome to take a break, if you like. Come back in an hour or so."

"Thank you, sir," she said and left the room, wondering why she feared some kind of criticism from his observance of her activities with the children.

Eleanore was stunned when her new wardrobe was delivered. While the dresses were conservative in color and design, she'd never imagined owning and wearing anything so fine. A dark cloak and two pairs each of gloves and shoes were also of the highest quality. And she was also provided with new underclothing and nightclothes. Mr. Barrington's generosity was difficult to comprehend. The first time she wore something new, she made a point of seeking him out to thank him. But before she could, he took notice of her attire and said simply, "You look very nice, Miss Layne." He made a contemplative expression and added, "Very much like . . . a governess." She saw the subtlest twitch of his lips and realized he'd meant it with some humor. She smiled in response and thanked him. He brushed aside the mention of his generosity and asked how the children were doing.

Days flourished into weeks while Eleanore grew so fond of the Barrington children that she wondered how she could ever be apart from them. While she continued to study her miracle book and dreamed of the day she could afford to go to America, she knew that day would be difficult simply because she might never be able to see David and Iris again. Still, her strongest desire was to search out and become connected to people who shared her love for this great book. She became increasingly dissatisfied with the sermons she heard on Sundays, but she attended church anyway, certain it was the best possible place for her to be on the Sabbath. And she looked forward to the day when even greater opportunities would open up to her.

The Barrington children were, as their father had said, not difficult by nature, and they were rather well behaved. She dealt with some occasional contention between them, or some whining or reluctance to do lessons now and then, but for the most part they did as she asked, and she thoroughly enjoyed her work. She wondered how she had ever believed herself content with the menial tasks she had been doing before when she'd already found such fulfillment in being a part of these children's lives. During the warm summer months they picnicked at least once a week, sometimes in the gardens and sometimes venturing farther afield. She asked permission of their father to take them into town, and every few weeks they would have an excursion to purchase new books and wander through the high street.

Eleanore grew to respect James Barrington as she observed his consistent involvement with the children and his kindness toward them. She recalled him saying when he'd initially hired her for the position that he wasn't necessarily a warm or tender man, but over time she had come to disagree with that. He was firm and expected obedience and respect from his children, but his discipline was kind and appropriate. In a way, he reminded her of her own father. Even though her memories of him were vague, she realized they would be near the same age.

At least once a week Eleanore was asked to meet with Mr. Barrington in his office to discuss the progress of the children. He always expressed his appreciation for her work, and never once criticized her methods. Still, she never felt entirely comfortable in his presence. She began a game of easing her nerves during such interviews by looking for some resemblance to his children. Now that she'd become so familiar with David and Iris, it was fascinating to see undeniable similarities to their father during the brief opportunities she had to speak with him. It would show up in a twitch of his lips or a certain expression. Eleanore had become familiar with their mother's face from the sketched portraits in each of the children's rooms, and she could see that they'd inherited their mother's fair coloring, but their faces were an intriguing combination of both their parents. As summer began to draw to a close, Eleanore felt so content with her position that she had to stop and wonder how her life could be so good. Of course, there were occasional challenges with the children, and she certainly missed her mother. But overall she was greatly blessed, and she thanked God daily for being so generous with her. She just couldn't imagine her life being any better—at least until she found the opportunity to go to America. Even that prospect now held a poignant edge, but her feelings on the matter hadn't changed. She knew more than ever that the book was true, and she would find the people who shared her beliefs or die trying.

Eleanore wondered if she'd been premature in thinking her life was close to perfect when, seemingly out of nowhere, David merged into a difficult stage. Incidents of minor contention between him and Iris over petty, ridiculous little things became more frequent. Then one morning while Eleanore was putting up her hair before breakfast, she heard David shouting from the other room. At first she hesitated to intervene, then she heard Lucy shouting back. Her tone of voice was nearly as disturbing as the words she said. Eleanore stepped into the room and asked in a calm voice, "What's the problem?"

That's when David ran from the room, and it took Eleanore nearly two hours to find him while Lucy watched out for Iris, who cried most of the time. Eleanore reported the incident to Mr. Barrington, as was expected, although she said nothing of the nanny's inappropriate behavior. She told Lucy, however, that if it happened again, she would report it. She questioned her own judgment when she sensed Lucy's defensiveness and feared she had made an enemy. A few days later, just before lunch, Iris said something about her mother, and David got angry with his sister for no apparent reason. When Eleanore sat close beside him and asked what he was upset about, he ran from the room. She considered reporting the problem to his father and enlisting his help, but he'd gone away for the day. Eleanore left Iris with Lizzie, and this time it took her nearly *three* hours to find David. He was sitting on the ground in a corner of the maze, damp with drizzle. She hurried to get him inside and warmed up, but he still came down with a cold and spent a few days in bed. His father was concerned, but he was apparently as baffled as Eleanore as to what to do about it. She prayed over the matter and observed his behavior closely, looking for clues, wanting to be able to understand what might be troubling him.

Once recovered from his cold, David ran off a third time, and then a fourth. Eleanore was always the one to go and find him. She'd discovered he had two favorite hiding places, and after the fifth time she realized that he wanted her to find him, but not too quickly.

Eleanore sat beside him on the grass within the maze, remaining in complete silence for several minutes before she began to talk. "When I was seven and my father died, for a long time after, sometimes I'd feel so angry. Even though I knew it wasn't my father's fault that he got sick and died, I felt angry with him for leaving me and my mother alone. And sometimes I'd think of things he'd said that I hadn't liked, and I would feel angry over that, too. He was a nice man and I loved him, but sometimes he made mistakes. One day I realized it was okay, even though he was dead, to admit that he hadn't been perfect, because I knew that God loved him anyway, and I knew that God loved me and He would send angels to watch over me, even though my father was gone."

She allowed more minutes of silence to pass before she said, "I would like it very much if you would tell me why you feel angry. You don't have to if you don't want to, but it might make you feel better to talk about it, and I promise not to tell anyone else if you don't want me to."

More minutes passed before he said, "You promise, really?"

"I promise," she said firmly.

Eleanore was both concerned and surprised to hear a very complex and confused oratory related to the child's feelings regarding his mother's death and his relationship with her prior to that. He also told her things Lucy had said that made her especially disconcerted. Eleanore did her best to talk David's feelings through with him, and he ended up crying in her arms. When he'd calmed down, she said carefully, "David, I meant what I said. I'm not going to tell anyone what you said about your feelings, but I want to ask your permission to talk to your father about what Lucy said." He looked concerned but said nothing. "Your father trusts her to take good care of you and your sister, and if she says things that are hurtful or unfair, I don't think he'd like that."

"Will Father have her dismissed?"

"I don't know."

David's insight and compassion amazed Eleanore as he added, "I don't want her to be without a job just because I don't like what she says."

"Perhaps I could suggest to your father that she be given a job elsewhere in the house, and someone else could help take care of you and Iris."

"Can it be Lizzie?" he asked eagerly. The children had gotten to know her somewhat when she'd occasionally joined them for lunch or one of their little escapades through the house on rainy days.

"That's up to your father," Eleanore said. "But if it's all right with you, I'd like to just talk to him about it. I won't say anything at all about the other things we talked about. I promise." He nodded, and she said, "If he wants to talk to you about Lucy, is that all right?" He nodded again. She stood up and held her hand out for him. They walked into the house together, but they were barely inside the door when Eleanore was informed that Mr. Barrington wanted to see her, and that David was to go up to the nursery.

Eleanore smoothed her hair and dress and entered his office. He didn't ask her to sit down, which was unusual. And his demeanor reminded her of the man she'd overheard that night in the library, even though she'd not actually seen him. He proved the comparison correct when his voice came harshly. "I've been informed of a most disturbing rumor concerning the care of my children."

"Have you?" she asked, decidedly nervous—and angry. She could easily guess what had happened. But she was determined to keep her composure. "And what might that be?"

At least he got straight to the point. "Lucy has informed me that she's overheard conversations between you and the children that give her cause for concern."

Eleanore swallowed carefully. Rather than trying to defend herself, she forced a steady voice and asked, "Are you accusing or asking me, sir?" A glimpse of confusion pressed through his angry countenance. She clarified, "Is this an accusation based on the assumption that Lucy is telling you the truth? Or might you be willing to give me the benefit of the doubt and acquire more information before you toss me into the streets?"

"I have no intention of tossing *anyone* into the streets, Miss Layne. But perhaps you could tell me what provoked you to speak so unkindly to my son."

"So, this *is* an accusation," she said.

He lifted his chin. "Are you saying that Lucy lied to me?"

She measured her words. "I'm saying that I have never spoken unkindly to your son. But since you obviously are taking Lucy's word above mine, perhaps you would like to consult a third party in order to determine whether or not I'm trustworthy."

"And who might that be?" he asked, sounding irritated. But was it with her, or with himself for looking like a fool by jumping to conclusions?

"Your son, of course. I assume you consider *him* trustworthy."

He looked thoughtful a moment. "Please sit down," he said and left the room. She could hear him speaking with a maid in the hall but couldn't tell what he said. Then he came back into the room, leaving the door open. The silence became horrid while they waited. Thankfully he kept his back turned to her, mostly looking out the window between bouts of methodical pacing. Eleanore heard someone enter the room behind her. He looked up and said, "Close the door. Sit down."

Eleanore felt a little sick to see David move to his father's side; Lucy took a chair nearby. This suddenly felt like a trial and she *didn't* want to be here. While she felt confident of her own innocence, she now knew Lucy was capable of lying, and she didn't at all like David being caught in the middle. She prayed his father would handle this well and not traumatize the child. Mr. Barrington sat in his chair behind the desk and urged David to stand in front of him, his back to the women. He said in a gentle voice, "It seems we have a disagreement in the household, David. I need you to be completely honest with me, no matter how you think it might affect people you care about." There was that methodical pause Eleanore had come to find common in her employer. "It can be difficult to be honest, especially when you need to say something that might hurt another person's feelings. I've taught you that it's important to be polite, and that some-times it's best not to speak opinions that might be hurtful. But right now I need the truth. Do you understand?"

David nodded. Eleanore breathed a little easier while her respect for James Barrington deepened. He then said to his son, "I trust Lucy and Miss Layne to take very good care of you and Iris, and you know that I expect you to be respectful of them." David nodded again. "I know that you've gotten angry sometimes, and I need to know if you've said anything to either Lucy or Miss Layne that might have been disrespectful." Hearing him use their names, Eleanore was reminded of the distinction of her position above others in the household. Apparently being a governess required a more formal usage of her name, as opposed to those with lower positions—a convention she wasn't necessarily fond of.

David was quiet a long moment. In a timid voice he said, "I . . . told Lucy that . . . she had no right to . . . say things like that about my mother . . . even if they were true."

Eleanore saw the alarm in Mr. Barrington's face, although he kept his focus completely on his son, perhaps hoping to keep the child's attention away from the audience in the room. "And what did she say?" he asked with a tightness in his voice that made it evident he was using restraint to hold back some degree of anger. The boy hesitated, and Mr. Barrington asked, "Did she say it to you, or to someone else?"

"I heard her talking to one of the maids; I don't know who."

"And what did she say, David?"

David hung his head and his voice became even more quiet. "I don't want to tell you."

"Why not?"

While Eleanore expected David to be concerned about getting Lucy in trouble, he said with a quaver of emotion, "I don't want to hurt your feelings, because you love Mama and miss her."

Eleanore sensed Mr. Barrington becoming unsettled. She felt sure this wasn't going the way he'd expected. He said with firm kindness, "I appreciate your concern, son, but you just need to tell me the truth, even if it hurts my feelings. We can talk more about it later if we need to. Right now just tell me what you heard."

David lifted his head. Once given the permission he needed, he apparently had no trouble stating the truth. "She said that Mama had gone to hell because she was a bad mother and she didn't love me and Iris."

Eleanore's heart pounded. She wasn't surprised by the confession since David had admitted it to her earlier. But she felt much like she had that night in the library when she'd overheard words she shouldn't have heard. She saw pain in Mr. Barrington's eyes, and he nonchalantly put a hand over his mouth that she knew was meant to conceal emotion. Then he moved his hand, and the pain disappeared behind a controlled anger. He swallowed hard, then asked in a strained voice, "Is there anything else that was said between you and Lucy I should know about?"

David gave a loud, hesitant sigh but apparently knew he wasn't going to get out of it. "Iris said that Mama was an angel in heaven watching out for us, and Lucy told her she wasn't. I told Lucy not to say things like that to Iris because it made her cry. Lucy called me a wicked child; she said I was like my mother."

Eleanore saw Mr. Barrington's nostrils flare and his face tighten. Still he didn't move his eyes toward her or Lucy. Eleanore kept her focus on David and his father, not daring to look at Lucy. In a voice that was surprisingly calm, Mr. Barrington asked, "Is there anything else?"

"No, Papa," David said. "Was it wrong for me to say what I did to Lucy?"

"We'll talk about it later," he said, then asked, "Is there anything you said to Miss Layne, or her to you, that I should know about?"

"No, Papa," he said again.

Mr. Barrington nodded, and Eleanore's relief almost left her breathless. Only then did she begin to shake as she realized how easily she could have lost her position due to someone else's lies. Mr. Barrington then tenderly took his son's face into his hands and said, "Thank you for telling me the truth. It was a brave thing to do. I want you to know that you are *not* a wicked child. You are a very, very good child. Do you understand?" David nodded. "And whatever anyone else might think or say, your mother loved you very much. Do you understand?" The child nodded again. "Good, then. Iris is upstairs with Jennifer. I want you to go and stay with them, and we will talk about this some more after supper. Is that all right?"

David nodded. His father hugged him, and he hurried from the room, not even glancing toward the governess or the nanny. Once the door had closed, Mr. Barrington's demeanor changed immediately. He stood and put his hands behind his back, exhaling loudly. His voice, barely calm, was deep with anger. "Tell me, Lucy, do you have anything to say to me?"

"No, sir," she said, and Eleanore finally glanced in her direction to see her head bowed, her hands folded in her lap.

"Might I take that as an admission that my son told me the truth?"

"Yes, sir."

"Then what are you still doing here?" he demanded.

She looked startled and stood abruptly, but he stepped directly in front of her, preventing her from leaving. "Look at me," he said in a voice that chilled Eleanore. She could see Lucy visibly trembling as she lifted her eyes to meet his. "Before you leave my employment, I want you to understand beyond any question the reasons for your dismissal. When you were hired, it was made inescapably clear that integrity was the most important requirement for working in this household. If this were simply a matter of your inappropriate comments to my children, I would have considered offering you employment in some other area of the house. But I will *not* tolerate such malicious lies in my home. You have one hour to pack your things and be gone. You'll be given conveyance into town and sufficient severance pay to meet your needs for two weeks. Get out."

Lucy all but ran from the room. The closing of the door startled Eleanore to the realization that she was now alone with Mr. Barrington, who was in a very foul mood. She was only grateful to know that his anger was not toward her. She was ready to excuse herself when he spoke with a complete absence of the anger he'd just leveled at Lucy. "I owe you an apology, Miss Layne. You were right. I was accusing you without sufficient information."

"Thank you, sir," she said without looking at him. "I humbly accept your apology."

"Now I need to ask you something." He returned to his chair behind the desk. "Were you aware of this problem?"

Eleanore looked at him then, forcing her confidence to the surface, praying he would understand her reasoning in what she needed to say. "I overheard Lucy saying to David part of what he told you. I addressed it with Lucy and told her if there was any further problem I would report it to you. Just before I came in, I was visiting with David in the gardens. He'd run off again, angry. He opened up to me over the reasons. I asked him if it would be all right if I talked to you about Lucy, and he gave me his consent to do so. I was on my way to speak with you when I was told you wanted to see me."

His silence implied deep contemplation. And she waited, trying to ignore her pounding heart and sweating palms. He finally asked, "So . . . is this what David's been upset about? Is this the reason for his . . . running off and hiding?"

"Partly," she said.

"What's the rest?"

"I'm not at liberty to say, sir." His eyes widened, and she clarified, "David told me his reasons in confidence. I promised him I would not repeat them to anyone."

"I'm his father. I can't help him if I don't know what—"

"I promised him, Mr. Barrington. Whether or not he chooses to share his feelings with you is up to him. I can only say that it's related to his mother's death. His feelings are complicated and fragile, and I would advise you to tread carefully. I don't feel it would be appropriate for me to say anything more."

Again there was silence until he said, "We're coming upon five months since you took this position. I asked you to give it six months and—"

"There's no need for you to be looking for a new governess, if that's what you're asking. I've grown very fond of the children and enjoy my work with them much more than I had expected. Given the chance to say so, allow me to express my appreciation for the opportunity."

She saw him smile, however subtly, a stark contrast to the other emotions she'd seen pass over him in the last little while. "So, my instincts weren't so far off then, Miss Layne?"

"No, sir," she said and returned his smile.

"May I take that to mean you would be willing to stay on indefinitely? Or at least until the children are grown?" She knew she must have looked panicked by the way he quickly added, "Do you have other plans, Miss Layne?"

"Nothing at this point, sir," she said, certain her desire to eventually go to America was not relevant to this conversation. It still would take years for her to save enough money. "I can only say that I . . . can't be certain where life's path might lead me."

"Marriage and children of your own, perhaps?" he asked, and she recalled that coming up in their original interview.

"Perhaps," she said.

"And do you have any prospects in that regard, Miss Layne?"

"No, sir. As of now I see no reason why I won't be able to work with your children for quite some time to come."

"Good. I believe that consistency is good for the children. And since I'll be needing to hire a new nanny, I'm glad to know they can find some stability in their governess."

"Would you like me to take over Lucy's duties as well, sir?"

"That won't be necessary. I don't want you responsible for them every minute of the day. It would be far too taxing; you need your own time."

"In most cases, a mother would be responsible for her children every minute of the day."

"But you are not their mother; you are their governess. Thank you for your offer, Miss Layne. Until I can find a replacement, you may need to put in a little extra time, but there are others who can help, including myself." He sighed and added, "You wouldn't have any suggestions, would you? Is there anyone in the household who might do well with the position? Someone with integrity?"

"You're asking me?"

"You've worked here for many years. I suspect you know the staff much better than I do. Yes, I'm asking your opinion."

Eleanore wanted to suggest Lizzie. She felt certain she would do very well and enjoy it, even though it would mean that their work schedules would directly conflict, and they'd rarely have time together unless they were both with the children. Instead she said, "Let me think on that. Perhaps you could ask the children what they think."

"I'll do that. Thank you, Miss Layne. You're free to go."

"Thank you, sir," she said and stood.

As she opened the door he added, "And thank you . . . for everything you do . . . and the way you do it. You are a great blessing to the children—and to me."

"You're very kind, sir," she said and left the room, but she couldn't help feeling warm inside over the outcome. She prayed in her heart that Mr. Barrington's talk with his son later would go well, and that Lucy would quickly find employment elsewhere and learn well from her poor behavior. And Eleanore thanked God for giving her the privilege to be a part of these people's lives. If she had to bide her time in order to get to America, she couldn't think of any better way to do it than this. She was truly blessed.

The following day David seemed in good spirits, and Eleanore had to assume the conversation with his father had gone well. Jennifer and Mrs. Bixby both helped with the children in addition to performing their usual duties in order to compensate for Lucy's absence, and Eleanore put in some extra time as well. In spite of what Mr. Barrington had said about the need for a nanny, she *did* believe she could handle the children all the time, and she wouldn't mind. They were old enough that they didn't need someone with them every single minute, and they were good children. There were other people available to watch them when necessary. But a new nanny would be hired and the routine would go on as it had before.

Early that evening she was called to Mr. Barrington's office. He was sitting on a couch some distance from the desk where he usually sat, his long legs stretched out, his ankles crossed. He was immersed in a book and remained distracted by it while he said, "Tell me about your friend, the woman you call Lizzie."

Although she suspected his reasons, she had to ask, "Why?"

He looked up, and subtle humor sparkled in his eyes. "Are you questioning my judgment, Miss Layne?"

"No, just asking a question, sir."

He looked back at his book and turned the page. "David tells me she spends time with you and the children on occasion, and he likes her. He wants her to be the new nanny. While I want someone the children feel comfortable with, there are obviously certain abilities and characteristics that are mandatory for the position. I'm simply asking you to tell me what you know about her."

"I've known her longer and more personally than anyone else on the staff, sir. She was a good friend to my mother, and we have remained close following my mother's death. I have never seen any evidence of unethical behavior in her. Her reading skills are very minimal, but she likes children and enjoys David and Iris. I believe she could handle the responsibilities easily enough. I do know that she previously served as a lady's maid."

"Really?" His surprise was evident. "Then why does she work in the kitchens?"

"She was not fond of working closely with ladies who were impossible to please."

"I see," he said. "Since Mrs. Barrington is dead, that won't be a problem."

Eleanore fought to keep from gasping. She'd never once heard him speak disparagingly of his deceased wife. She made no comment.

"In your opinion, do you think she's right for the position, then?"

"I think she would do well, sir."

"Do you feel the friendship you share would be an advantage to your sharing responsibilities with the children?"

"I believe we could work well together. I suggest you talk with her and make your decision."

"I intend to. Please tell her to come and see me right away."

"Yes, sir."

She waited for him to dismiss her, but he said, still looking more at the book, "David doesn't want to tell me his reasons for feeling angry and wanting to run away."

"Perhaps he will eventually."

Mr. Barrington looked at her. "You're not going to tell me, are you?"

"No, sir."

He sighed loudly. "You can be terribly stubborn, Miss Layne."

"If you mean I won't be wheedled into breaking my promise to David, you're absolutely right. If *you* had told me something in confidence, Mr. Barrington, I dare say you would not want someone else wheedling it out of me."

He exhaled loudly. "Your point is well taken, Miss Layne. That will be all. Thank you."

Eleanore left the room and went straight to find Lizzie, announcing without preamble, "Mr. Barrington wants to see you."

"Me?" Lizzie squeaked. "What on earth for? Did I do something wrong?"

"No, of course not," Eleanore said. "Just . . . wash up and take off your apron. Hurry. He's in his office."

Eleanore saw Lizzie an hour later and had never seen her so happy. She couldn't stop talking about what a miracle this was for her. She'd always wanted children of her own and had never married, and she'd grown terribly weary of her work in the kitchen, even though she'd never complained enough for Eleanore to realize that was the case. That very night Eleanore helped Lizzie move her things into Lucy's old room, and the next day they went together into town so that Lizzie could order a new wardrobe. They took the children with them and made an outing of it.

It took no time at all for Lizzie to work herself comfortably into the children's lives. And while Eleanore and Lizzie had very defined shifts and responsibilities with David and Iris, they often spent time as a foursome. One benefit of this was Eleanore's opportunity to help Lizzie improve her reading skills. With her own money she bought Lizzie the gift of a journal so that they could all do journal time together. And when the children were reading, Lizzie began reading as well, occasionally asking Eleanore what a word meant or how to pronounce it.

Mr. Barrington checked in on the children regularly, as always. He was apparently pleased with the new arrangement and commented more than once to Eleanore that David and Iris seemed to be doing well. And Eleanore agreed.

Autumn merged into a winter that was long and cold, but Eleanore always managed to find ways to keep the children busy indoors, and they had great fun together. She helped them make silly and sentimental gifts for their father for Christmas, which he told her later were absolutely the best gifts he'd ever received. She noticed that he'd hung the plaster impressions of his children's hands on his office wall.

While Eleanore celebrated Christmas with some of the other servants, as she always had, she was surprised to receive a gift from the children. They brought it to her the morning of Boxing Day, and their father hovered in the doorway while she opened the beautifully wrapped box. Inside was a set of two of the most exquisite journals she'd ever seen. Never had she imagined such fine leather binding, such quality paper, edged with gold. Also in the box were two elegant pens and a supply of ink. She made a genuine fuss over them, which left the children beaming. While she was hugging the children, one in each arm, she looked up at their father and said quietly, "Thank you."

He just nodded and said, "Merry Christmas, Miss Layne." Then more loudly, "Come along, children. Today is Miss Layne's day off. You get to spend the day with *me*." He laughed as if nothing in the world could make him happier.

"Best of luck to you," Eleanore said as the children ran past him and down the hall. He mocked an expression of terror that made Eleanore laugh. He smiled and followed after David and Iris. Eleanore pressed a reverent hand over her gift, anxious to finish filling up her current journal so that she could begin using these. She wondered what course her life might take, and how it might fill these pages.

Chapter Four
THE PROPOSITION

Spring arrived suddenly. Warmer air beckoned Eleanore and her young charges into the outdoors. As the days stretched toward summer, her contentment deepened with the realization that she had been the governess for a year; perhaps the best year of her life—made better by being able to read daily from her precious book. She memorized passages and deeply pondered their meaning, while she frequently went to the library to read from the Bible, occasionally making comparisons that only strengthened her belief that both books were undoubtedly the word of God. And while a part of her longed to go to America, the serenity she'd found in her life here left her patient and willing to let life take its course and allow future events to be guided by God's hand.

Eleanore's first serious challenge with the children in months came up when David got into an argument with his sister and ran from the house. She checked the usual hiding places and found him in the third place she looked. They sat on the ground and talked for a long while, then returned to the house. She felt concerned for him but not certain how to help. Once her shift ended she wanted to talk to Mr. Barrington to let him know where the matter stood with David, but he was away. She left the house for a long walk, praying as she ambled over the moors that she could help David finally come to terms with his feelings over his mother's death.

A rainstorm moved in unexpectedly while Eleanore was some distance from the house. She was thoroughly wet when she returned and walked through the door to find Mrs. Bixby waiting for her.

"Mr. Barrington wants to see you," she said.

"I'll just hurry to change and—"

"No, he said immediately."

"But look at me. I'm—"

"No matter. Don't leave him waiting."

Eleanore attempted to smooth her hair and dress before she knocked at the office door.

"Yes?" he called, and she went in. He glanced at her, then looked again. "Good heavens, child. What *have* you been doing?"

"I simply went for a walk, sir, and it started to rain. I was going to change, but Mrs. Bixby said you wanted to see me immediately."

"I do, yes," he said. "But it's not *that* urgent. For heaven's sake, go change into some dry clothes."

"Thank you, sir. I'll be back shortly."

Eleanore hurried as quickly as she could and tried not to feel nervous over wondering what he might want to discuss. She returned to the office, and he said, "Well, sit down, Miss Layne. I should think you've been in this room often enough that you know you don't need an invitation."

"Thank you, sir," she said and took the usual seat.

"I understand that David ran off again this afternoon."

"That's right. You were not here when my shift ended, and I was prepared to discuss it with you as soon as I returned."

"So you've returned. I thought this habit had been resolved."

"Apparently not."

"Do you know why he's prone to getting so upset and hiding away like this?"

"It's the same as it's always been, sir."

For a moment he looked as if he had no idea what she meant, then he leaned back in his chair. "You're not going to tell me, are you?"

"Actually," she said, "I asked David today if I could have permission to discuss his feelings with you." Mr. Barrington's eyes widened. "He said that would be fine, but he was worried about your being unhappy with him. I promised him that you would not be angry. I repeated what I once heard you say to him, that he needed to be honest even if it might be hurtful to someone he cares about."

He looked thoughtful, perhaps a little stunned. "So tell me, Miss Layne, what is it that causes my son such grief that he would be so hesitant to share with me?"

Eleanore began at an easy point. "Apparently David and Iris liked to play in their mother's room when she was resting. Correct me if I'm mistaken, but I assume they wanted to be near her and would sometimes be mildly mischievous to get her attention."

He leaned back in his chair. "That would be a fairly accurate assumption. Go on."

"David tells me that his mother was lying down and he kept asking her to play a game with him and she wouldn't. When he told her that she never played with him and Iris, she got angry. She got out of bed, took hold of their arms and dragged them to the nursery. She shouted at them to stay there and be quiet and slammed the door. An hour later you had sent for the doctor."

Eleanore saw him close his eyes, heard him blow out a harsh breath. "And apparently David's perception of this is . . ." He didn't finish.

Eleanore suddenly hated being in this position, until the thought occurred to her that someone like Lucy could be in this position. At least Eleanore could recognize in herself the ability to be compassionate and appropriate. She cleared her throat carefully and just said it. "He believes he is responsible for his mother's death."

Mr. Barrington's astonishment didn't surprise her. He stood abruptly and went to the window, leaning his hands on the sill, breathing sharply. Eleanore felt near tears to see the evidence of his concern for his son.

"Apparently," Eleanore went on, wanting to have all of this in the open and over with, "David has done well at pushing his guilt aside except for when Iris says something about missing her mother or feeling sad. And combined with the things that Lucy said . . . well, his feelings are complex at best."

"Of course," he said, distracted.

"If I may offer my opinion . . ."

"Of course," he said again, as if he would welcome it.

"I don't believe something like this will be solved quickly. Over time, we can help him understand. This is just a part of his grieving for the loss. I believe grief is relative to the individual. Neither of us truly knows the relationship he shared with his mother. He's told me very little in that regard. As I see it, we simply must allow him to grieve in his own way, and give him the time he needs to come to terms with it. But understanding the complexities of his grief makes it possible to help him know what's true and what isn't."

He was silent a long moment, then returned to his chair. "You're very insightful for one so young, Miss Layne. What lessons on grief has life given *you?*"

She wanted to tell him that such a question felt too personal and probing, but she just answered it. "My father died when I was seven; my mother died two years ago."

"And you cared very much for them."

"I did; I do."

"Well, David may not appreciate the fact that his governess has empathy for his loss, but I do. I can try to help him understand what really happened, but as you said, it could take time. I'm concerned that one of these days he'll run off and get lost or caught in a storm."

"I've talked to him about that. I'm coming to learn his usual hiding places. I will do my best not to let him go too far."

He was quietly thoughtful, but she knew it wasn't appropriate for her to leave until he dismissed her. She just waited until he said, "I'm going to talk to David and be forthright. I need to tell him what happened . . . medically . . . so he knows that it had nothing to do with him. Even if her getting angry and physically removing the children from the room *had* caused a problem, her actions would not be his responsibility. But I can assure him the problem existed long before the incident. I think that *you* need to know what happened, as well. He trusts you and talks to you. If it comes up again, you can help reinforce the truth."

"Of course."

He looked directly at her. "There was a problem with the placenta."

"I'm sorry?" Eleanore said, having never heard the word.

He looked astonished by her ignorance. "Have you never been taught the basics of childbirth, Miss Layne?"

"No, sir," she said, trying not to sound embarrassed—especially when she realized that *he* was going to tell her.

She felt like one of his children as he leaned his forearms on the desk and stated plainly, "The placenta is attached to the inside of the womb where the baby grows. The baby is connected to the placenta with the umbilical cord, which feeds the baby everything it needs in order to grow. After the birth, the cord is cut, and the placenta breaks loose when it's no longer needed. According to one of her maids, Mrs. Barrington had been bleeding for a couple of days and hadn't wanted it reported. In case you didn't realize, Miss Layne, there should be no bleeding during pregnancy."

She felt her eyes widen but refused to show her discomfort any further. She *hadn't* realized that. No one had ever told her such things. But she was more astonished to realize that a man was this clearly aware of the nature of a woman's cycles, and he was frankly discussing the function of a woman's body as naturally as he might have told her that his children should get more fresh air.

"Her reasons for not reporting the problem are irrelevant. The point is that she didn't, and then it got out of control and couldn't be stopped. The placenta had broken loose too soon. The baby was dead inside of her long before she got angry with David. There is no connection whatsoever."

Eleanore swallowed carefully and had to admit, "I'm glad to know that, Mr. Barrington, and I'm certain David will be too." She didn't add that she was also glad to know his father would be the one to explain it.

With no further attempt at conversation, he said, "Thank you for your time and insight, Miss Layne. Let me know if anything changes."

"Of course, sir."

The following morning, David took Eleanore aside and told her very maturely that he was glad she'd talked to his father, because they'd had a long visit the previous evening. He cried a little as he admitted he was glad to know he hadn't hurt his mother. She sensed that he still had some confused emotions related to his mother's death, but he was making progress. She hugged him and told him she was proud of him for his grown-up attitude in handling the situation.

Over the next several days, Eleanore saw a lighter side of David than she had ever seen. He'd certainly seemed to be a happy child in the past, but she realized now that he'd been some-what subdued for as long as she'd known him. He was now prone to more laughter and to teasing his sister in ways that made her giggle, as opposed to feeding contention between them.

On a gray afternoon, Eleanore had a world map spread over the table in the sitting room, talking with the children about how far different countries were from England. Lizzie was there as well. Eleanore couldn't help gazing at the eastern shore of America, more specifically New York. That was where the book had been printed; it said so inside. She distracted herself by asking the children where they would like to travel if they could go anywhere. David wanted to go to India to see a real elephant. Iris wanted to go to France because Lucy had told her about the fine pastries there.

"Where would you like to go?" David asked her.

"America," she said without hesitation.

"Oh, that would be grand!" Lizzie added.

"And what do you think is so grand about America?" Mr. Barrington asked from the doorway, startling them all. But Eleanore had gotten used to the way he purposely arrived in silence in order to observe his children without them being aware. She'd gotten past her concern that he was trying to scrutinize her performance, mostly because she knew she had nothing to hide from him. He stepped into the room and added, "Tell me, Lizzie, why would you want to go to America?" His tone expressed genuine curiosity, likely for the sake of making conversation.

"It would be a great adventure, sir. Would it not?"

"Indeed it would," he said and sat down. Iris climbed onto his lap while David closely examined India on the map. "And what about you, Miss Layne? What in America lures your wishes there?"

Eleanore felt caught off guard. She didn't want to answer honestly; she'd never told anyone about her desire to go to America, let alone her reasons. She settled on generalities rather than a specific purpose. "I would very much like the opportunity to explore new beliefs and a way of life that does not hold some of the restrictions we have here in our society."

His eyes widened, and she wondered if he would think her too bold. Before he could comment, David said, "Tell me again where you've been, Father."

"Well," he said, scooting his chair closer to the map, "I *have* been to America, but only briefly." He pressed his finger over New York City, and Eleanore's heart quickened. "I was here for a few weeks, but didn't go far from there." He then pointed out Jamaica, three different ports in Africa, and two in Asia. He'd also been to Australia and New Zealand.

Eleanore became thoroughly enchanted by listening to him answer the children's questions about these exotic places and the things he'd seen and done. David seemed disappointed that he'd not gone searching for strange animals, although he admitted to having once ridden an elephant. What Eleanore heard in his explanations of his travels was his apparent fascination with the customs and behaviors of people in different cultures. She couldn't help thinking she would have liked to ask him more on that count, but such questions might have bored the children, and suppertime was approaching.

Less than a week after the world-travel discussion, Eleanore was called to Mr. Barrington's office. She'd not seen him since that day and wasn't surprised by his request for an interview. He never went too long without privately asking her about his children's progress. She was prepared to report that Iris was reading excellently for a child nearly five. And David showed a great deal of intelligence and, for a boy of seven, was eager to learn.

Once seated in his office, Eleanore was completely stunned to hear him say, "I need to inform you, Miss Layne, that I have made the decision to move to America."

Her heart quickened with both envy and dread. He was telling her that she would no longer be needed. If only she had enough money saved for passage, that would be fine, but . . .

He continued. "It's been a longtime wish of mine. I've always had a fascination with politics, and the history and workings of American politics have especially intrigued me. It's somewhat of a hobby, I suppose. My late wife had no interest in ever leaving her home, and I respected that. Truly, I had come to accept that my wish would never be fulfilled. Now, with her gone, I struggle with the memories of this place in relation to her. So, I've made the decision to sell the estate. I have an interested buyer.

Everything is coming together, and I know it's the right course for me and my children."

She looked down and clasped her hands to keep them from trembling. "I understand, Mr. Barrington. I wish you all the best."

"The purpose of this meeting is not to relieve you of your position, Miss Layne. I'm asking you to come with me." She looked up, startled, heart pounding. He was serious. *A miracle!* "The children have grown very attached to you—for good reason. I can't possibly care for them on my own. Most of the servants will stay with the estate when it is sold. I understand you have a desire to go to America. I'm hoping that your wish might be the same as mine in that regard."

Eleanore could hardly breathe. It was her every prayer answered, her every dream come true. In all the times when she'd felt torn between America and the children, she'd never even considered that such an opportunity as this might cross her path. She had no trouble being completely honest with Mr. Barrington. "I'm honored that you would ask me, sir. And I could not possibly turn down such a grand offer. It's true that I have dreamed of it, for reasons I consider personal. But I've come to dread the day I would leave, not wanting to be separated from the children."

He smiled slightly. "Then it would work out nicely. Of course, I will see that your every need is met. There is only one problem, as far as I can see."

"What is that, sir?"

"Some might not consider it appropriate for us to be traveling together in such a way, even though we will have others with us. I'm not a man to set much regard on what others may think, which makes that the least of my concerns. However, I believe there are a number of reasons why it would be most advantageous in every respect if we were to be married."

Eleanore sucked in her breath. Surely she had misunderstood, or misheard. The only other possibility was that he

suffered from some degree of madness. Through heart-pounding
silence she countered his fervid gaze, waiting for him to offer
some kind of explanation. When he didn't, she asked, "Did I
hear you correctly, Mr. Barrington?"

"If you heard me say that we should be married, then you
heard me correctly."

"Then surely you jest, sir."

"If you think I would make light of such a thing, then you
do not know me at all."

"That is precisely correct. I do *not* know you at all." Her
voice sounded far more agitated than she'd intended. "Neither
do you know enough about me to make me believe that this
proposal has any validity, that it has anything to do with the
purpose of marriage."

The silence that followed her little outburst made her
wonder whether he would be angry or reprimand her for
speaking so boldly. But his countenance was calm; she could
almost believe he'd expected her to protest. But what woman
wouldn't protest? In all practicality, he was old enough to be her
father. But more importantly, they shared no degree of the relationship that she had always believed should preclude marriage.
When he spoke, his voice was kind but firm. "Miss Layne,
please allow me to explain myself, and then you are certainly
entitled to accept or decline my offer. Although I would ask you
to take some time to think about it and not make a decision too
hastily."

She swallowed hard. "Of course."

"First of all, I would like to tell you what I know about you
that enforces the validity of my proposal. You know how to work,
and you do not expect something for nothing. You find happiness
and pleasure in life, no matter what a day might entail. You have a
passion for the literary arts that is much like my own. You believe
in God, and you pray. You live by your instincts, and you honor
your feelings and beliefs. You have integrity and dignity. Your

reasons for wanting to go to America echo my own in a way that is almost eerie, Miss Layne. And most important of all, you are a better mother to my children than their own mother ever was. I'm asking you to marry me because I believe we are compatible at the deepest roots of ourselves. I believe we can follow the same dream and find fulfillment and contentment in the life we can create together." He let out a deep sigh. "Or if you prefer to keep the arrangement simple . . . I need a mother for my children, and you want to go to America. We are in a position to help each other, Miss Layne."

While Eleanore couldn't help but be impressed by his observations of her—and deeply complimented by his regard—she felt the need to point out, "It certainly has all the makings of a practical arrangement, Mr. Barrington. But what of love?"

He didn't look ruffled by the question; he seemed to have anticipated it. "Miss Layne, I don't pretend to be any more or less than I am. I readily admit that I am not necessarily prone to tender emotions or sensitivity. I believe that being content and fulfilled in a relationship is far more important than the romantic, simpering notions that bring two people together and more often than not leave devastation in their wake. I have yet to see a successful marriage based on two people falling in love. That kind of love is like chaff, Miss Layne." Something hard showed in his eyes; his voice became tight. "It blows away with a change in the wind. And I have no use for it. If you decide to marry me, I can promise you respect and total commitment. I am not, nor will I ever be, a philandering man. I will commit myself to you, body and soul. I will give you anything you ask of me; anything—for the asking, so long as it is in my power to give." As he paused methodically, his eyes hardened further. "However, love is not part of the deal. Hold no delusions on that count. I will give you a good life, wherever that life may take us. I will protect, honor, and defend you. I will provide for your every need and whim. A thousand women would envy your position right now."

While she tried not to be appalled by such arrogance, she couldn't hold back the urge to say, "Then why are you not proposing to one of *them?*"

He looked surprised. Was it her question or the audacity of it that took him off guard? He stated firmly, "I have no interest in a simpering female who sees in me nothing but the means for wealth and the opportunity for new adventure."

"Yet you just made those points very clear in your proposal, Mr. Barrington."

"Only because I know you're the kind of woman who would be reluctant to accept a proposal of marriage based only on such things."

He *did* know her. Eleanore felt unnerved by his insight and perception but didn't have time to think about it before he continued, "Now, as long as we're taking a practical approach, allow me to point out some things that you might not have considered. What do you think the likelihood might be of a woman in your position to receive *any* proposal of marriage, let alone one based on *love?* How many eligible men do you come in contact with, Miss Layne? While you repeatedly devour such books as those penned by Jane Austen, do you truly believe that such romantic endings really exist in your limited world? *If* you were given the opportunity for marriage, it would most likely be among your own class, and you would spend your life continuing to do what you do now: work for others. The dimensions of our society, and the need for survival in it, may not be fair or equitable, but they exist nevertheless. I'm offering to care for you in every way. I can assure you that in spite of your charm and beauty, Miss Layne, you will *not* receive any such offer again."

"How can you possibly know the path of my future, Mr. Barrington?"

"I'm no prophet, Miss Layne. But I have spent nearly forty years watching servants come and go, but mostly they stay and stay, because that's the fact of their lives. The ones who left here chasing after romantic love usually came back brokenhearted and the worse for it."

Eleanore felt an inner trembling overtake her as his words began to settle in and make sense—far too much sense. He was right, and she wanted to hate him for it. He was offering her the chance of a lifetime. For the first time ever she looked at him as a man, not her employer or the father of the children in her care. He was undoubtedly attractive, but she didn't feel attracted. Her stomach tightened as she considered aspects that she knew were a part of marriage. She couldn't possibly consider marrying a man without asking herself if she was prepared to be a wife to him in every respect. Could she share this man's bed, have his children? She knew little about the actuality of such things. But she did know that the relationship between a husband and wife was a part of human existence, and no human adult could be unaware of that or ignore it. But thus far it had been ignored in this conversation. Was it simply to be taken for granted but never discussed? He was asking her to be his wife, not his mistress. What he offered was noble and sanctioned by God. But could she go through with it? She almost felt angry with herself to realize how deeply she was considering it. He'd offered her time to think about it, and she hadn't even left the room.

She wondered if he *was* a prophet, or at least capable of reading her mind, when he said, "You once told me that you would like children of your own. Would you prefer to see them born and raised as part of a serving class? Or born and raised Americans, where there is no distinction of class? Would you want to wonder if your children might have their simplest needs met, or be assured that they would always be cared for in the best possible way?"

Eleanore drew in a ragged breath. There. He'd said it. He intended for this to be a marriage in every respect, for them to have children together. And again he was right. She had always been observant of the world around her and the people in it. She'd seen much evidence of suffering and poverty. Those who served in the Barrington household and worked the farms on his estate were treated fairly and never went without. It wasn't always the case with others of her class, and she knew it. And if he was leaving and selling his property, would she have any control over her life while in the employment of someone else? She wanted to scream and curse at him for making his offer so neat and convenient in every respect. She wondered how long he had pondered the presentation of his case in order to leave no room for a rebuttal, and no sensible reason for refusing. Still, she *did* need to think about it.

She stated with the same firmness he had used with her, "It seems you've thought of everything, Mr. Barrington. If I don't accept your proposal, what will you do?"

"I don't know. I'll consider that once I have your decision."

Eleanore quickly contemplated the implications of their conversation and urged herself to take advantage of this opportunity. In spite of his declaration that she could never expect him to love her, she couldn't help feeling disappointed on that count. In that moment she certainly had no comprehension of ever loving *him*, but the very idea of sharing a lifetime—and children—with a man, and having no love between them, left her empty somehow. Could she live each day of her life with that one element missing? He'd said that he'd never seen a successful marriage based on that kind of love, but *she* had. Her parents had loved each other deeply, and that love was instilled into the deepest part of her spirit. She wanted to tell him, but at the same time she didn't want to expose such feelings to have him mock or discredit them. Instead she asked, "Did you love her?" He looked confused, and she clarified. "Did you love Mrs. Barrington?"

For the first time since she'd entered the room, he was visibly agitated. "She's gone. That's irrelevant."

"You're asking me to be your wife, yet you refuse to answer a simple question in regard to yourself. What am I to make of that?"

Their eyes met intently, and Eleanore realized that his answer—and his attitude—could have great bearing on her decision. She'd seen him take heed to her suggestions regarding his relationship with his children. She believed him to be humble and teachable—at least in relation to being a father. If he couldn't be that way with his wife, then she didn't want to be in that position. She almost wanted him to snap at her and refuse to answer the question. It would give her the just cause she wanted in order to disregard his proposition. No matter what kind of life he offered, if they couldn't communicate at a level that was honest and real, she could never live with him day in and day out.

In response to his stunned expression, she repeated the question, "Did you love her?"

Eleanore's heart quickened for different reasons when she saw stark sorrow in his eyes. She expected some confession of how his love for her had been so deep that he could never love again. Instead he said in a quiet voice, "No." He inhaled sharply. "But I trusted her."

Eleanore imitated his sharp breath as the underlying message struck her. She hoped she wouldn't regret asking, "And she broke that trust?"

She saw him swallow. "You know enough about her behavior as a mother to know the answer to that question."

"I know what kind of mother she was. I'm asking about her being your wife."

She knew he didn't want to answer, but he said, "Yes, she did." He stood up as if to end the conversation. "Take some time to think about it. Will two days be sufficient, or do you need more?"

She stood as well. "That will be fine. I'll let you know in two days." She paused and asked, "Have you discussed this with anyone else?"

"No," he said. "No one. Until you've made a decision, it will be left between the two of us."

"Thank you."

"Thank you for your time, Miss Layne."

She nodded toward him and left the room, just as she had more than a hundred times before, as if a marriage proposal were no different than any other conversation they'd had over his desk.

Eleanore was grateful to leave the children in Lizzie's care for the rest of the evening. She felt such a need for fresh air that she feared suffocation if she didn't get it. Once outside, she ran to a secluded spot in the gardens where she sat on the ground. Allowing herself to fully grasp the implications of the conversation, her chest constricted, and she heaved for breath. *James Barrington had proposed marriage!* Her heart pounded, and her insides trembled. It was ludicrous! Wasn't it? How could she accept such an offer? But how could she turn it down? His defense of the arrangement went round and round in her mind while she prayed in silence to be guided in the path of her life. No decision she had ever made, or would yet make, would influence her life so greatly—one way or the other.

She forced herself to her senses and fought for enough composure to go into the house for supper. Most of the servants were gathered for the usual meal when Mrs. Bixby announced that Mr. Barrington was making plans to sell the estate and move to America. She became mildly emotional as she repeated to the staff, who were all obviously concerned, that he'd assured her he wouldn't sell the estate to anyone who would not treat fairly those entrusted to his care. The conversation turned naturally to speculations over Mr. Barrington's reasons for going. Many felt sure that the memories of the house were difficult for him with his wife gone. They talked as if the two of them had shared a deep and abiding love. Eleanore considered all she knew from her perspective. And just this evening he'd admitted to struggling with memories, but he'd also said he hadn't loved his wife.

Eleanore was drawn from her thoughts when one of the maids said, "Do you think Mr. Barrington will ever remarry?"

"I should hope so," Mrs. Bixby said. "He's far too young to spend the rest of his life alone, bless his soul."

Eleanore couldn't resist asking, "And what kind of woman do you think he might choose?"

She then listened to their speculations while her insides knotted tightly, and she regretted the attempt to ease her curiosity. Not one of them surmised that the enigmatic Mr. Barrington would choose a seventeen-year-old governess to be his second wife. She was surprised, however, to hear the conversation turn to giggling conjectures from the women on what it might be like to marry such a fine man. It became clearly evident that every woman in the room would fall at his feet if given such an offer as she had been given. While Eleanore wondered what was wrong with her that she couldn't share their enthusiasm, she recalled his saying, *I have no interest in a simpering female who sees in me nothing but the means for wealth and the opportunity for new adventure.* She could see now what he'd meant, but she could also see something else. They were openly discussing how handsome and virile he was, a thought that had never once crossed Eleanore's mind during all the times she'd encountered him. She wondered if the timing of the conversation might be God's way of giving her some added perspective to consider. Or perhaps it was just coincidence. Either way, she had far too much to consider as she lay in bed that night, staring at the ceiling, holding the bedcovers tightly in her fists while the conversation with Mr. Barrington repeated over and over in her mind, like some kind of eerie dream. Logically assessing everything he'd said, she could only think of one reason to turn down his offer. His bold declaration of having no interest in love left an apprehensive emptiness inside of her. Could she spend her life craving love and never being satisfied? On the other hand, if she did, in spite of all odds, fall in love and marry for that reason, how much meaning might it have amidst the inevitable challenges of the life she was destined to live? And what if another opportunity to marry never came at all? As always, when a difficult situation arose, Eleanore asked herself what her mother might advise. Memories of her mother's wisdom answered the question clearly. *Always honor your deepest feelings, my precious. They will guide you in the path God wishes you to follow.* Eleanore then recalled her mother's lengthy explanations of how important it was to know that a choice was made according to such feelings. Then, no matter how hard it became, she would know she had taken that path for the right reason. *God does not always guide us along the easiest path, but we must follow the right one.*

With her mother's advice close to her heart, Eleanore prayed silently, on and on, for God to guide her path. Somewhere in the middle of the night she finally found the courage to audibly ask the question. Perhaps she feared that letting it come into the open might make it too real. "Please God," she muttered, her eyes squeezed tightly shut, "tell me, give me an answer. Would you have me marry this man? Is this the right path for me?" The thought that occurred to her felt strange, and she tried to ignore it, but an hour later—when it was the only thought that wouldn't leave her mind—she had to stop and hear it fully. *You already know the answer. Honor your deepest feelings.*

"What *are* my deepest feelings?" she asked aloud, hoping in her heart that she wasn't deluding herself to believe that God Almighty would actually take the time to listen to her, in her own insignificance in this vast world, and give an answer with consideration to her deepest wishes and hopes.

Eleanore fell asleep with the question still hovering in her mind. Her first habitual thought when she awoke was to wonder what she might do with the children today. She didn't even recall the dilemma she'd gone to sleep with, or the turmoil of the previous day, until after the idea came to her mind, seemingly out of nowhere, of seeing herself as Mrs. James Edward Barrington. She gasped from the impression, then moaned when she realized that the idea was not uncomfortable or negative in any way. The very notion of being his wife had never occurred to her prior to last evening, and now it seemed to have settled into her every cell with perfect ease, as if it were as natural as the rising and setting of the sun.

"Dear God, help me," she murmured, knowing that He had. And somehow she knew that God would give her contentment and security enough to compensate for the wishes she had that would never be fulfilled. A flow of tears accompanied her lengthy prayer of gratitude for the answers and guidance she'd been given, and she pleaded for the strength and courage she would need to embark upon this journey.

Chapter Five
THE AGREEMENT

Eleanore felt as if she were sleepwalking. The normal routine of preparing for the day and going to the kitchen for breakfast became dreamlike as she considered all that had changed since she'd last gone through these normal motions of routine living. She quietly observed both the familiarity of the people who were a part of her life and the tiny community of this household in which they lived and worked. Trying to imagine herself as the wife of James Barrington put a knot in her stomach. How could she ever do it? She began to doubt the reasoning behind her decision until she recalled the undeniable feelings that had accompanied her knowledge of what she needed to do.

Being with the children took on new meaning for Eleanore. More than once during the day she had to fight back tears to think of officially taking on the role of stepmother and maintaining it for a lifetime. In that respect, her peace deepened. She had trouble reconciling herself as the wife of James Barrington, but she had no trouble with being a mother to David and Iris. To be given such a privilege felt miraculous, if only she didn't have to contend with everything else that would be required of her to make such a miracle happen.

"Is something on your mind?" Lizzie asked, bringing her to the realization that her friend had been talking to her over lunch in the nursery. The children had finished eating and were playing nearby.

Eleanore couldn't lie, but wasn't ready to discuss it yet. "Actually yes, but . . . we'll need to talk later."

Lizzie looked concerned but said nothing more. They would never discuss private matters in front of the children, but Lizzie had no idea that Eleanore first needed to speak with Mr. Barrington before she could talk about the situation to anyone else.

The perpetrator of her turmoil checked in on his children in the middle of the afternoon. After the usual greetings had been exchanged, he looked directly at her. "And how are you today, Miss Layne?"

She turned away, unable to look at him. "I'm well, Mr. Barrington, and you?"

"Quite well, thank you. Although, I dare say you seem a bit . . . distracted."

She tossed him a sharp glance, noting the mild humor in his eyes.

"I was thinking the same thing," Lizzie said, and Eleanore resisted glaring at her.

"Perhaps some fresh air would do me good," Eleanore said and left the room. Once outside she breathed deeply and walked slowly while she attempted to merge James Barrington, the man, with the lord of the manor and her employer. She found it difficult, if not impossible, to adjust the two in her mind. The man she had come to know was, by all appearances, kind and decent. If not for the conversation she'd overheard long ago with his first wife, she might have had no reservations in regard to his character. But she *had* overheard it. In spite of the evidence she'd gained concerning Mrs. Barrington's shortcomings as a mother, she had no idea of their marriage relationship beyond his minimal confession related to love and trust. But that had been cryptic, to say the least. She wished that she understood better the situation between him and Caroline Barrington, if only to find peace over the incongruities in her mind. Still, she couldn't deny that even given such concerns, her decision was clear and firm.

Considering the changes this marriage would bring into her own life, she had trouble mentally merging herself from serving in this household to being Mrs. Barrington. Being raised to the level of governess had been a challenge, but this . . . She couldn't even imagine. Of course, they would be going to America. She wouldn't be staying here where she had worked for so long. But the weeks between now and then could be difficult. She felt disconcerted and uncomfortable but not enough to dispel the strength of what she knew to be right. And now that she did know, she had to give him her answer and be done with it. She knew he'd not be expecting to hear from her until tomorrow, but she couldn't wait that long. She knew it was right, but she couldn't deny that she also felt afraid. She wanted the next step behind her so that she could stop dreading it. And then perhaps she could get a better idea of what to expect so that she could become accustomed to the dramatic changes in the path that lay ahead.

Eleanore was relieved to go back inside and find that Mr. Barrington was no longer with the children. Lizzie asked if she was all right, and she simply said that she was. Late in the afternoon, as soon as her time with the children was done, Eleanore had to ask three servants before she discovered that Mr. Barrington had gone riding. She paced an upstairs hall where she could see the stables from the window. Her anxiety tightened when she saw him ride in, and a few minutes later he walked toward the house. Knowing his office was his most common place of respite, she waited a few minutes, then went downstairs and knocked at the door, relieved to hear him call, "Yes." She wanted to have this over.

She expected to find him reading, as he often was, but he was standing at the window, his forearm resting above his head against the window frame. He made no effort to see who was there, and looked startled when she said, "Forgive me for disturbing you, Mr. Barrington."

He turned toward her abruptly. "Miss Layne," he said. "You're not disturbing me. Would you like to sit down?"

"No, thank you, sir." She looked at the floor. Combined with the thought of becoming his wife, looking at him had suddenly become difficult. She couldn't deny his handsome face and the charisma of his stature. But she felt absolutely no attraction to him whatsoever. Considering what she'd heard the maids saying about him the previous evening, she wondered again what might be wrong with her in not being able to share their way of thinking.

"What do you need?" he asked. "Is there a problem with one of the children?"

"No, of course not," she said. "They were delightful today, as always. They are counting on your finishing that story with them after supper."

"Of course," he said. Then there was silence, and she knew she had to say what she'd come to say.

Drawing courage, Eleanore lifted her head so that she could meet his eyes. She didn't want him to think that she had any hesitance or doubt in her answer. "I've come to give you my decision, sir," she said.

He looked surprised; his brow furrowed in concern. She wondered how disappointed he might be if she refused him. Would it deeply trouble him? Or would he quickly pass it over and move on? She told herself it didn't matter. She was more concerned with what level of relief he might feel at her acceptance. She reminded herself not to have expectations. She might never know how much or little this marriage meant to him. And perhaps it was best she didn't.

"And how long will you keep me in suspense, Miss Layne?" he asked, and she felt embarrassed to realize the length of her silence.

"Forgive me," she said again. "I wish to accept your proposal, Mr. Barrington." She saw him draw a deep breath, as if he'd been holding it. There was no denying the flicker of relief in his eyes, and she was grateful for it. She hurried to add, "I am honored that you would give me this opportunity, and I will do my best to be an acceptable mother to your children."

"*Our* children," he corrected, his voice gentle. She didn't know if he meant that she would officially become a mother to David and Iris, or if he wanted to remind her that they would have children together. Both perhaps.

"Our children," she repeated. Then asked, "Do you have specific plans that I should be aware of, sir?"

"I will announce our engagement right away. I would like to leave the country in approximately one month, and I want to be married before we leave. I will post the banns on Sunday; we should be able to marry the week before our departure. You'll be fitted for a new wardrobe in the next few days so that it can be ready in time. In addition, I would like you to choose one of the servant girls to accompany you to America."

"Why, sir?"

"I don't want you to be responsible for the children every minute of the day. We need someone to help watch out for them, and it should also be someone who can help with your needs, as well."

"*My* needs? I don't—"

"Miss Layne, listen very carefully. Once our engagement is announced there is only one thing that will remain the same for you in this household. You will continue to spend time with the children as you have been. You will need someone to work with you as a lady's maid, and as I said, that same person should also be able to help with the children. They're getting older and don't need constant attention, so it shouldn't be terribly difficult to balance both duties. As long as she meets those requirements, it's up to you to choose the right person. I'm assuming you would choose Lizzie, considering your present relationship. It should be someone you feel comfortable with and can trust. I'll leave that decision up to you. Mr. Higgins will be going with us, as well.

"I will let you work out the details of the wedding with Mrs. Bixby. She'll know what to do. It's your wedding, and you may have it any way you want. She will also help you pack and prepare for the journey. Do you have any other questions for me?"

"Not . . . at the moment," she said, so overwhelmed she almost felt heady.

"I'm available any time of day should you need to discuss anything at all."

"Thank you, sir," she said.

She turned to leave the room, and he said, "Miss Layne." She hesitated but kept her back to him. "If you have any reservations whatsoever, they should be addressed now. I want to know that you're absolutely certain this is what you want. Once I make the engagement public, I will consider the decision final. If you have any concerns or cause for hesitation, I need to know."

Eleanore swallowed carefully, wondering if he sensed that she *did* have concerns, though obviously not enough to keep her from marrying him. She appreciated his perception, and couldn't deny gratitude for an opportunity to address her feelings openly. But actually doing so would not be easy. Not certain such an opportunity would ever come again, she prodded her courage to the surface and turned to face him. "Do *you* have any concerns or reservations, sir?"

"Not beyond what I just mentioned. I don't want you to ever regret your decision, and once you've made it, I don't want you to back down."

"My decision is final, sir. And I know in my heart this is the right course for my life. I can't explain how I know; I just know."

She saw relief in his eyes and that barely perceptible smile that was typical of him. Then he said, "But?" She felt confused, and he clarified, "Your decision is final and you know it's right, but . . ." He motioned with his hand for her to finish.

"May I be frank with you, sir?"

"I would not want my fiancée to be any other way, Miss Layne. Please sit down and talk to me." Eleanore took her usual seat across the desk from him. For a moment she was taken back to their first interview in this room. She imagined him asking about her goals and aspirations for the future, and she wondered how it might have gone from there if she'd said, *I will be marrying you and bearing your children.* The irony quickened her heart while she found herself staring at him, attempting to grasp the reality that she *was* his fiancée, that she *would* marry him and bear his children. The silence grew long but surprisingly not uncomfortable. She sensed him accepting the change between them, just as she was, and the gentle kindness in his eyes made it easier to think of saying what she needed to say.

"Your concerns?" he said to spur the conversation on.

Eleanore looked down at her hands clasped in her lap. She cleared her throat. "You know, of course, that I had a habit of sneaking into the library at night to read from the Bible."

"Yes," he drawled.

"Some weeks before Mrs. Barrington died, I . . . was in there when . . . the two of you came in and . . . you were arguing." She looked up enough to gauge his reaction. He winced slightly as if something painful had pricked him. His face tightened, and the hollow line of his cheek became more prominent. She clearly saw David in his face.

"I see," he said.

"Obviously I could not have made myself known, but I never said a word to anyone about what I overheard. Not a word."

He looked at her firmly, but she saw no anger in his eyes. Concern, perhaps. "And what exactly did you overhear, Miss Layne?"

"Is that relevant?"

"Apparently. You're the one who brought it up."

"It's not so much the things that were said, Mr. Barrington, as the indication of your relationship with her. I admit to being startled by what I heard. Prior to that time I'd always had the impression from things the servants said that the two of you shared a loving marriage." He lifted his brows, and she went on. "I can assure you that when I heard what I did, I never would have imagined myself ever being in the position I'm in now. I'm not the kind of person to jump to conclusions or pass judgment over circumstances I know nothing about. But if I'm going to be your wife, I would like to understand the cause for such animosity. Whatever our reasons for marrying may be, Mr. Barrington, I would never want such discord between us."

"Rest assured, we are in complete agreement on that, Miss Layne. If I had even the slightest inkling that you were anything like my deceased wife, I most certainly would not have proposed marriage."

He sighed and looked the other way, giving her a perfect view of his profile. She took notice of his appearance as she never had before. His chin and nose were strong but not overly prominent. His cheekbones were firm. His hair looked nearly black in this light. Iris had his lips, and her nose was shaped exactly the same. He briefly rubbed a hand over his face and left his fingers against his chin. She observed, "You're not comfortable talking about her."

"No, I'm not," he admitted readily. "But I certainly cannot dispute your concerns, or your right to know. I would like to be able to say that her bad behavior excused mine. But truthfully, I regret the way I treated her at times, in spite of the circumstances."

Eleanore desperately wanted to ask what those circumstances might have been. No matter how she tried, she couldn't forget hearing him say, *If children are such a burden to you, my dear, I wonder you don't figure out what causes them and put a stop to it.* A part of her wanted to repeat what she'd heard and ask him to explain why he would have spoken words so cruel, but something deeper cautioned her to keep her concerns vague. She wanted to hear an explanation that was genuine, not an attempt to smooth over a particular comment.

"So, tell me, Miss Layne, what exactly *did* the servants say about my marriage?"

She shrugged and looked down. "I just . . . got an overall impression that . . . the two of you cared very much for each other; that you were happy together."

He made a noise of mild disgust. "It would seem that people in this house only choose to see what they want to see, or that I'm a much better actor than I thought I was."

Eleanore felt the need for clarification. "Are you saying, then, that the marriage was not good?"

"I should think that would be obvious from whatever you overheard, Miss Layne. Mrs. Barrington and I had not had a congenial conversation in years. I never cared what the servants thought and made no effort to hide the way I felt. My only concern was for the children. I wanted them to feel secure. But they were far too sharp to miss the truth, I'm certain."

"After working with the children, it's easy for me to understand why you were displeased with her behavior as a mother."

"Disgusted would be more accurate," he said and leaned his forearms on the desk. "Miss Layne, you *do* have a right to know about the situation in my first marriage, but let me make it perfectly clear that I am *only* telling you this because you just agreed to be my wife. What I'm about to tell you will not go beyond the two of us. Do I have your word?"

"Of course."

"I'm not going to give you details of the problems; she's gone and those things are irrelevant. But my greatest source of anger was simply the fact that the baby who died with her was not mine." Eleanore sucked in her breath and held it. "I had not shared a bed with her since prior to Iris's birth."

Eleanore forced her breath out slowly. Everything now made perfect sense. His anger in the library and the things he'd said now seemed more than justified. "I had no idea."

"No one did. Thankfully, she was discreet. The children have enough to contend with in the way she treated them; they don't need to know she was unfaithful." His face twitched, and his lips tightened as he looked down.

"I don't know what to say."

"There's nothing to say, Miss Layne." He met her eyes firmly. "I just want you to know that the evidence I've seen of your integrity has immeasurable value to me. More than anything else, I need this marriage to be based in complete honesty. Her being unfaithful didn't hurt nearly so much as the lies she told me to cover it up. Promise me that you will never be anything less than completely honest."

"Yes, of course. And might I expect the same in return?"

"Yes, Miss Layne. I will never expect anything more or less from you than I myself am willing to give."

"Can you believe me when I promise to always be honest?" she asked, hoping to prove a point.

He countered it quickly. "Can you believe *me?*"

She evaded his question as easily as he'd evaded hers. "You just admitted to being a very good actor. Should that concern me?"

He drew a loud breath. "You have never given me any reason to believe you are not trustworthy. I would hope you have seen the same in me. In spite of my history with Mrs. Barrington, I do my best to take the attitude that a person should be trusted until proven otherwise."

"I would agree," she said. "Then I suppose we will simply have to trust each other."

"Yes, we certainly will," he said. Silence preceded him adding, "Do you have any other concerns that we've not yet addressed?"

"No, sir," she said and stood.

"Thank you for your candor, Miss Layne."

"And yours."

"No matter how difficult something might be to address, I would far prefer talking it over rather than silently wondering and making incorrect assumptions."

"Of course," she said, marveling that her respect for him had deepened steadily for as long as she had been interacting with him. And their most recent conversations had left her feeling that this intense respect and admiration she felt toward him could surely compensate a great deal for the inevitable lack of love.

Once beyond his office, Eleanore hurried outside, needing a brisk stroll through the gardens to clear her head and allow it to catch up to all she had just learned—and committed to. Finally, she couldn't keep from crying as the full reality took hold. She knew it was right; she absolutely knew. But that didn't make her any less terrified or overwhelmed. She now better understood this man she was going to marry, and her heart ached on his behalf. Never in all her speculations on the source of contention between him and his wife had she considered such an atrocity. As she walked, she prayed for Mr. Barrington, for the children, and for herself—that she might be an instrument in God's hands to help this family heal from the wounds left behind by Caroline Barrington's shameful behavior.

On her way back to the house, Eleanore was surprised to see Lizzie approaching. "I thought I'd find you here," she said.

"Where are the children?" she asked, once they were standing face-to-face.

"With their father. He said that I should talk to you."

"Did he?" she asked, not entirely surprised.

"He said that he knew you and I were close and that it might be good if we had a long talk." Lizzie sounded suspicious. Eleanore could only look at the ground. "I didn't bother to mention to him that his concern seemed just a wee bit beyond his place as our employer. But I'm guessing he knows something I don't, perhaps the same something that's had you . . . how did he say it earlier? Distracted?"

Eleanore turned back the way she'd come and started walking. Lizzie walked beside her. They'd only taken a few steps when Lizzie said, "Whatever it is, just tell me and get it over with."

"Mr. Barrington has informed me that he's selling the estate and moving to America."

"Then it's true?" Lizzie asked.

"It is."

"So, you're understandably upset about having the children leave," she said. "I'm not looking forward to that myself. And then we'll have to adjust to a new employer and—"

"That's not the problem, Lizzie," Eleanore interrupted, and she stopped walking so they were facing each other again. Feeling a little weak she took Lizzie's arm and guided her to a nearby bench where they sat side by side. "He's asked me to go with him."

Lizzie gasped, then laughed, then cried, all in the space of a minute. "Oh, that's wonderful!" she said, wiping at her face. "I mean . . . wonderful for you. I'll miss you dreadfully, but—"

"Lizzie," Eleanore interrupted again, "if you had the chance to go to America, would you want to go?"

"Oh, it would be grand!" she said with enthusiasm.

"It would mean never coming back here."

"I've got no one here I'd miss any more than you do. But . . . what has this got to do with me?"

Eleanore mustered some enthusiasm for this aspect of the arrangement in order to approach the topic more comfortably. "What if you had the opportunity to go to America in return for serving as a lady's maid to some extent, and also helping with the children?"

Eleanore could see Lizzie's mind working. "Did he ask you to ask me?"

"He told me I could bring someone to fill those duties, anyone I chose. He did mention your name. I believe I mentioned when he took you on as the nanny that you'd had some lady's maid experience."

"He certainly trusts your judgment."

"Yes, it seems he does."

"Don't tell me. Let me guess. He's getting married again. He needs help with the children *and* someone to help care for the new Mrs. Barrington."

"Yes, that's true."

"I thought so!" Lizzie said eagerly. Then with dismay she added, "I'm qualified, but I'm not certain I want to work with this woman, whoever she might be."

Eleanore took a deep breath. This was the hard part. "It could be difficult," she said, "to suddenly be working for someone who has always worked by your side. But I don't know how I could ever do it without you."

Lizzie's mouth came open but no sound came out. Her brow furrowed; her eyes narrowed. Eleanore reversed the conversation and said, "Don't tell me. Let me guess. There's only one possibility that could make sense, but you can't believe it's possible because it doesn't make sense at all for a man like James Barrington to propose marriage to his governess."

Lizzie gasped. Then there was silence. She caught her breath and then sighed hugely before she was able to utter, "Well, bless my soul and knock my feet out from under me. Who'd have dreamed?"

"Indeed."

She let out a burst of laughter. "It's the most wonderful thing I've ever heard. He's a good man, you know."

"Yes, I know."

"And to think that he's fallen in love with you and—"

"No, Lizzie." Eleanore took her hand. "This is a marriage of practicality and convenience. He made it very clear that love would have no place in it."

"I see." Lizzie sounded less enthused. She knew better than anyone that Eleanore dreamed of finding the kind of love her parents had shared.

"Beyond that he's offering everything a woman could ever dream of. I will make the most of it, and I will not complain.

Better this than marrying into poverty, or never marrying at all."
Lizzie looked down, and Eleanore hurried to add, "I didn't mean
anything by that. I just—"

"I understand, my dear. It's no secret that if I'd had my way
I'd have married. I would have loved to have my own children.
But opportunities can be scarce. And you would be a fool to
turn down this one. I just have to ask . . . if you're sure. No
matter how grand his offer might be, you mustn't do it if you
don't know that—"

"I *do* know, Lizzie."

"Then all will be well." Lizzie touched Eleanore's face, much
as her mother might have, and they embraced.

"You'll go with me, then? Won't you?"

"Of course!" Lizzie said. "How could I not?"

They talked a while longer, and Eleanore appreciated Lizzie's
frank way of helping put her decision into perspective. Having
Lizzie by her side through the forthcoming challenges would
certainly make them easier to face. Eleanore expressed her
concern about Lizzie being expected to act as a servant, while
Eleanore was being promoted to lady of the house. But Lizzie
just laughed and said she couldn't be more delighted, and that
there was no one she would rather work with. And they agreed
that no matter what changes took place, they would always be
friends. Considering that Lizzie was actually old enough to be
her mother, and knowing the depth of friendship they shared, it
made marrying a man near Lizzie's age seem a little less strange.

As they were walking into the house, Eleanore felt panicked
to recall Mr. Barrington saying he would announce the engagement soon. She wondered exactly what that would entail and felt
decidedly nervous. Lizzie went upstairs to check on the children,
and Eleanore went into the kitchen to find only Miss Gibbs
there. She was one of the few people in the household that
Eleanore shared any kind of personal rapport with, and she occasionally helped her a bit here and there just for the opportunity

to converse. The simple task of scrubbing a stockpot felt comfortable and allowed her mind to settle somewhat.

"So how are the little darlings?" Miss Gibbs asked.

"They're well. They really are good children. I've become very attached to them."

Miss Gibbs looked concerned and said, "That could be a problem if Mr. Barrington truly is planning to take them to America."

"I understand that he is," Eleanore said. "He's told me himself that he's firm on leaving."

"Mercy me," the cook said, sounding mildly upset. "I just can't imagine what it will be like to have all of this change hands, to be working for someone else."

Eleanore swallowed carefully and looked down. "Yes, it would seem some big changes are in the wind. I—"

She halted when Mrs. Bixby rushed into the kitchen, straight toward Miss Gibbs, agitated and concerned. "Oh good, you're here," she said. "Mr. Barrington has just informed me that he's having a guest for dinner and we're to set the table for two."

Miss Gibbs wiped her hands on her apron, asking with excitement, "Is it a lady?"

"I believe it is," Mrs. Bixby said.

"Oh, my." The cook put her hands to her face. "Perhaps he's found someone, bless his soul."

Eleanore sat down at the nearby worktable and pressed her head into her hands, listening while her stomach tightened. Should she tell them? How could she when she felt incapable of even speaking?

"Perhaps his time out of the house hasn't been all about hunting and lounging at the gentlemen's club," Mrs. Bixby said. "I wonder if—"

She stopped when a male voice broke in. "Excuse me," Mr. Barrington said, and they all looked toward him as he stood in the doorway. Eleanore wondered how much he might have overheard, although the other women were quite some distance from where he stood. His eyes focused on Eleanore just before he said, "Miss Layne. I'm glad I found you. You will be dining with me this evening. I'm certain you can figure out when and where that would take place."

"Yes, of course, Mr. Barrington," she said. He smiled subtly and left the room.

Eleanore drew courage and turned to look at the other women, not surprised by their visible astonishment. In fact, they looked almost humorous with their mouths hanging open. Miss Gibbs was the first to speak. "What is *this?* Have you been keeping secrets?"

Eleanore cleared her throat and turned away, pressing her hands flat on the table to keep from wringing them. "It only came up yesterday, and we . . . agreed not to say anything until . . . the arrangement was . . . decided upon and . . ."

"*What* arrangement?" Mrs. Bixby gently prodded while she and Miss Gibbs stared at her, aghast.

Eleanore decided to work into this slowly. "Mr. Barrington has asked me to go to America with him. He wants me to help care for the children . . . permanently."

"America?" Mrs. Bixby echoed, sounding dismayed. "You're . . . leaving, then?"

"I am," she said.

"What a wonderful opportunity for you, dear," Miss Gibbs said, but she sounded sad. Or was it concerned?

Mrs. Bixby asked, "What do you mean by permanently, dear?"

She cleared her throat again and just said it. "He's asked me to marry him."

Both women fell onto chairs and stared as if she'd sprouted wings. Miss Gibbs was the first to speak. "I hope you had the good sense to accept."

"Yes, I have," she said. "But no one else knows yet except Lizzie. Please don't say anything until . . . he announces it."

"Well, you'll be having supper with him," Mrs. Bixby said. "That will have the whole house talking. You should be changing into something nicer." She sounded pleased and excited. "This is wonderful news, dear. You'll soon be the lady of the house."

"I'm not sure I *want* to be the lady of the house," Eleanore admitted. "I don't think it's in me to be the one giving orders."

"It's right and proper, and you mustn't concern yourself with that."

"I think it's marvelous," Miss Gibbs said, but Eleanore found it difficult to agree.

Mrs. Bixby insisted Eleanore go upstairs to freshen up and change for supper. She put on a dress she normally saved for Sundays, wondering about the new wardrobe she would be acquiring. That thought—along with a hundred others—left her frightened and uncertain. She took her hair down, smoothed it carefully and put it back up, winding the long braid into a circle at the back of her head, and pinning it into place. Studying her reflection, she tried to imagine herself as Mrs. James Barrington. He was titled, for the love of heaven! She was grateful that he brought no attention to that fact and preferred to avoid it. Still, what did that mean in relation to her marrying him? Once they got to America it would mean nothing. She tried to focus on this fulfillment of her deepest wish, rather than her anxiety over the means that would make it happen.

Chapter Six

THE FUTURE
MRS. BARRINGTON

Eleanore had never felt so nervous in her life as when she approached the door to the formal dining room. Even telling him earlier that she would accept his proposal had not unnerved her as much as now being alone with him, officially engaged. She took a deep breath and pressed her hands over the tremor in her stomach, willing it to settle. She uttered a brief, silent prayer before opening the door. She had only been in this room to clean it, but she'd forgotten its beauty and elegance. The man she was going to marry sat at one end of the long table, reading a newspaper, apparently relaxed and unruffled. An extra place was set just to his right. He looked up at the sound of the door and quickly folded the paper, tossing it onto an extra chair as he came to his feet.

"Miss Layne," he said, showing a hint of a smile as he stepped toward her. "How lovely you look this evening."

"Thank you, sir," she said. Then, for the first time since her father's death, a man touched her. He took her hand and lifted it to his lips. She watched with fascination as his lips came in contact with her fingers. Without letting go of her hand he met her eyes and said with mild alarm, "You're trembling, Miss Layne. Am I so frightening?"

"No, sir," she said, wishing he'd let go of her hand if only to make him less aware of her trembling. His eyes silently asked for an explanation, and she could only be grateful for the established code of honesty between them. In spite of the dramatic changes in the state of their relationship, she had become comfortable speaking candidly with him in regard to the children, which made it easier to say, "I'm simply unaccustomed to the situation. This is all very new and strange. I have no idea what to expect, or what might be expected of me. I don't want to embarrass you or—"

"That is not possible," he said with a perfect confidence she had difficulty sharing. "Come." He pressed her hand over his arm and put his over where it rested, as if to keep her from retracting it. "Let's talk about this."

He guided her to the table and helped her with a chair. Again, this was something she'd never experienced before. He sat down and smiled at her, but she glanced away, feeling timid and uncertain.

"Talk to me, Miss Layne," he said gently. "Tell me why you feel . . ." He stopped when the first course was brought into the room by maids she had worked with, shared servants' meals with. And they were now serving her.

"Thank you," Mr. Barrington said before they left the room, and Eleanore couldn't help but think how kind he was. Then without any prior notice he bowed his head and verbally thanked God for the food before them and asked a blessing upon it. She spoke her amen following his, and he began to eat. The beautiful dishes and varied pieces of silver left her intimidated. She'd washed and polished and stacked them neatly away, but she'd never dreamt of personally using them. Not certain what utensil to use first, she just watched him and followed his example. That eased her nerves slightly. Surely she could learn a great deal by simply following his lead.

She'd barely taken a careful sip of bisque when he said, "I believe you were going to tell me why . . ." Again a maid came in to interrupt him. He sighed, but his expression was more amused than annoyed as she placed a silver bowl of hot buns on the table and left the room.

Eleanore spoke her most prominent thought. "They're all whispering and speculating, you know."

"Are they?"

"Some of them take great pleasure in every possible opportunity to discuss what might be taking place in your life. They sit in the kitchen between duties and talk of things that have nothing to do with them, and much of it is grossly distorted because they have no idea what they're talking about." He said nothing, and she added, "Doesn't that bother you?"

"Should it? Servants gossip. I have no reason to care what they think."

"Well, now they're talking about *me*. They're wondering what on earth you're thinking."

He chuckled softly. "Are you questioning my judgment again, Miss Layne?"

"Perhaps," she admitted. "But whether or not *I* question it, I'm absolutely certain there are many in this household who will."

"Their opinions are irrelevant to me, Miss Layne."

"It's not so much their opinions that concern me, sir, as their behavior toward me. I have worked *with* these people for most of my life, and now I'm expected to have them working *for* me. To say that the situation is likely to be awkward would be a gross understatement, Mr. Barrington."

Before he responded, he paused methodically, something that she had come to realize was typical of him. He was clearly a man who weighed his words carefully. "I can understand why this would be a . . . challenge for you, Miss Layne. However, it won't be long before we leave for America, and we will be leaving all of this behind."

He reached across the corner of the table and took her hand. Eleanore looked at their clasped fingers, then at his face. She wished they could leave for America tomorrow, but that wouldn't happen until they were married, and she felt thoroughly unprepared for all that would happen between now and their departure.

"Of course," she said and forced a smile. She silently reminded herself of all that was important and good for her in this arrangement, and the list was long. She needed to keep this perspective, every hour of every day. It was all that would get her through the coming events.

While they ate, he encouraged her to maintain a comfortable relationship with the people she interacted with, and not worry too much about the changes. Although he did clarify that it was still right and appropriate that she should not hesitate to expect any of the servants to do as she asked of them, especially after they were married. With his point made, he steered the conversation toward her greatest passion. He asked her questions about the books she'd read that had left the deepest impressions on her. She avoided bringing up the book of scripture that had changed her life, but she became more relaxed as she talked of many other books that had moved and touched her. She was pleasantly surprised to learn that he too had a passion for books. She realized now that she had seen him reading many times but hadn't given it much thought. Now she knew they had read many of the same books and had much to talk about. He spoke of his passion for history and politics, and she enjoyed hearing him talk of them. By the end of their slowly eaten meal, Eleanore felt more at ease with him than she ever had, and the prospect of marrying him didn't feel quite so challenging. Just being able to share comfortable conversation with him soothed something inside her. If nothing else, they could grow old together reading side by side and talking of what they'd read.

When they had finished eating, he stood and helped her with her chair. He guided her hand over his arm and walked with her while they continued to talk. She felt the hint of a thrill when he brought her to the door of the library. The ironies of their past encounters here struck her as he opened it and motioned for her to go in. Once inside the door, she closed her eyes and inhaled deeply, as she always did.

"What is this?" he asked, and she opened her eyes to find him watching her.

"I love the smell of books," she said. "I could never come in here without just . . . smelling them."

His lips twitched with the hint of a smile, and he closed the door. He said nothing but sat down, making himself comfortable. Eleanore didn't know if he expected her to sit as well, but she far preferred to peruse the books. In fact, she reveled in the opportunity to look them over in better light than she ever had, and without the fear of being caught. After several minutes with no conversation, she stole a quick glance at him, only to find him watching her. She ignored his unnerving observation and focused instead on the books, paying attention to that little voice in her heart that might call out to one book in particular.

"You're welcome to read anything you like," he said.

"Thank you." Then a minute later she asked, "All of this will stay behind when we go to America?"

"There are a few favorites that will be going. We can purchase more books there."

"Do you think they're readily available?"

"In the cities, yes. Nearly anything can be ordered. There is much export from here to there."

"I suppose there would be."

Again there was silence while Eleanore slowly ambled the perimeter of the room, taking in the titles and authors' names on the spines of books that caught her eye. But it was only when she came to the Bible that she had any desire to remove a book from the shelf. As she drew the heavy book carefully into her hands, he said, "Is it more alluring to you than any other book in the room?"

"Yes," she said and sat down on the couch with the Bible on her lap. She'd never sat on the couch before. Again she became aware of him watching her. Was he trying to figure her out? Was he wondering what he'd gotten himself into?

"How much of it have you read?" he asked.

"It's hard to tell. I've only read in snatches here and there." She gave him a brief smile. "Sneaking into the library in the night doesn't allow for lengthy bouts of reading." She pressed a hand over the elegant cover, then opened the book, idly flipping through pages. "I just . . . look until something . . . catches my attention. It's as if . . . my feelings draw me to a concept or story that will benefit me at that particular time."

"Truly?" he asked, with no trace of mockery. "And what is your favorite Bible story, Miss Layne?"

"Oh, there are so many!" she said, unable to hide her enthusiasm. "I love Queen Esther, and Moses parting the Red Sea. I love it when Joshua's people have to step into the river before the water stops so they can cross into the promised land. But I think I love most of all the parables that Jesus teaches in the gospels of the New Testament."

A glance showed her a sparkle of intrigue in his eyes. "Then . . . you would consider yourself truly a Christian woman? Not just because it's the social expectation, but in your heart?"

She met his gaze firmly. "Yes, I suppose I am. Although . . . I'd never really stopped to think about it that way."

"You live that way," he said. "Your passion for His teachings shows in your conduct."

She only had to think about it for a moment before she said, "I could say the same of you."

He looked away, perhaps embarrassed. "I try, but . . . as you have seen in the past, I have often fallen short."

"We all fall short, Mr. Barrington; otherwise there would be no need for our Savior when this life is over." He looked at her quickly, surprised. She wondered if she'd spoken too boldly, or if he didn't agree. She broke the tension by asking, "Was it important to you, then?"

"What?"

"Had you determined that I was a Christian woman before you asked me to marry you?"

"It was very high on the list."

"You have a list?"

He chuckled. "Not literally; just in my mind."

She recalled that during the conversation when he'd proposed, other items on that list had come up. Reminded of the very fact that she had become his fiancée, she turned her attention more to the Bible, needing a distraction from the reasons for quiet, intimate conversation with James Barrington.

Eleanore felt drawn to the page where the book had fallen open. Her eyes focused immediately on the words, *And Leah conceived, and bare a son . . . for she said, Surely the Lord hath looked upon my affliction; now therefore my husband will love me.* She slammed the book closed, having no idea of the reference should she ever want to find it again.

"Is something wrong?" he asked.

"No," she lied, while her heart pounded. Her reaction more than the words she'd read left her inwardly reeling. Could she possibly consider such words merely coincidence in light of the present circumstances in her life, and her attempt to come to terms with them? She had an inkling of once having read something about Leah, but in that moment she couldn't recall anything about the story. She felt both a desire to read more about her, and an inclination to avoid a story that had provoked such a reaction in her from one line alone.

"You're welcome to take the Bible to your room, if you like," he said, and she knew her surprise was evident. "In fact, I think it wise to just officially put it in your keeping. After all," he said, smiling, "your name will very soon be written in it."

The thought left Eleanore warmed and chilled at the same time. She recalled the night she'd found Caroline Barrington's death date written in the Bible. If she had only known!

"Come along," he said and stood, taking the Bible to carry it for her. "It's nearly bedtime for the children. I need to tuck them in, and we've got something important to tell them."

He put her hand over his arm, and she kept it there as they walked up the front stairs, mostly in silence. He waited for her to put the Bible in her room before they found David and Iris in the sitting room with Lizzie. The children were dressed in their night-clothes and were reading together with Lizzie's arms around them.

"Oh, look who's here," Lizzie said and discreetly winked at Eleanore as the children greeted their father with hugs and laughter. "I'll be off then, sir," she added. Eleanore hadn't realized it was normal for him to be the one to put the children to bed.

"Thank you, Lizzie," he said. "We'll see you in the morning."

"Good night, Lizzie," the children both said and waved at her as she left the room. Except that Iris called her Wizzie.

David and Iris sat back down, with their father taking Lizzie's place. He glanced up to see Eleanore still standing and nodded toward the couch, indicating that she should join them. She sat on the other side of Iris and listened while he finished the story they'd been reading with Lizzie. When it was done, he said with an eager voice, "I have some exciting news to tell you." They both looked up at him. Eleanore's heart quickened.

"Is it about going to America?" David asked.

"Can we go soon?" Iris added. The children were obviously pleased with the prospect.

"It's even more exciting than that," James Barrington said as if he truly meant it. Eleanore couldn't help wondering if he felt so much enthusiasm for their marriage, or if he was simply a very good actor. "I'm going to be married again," he said, glancing briefly at Eleanore before he looked at each child squarely. "You're going to have a new mother, and she will be going with us to America."

Neither of the children spoke. Iris looked intrigued; David looked skeptical. He made clear his reservations when he simply asked, "Who?"

"Miss Layne, of course," he said. "So, what do you think of that?"

Iris giggled and threw her arms around Eleanore's neck, which provoked a chuckle from her father. David proved to be much like his father when he spoke with methodical pleasure. "I think it's grand."

"It think it's gwand, too," Iris declared. "Does this mean she will be with us fowever?"

"Forever," her father said and reached for Eleanore's hand, squeezing it as if there existed a tender love between them. But the smile he gave her at the same time had no air of false diplomacy. She knew he'd meant the gesture as evidence of the common bond they now shared. They were embarking on a new life together, with a unified purpose and common goals.

"Is she twuly going to be our new mama?" Iris asked her father.

"She truly is. In a few weeks there will be a wedding at the church, and after that she will be your mother."

Eleanore counted one more aspect of the situation she'd never thought of. A church wedding. It was what she'd always dreamed of, but under the circumstances she felt so unprepared. She could easily imagine the church filled with people she didn't know, and all eyes would be on her. But she couldn't think of that right now.

"Will we be at the wedding?" David asked.

"Of course you will," his father said. "If it's all right with Miss Layne, I think that you should be the best man, and you shall stand beside me and hold the ring. And you," he turned to Iris, "should be the bridesmaid and walk down the aisle with Miss Layne, and hold her bouquet for her during the ceremony." He looked at Eleanore. "What do you think, my dear?"

My dear? He'd called her his dear. "That sounds perfect," she said, sticking to the point of the conversation. To Iris she said, "And you shall need a new dress, and flowers in your hair."

Iris beamed, then asked, "What's a cewemony?"

Eleanore was glad when Iris's father answered, and she turned to look at him. "A marriage ceremony is when two people go before the vicar and promise to be married and take care of each other for as long as they both live. And then they are married. After the ceremony Miss Layne will become Mrs. Barrington. She will have the same name as the rest of us, and that will make her officially a part of our family."

He answered a few more questions, then insisted that it was time they went to bed. He made it clear with glances and subtle gestures that he wanted Eleanore to accompany him to each of the children's rooms, and she hovered nearby through a well-practiced ritual of bedtime prayers and being tucked tightly beneath the covers by their father. He then walked her to the door of her room, took her hand and kissed it, concluding their time together with the same gesture that had begun it.

"I wonder," he said, "if you might accompany me in the morning before breakfast."

"And where might that be?" she asked, nervous.

He smiled in that subtle way of his. "Meet me in the nursery as soon as you are dressed," he said. "Good night, Miss Layne."

"Good night," she said and watched him walk away before she went into her room and spent the next few hours trying to convince herself that this was not a dream. The dreamlike quality of these circumstances was only enhanced by her conflicting emotions. Fear and uncertainty were woven irrevocably into the joyful prospect of going to America and never having to be parted from David and Iris. But even her deepest fears associated with becoming the wife of James Barrington felt less daunting than they had at the beginning of the day. She could tally a long list of reasons why he would be a good husband, and only one truly defensible cause for hesitation. But her desire for love seemed irrelevant when balanced with all he offered, combined with the evidence of his fine character. She smiled, recalling his mention of the mental list he had of reasons for making her his wife, realizing she'd now done the same. It seemed they were well suited in many respects; they even seemed to think alike. Had he noticed that long before she'd ever thought to consider such a possibility? Was that on his list? It was now on hers.

Eleanore fell asleep wondering what adventure lay ahead of her in the morning with her fiancé. She was pleased to note when she woke up that she felt more thrilled than apprehensive. She hurried to get dressed and ready for the day, wanting to be in the nursery before he arrived, but she entered to find him standing at the window, leaning his forearm on the frame above his head. She could hear Lizzie across the hall with the children. When it became evident he hadn't heard her come in, she took a long moment to observe him while he was unaware. *Her fiancé.* She put a hand over her quivering stomach and forced away her nerves in order to enjoy whatever he might have in mind.

"Good morning, Mr. Barrington," she said, and he turned, showing pleasure to see her.

"Miss Layne," he said and stepped toward her. "Shall we?" He took her hand and put it over his arm. While she'd had no idea what to expect, she had to suppress her panic when he headed toward the kitchen where the majority of the servants were gathered for their usual early breakfast. Was this the moment when he intended to make their engagement common knowledge? He hesitated outside the door as if something had occurred to him. She was hoping he might say that perhaps this could wait, or that maybe she would rather be absent when he made the announcement. Instead he asked, "Would you like something to eat before we go out? I believe you're accustomed to eating earlier than I am."

"No, thank you," she said. "I'll be fine."

He smiled. "We'll eat together later." He then walked into the kitchen, holding her hand over his arm as if to make certain she had no option to retreat.

"Good morning," he said loudly enough for everyone to be made aware of his presence. "Please, don't get up," he added quickly, and those who had been sitting halted in their efforts to stand. An austere silence fell over the room, as if he were royalty and they were honored just to be in his presence. The silence grew deeper while she felt their eyes taking in the fact that she was at his side, her hand on his arm, his hand over hers. Their expressions wore varying degrees of surprise. Some had surely heard rumors that she'd had supper with him the previous evening; some had heard nothing. All couldn't believe what they were seeing. *It's really true,* she imagined them thinking. *He has indeed lost complete control of his senses.*

"You can now put all rumors and gossip to rest," he said. "If you hear the truth straight from me, there will be nothing to speculate over. I will be marrying Miss Layne within a month's time. I am in the process of finalizing the sale of my estate, and it will be changing hands once I leave for America, which will be as soon as it is feasible following our marriage. Lizzie and Higgins will be going with us. The rest of you will remain in the employment of the new owner, who has wholeheartedly agreed to maintain your wages and fair treatment. I would ask that you all give your support to Mrs. Bixby in planning and preparing for the wedding celebration, and also in helping us prepare for our journey. I thank you for your ongoing loyalty and service. I believe that's all. We'll leave you to enjoy your breakfast."

He turned and walked out of the room, keeping her at his side. In the hall he said, "Now, that wasn't so hard."

Eleanore didn't comment. She just tried not to think about the conversation now taking place in their absence. She focused instead on the fact that they were walking toward the stable while he pulled on black leather gloves. She didn't express her panic until he actually began to saddle a horse.

"I'm not certain what your plan is, sir, but I have never in my entire life been this close to a horse, let alone ridden one."

He chuckled. "High time you had the experience."

"But, sir, I—"

"Miss Layne," he said while tightening a strap on the saddle, "do you think I would do anything to put you in peril, or even frighten you?"

She thought about that for a moment and had to say, "No, sir."

"Then I assume you trust me," he added with that little smile of his.

"I've agreed to marry you, haven't I?"

His demeanor soured slightly. "In my experience, the two don't necessarily go hand in hand."

She felt tempted to apologize for saying something that brought up an uncomfortable issue for him. Instead she chose to give a counterpoint. "For me they do."

He paused in his task long enough to meet her eyes. "How refreshing," he said and turned his attention back to tightening a strap beneath the horse's belly. A minute later she was amazed at how gracefully he helped her into the saddle, and she was relieved to realize that the full gathers of her skirt allowed her to straddle the animal and remain completely modest. Before she had a chance to accept where she was sitting, James Barrington immediately mounted behind her. It was startling to feel him so near, but she was more concerned about actually being on a horse. When it first moved, she let out a startled gasp and heard a chuckle behind her ear. But within a few minutes she had become accustomed to the sensation. They rode mostly in silence to all the places on the estate where she had walked, and more. When they returned to the stable she couldn't deny that the past hour had likely been the most exhilarating experience of her life. He had certainly proven that life at his side would give her the opportunity for more adventure than any girl of her station could ever hope for.

They shared a simple, quiet breakfast together. Not much was said, but she was glad to note that she already felt more comfortable with him than she had the previous day. Perhaps being his wife wouldn't be so terribly difficult.

After breakfast, he informed her that they were going into town to accomplish a number of errands, including her approval of a new wardrobe. In essence, he diplomatically told her that the dressmaker would know more what she would need, and her measurements were already recorded from her previous orders. Eleanore's opinion would only be needed on the choice of some fabrics. She was relieved not to have to endure a tedious fitting, or be asked questions about wardrobe items that had no meaning for her.

An hour after breakfast they headed into town in the carriage, taking the children along. Eleanore enjoyed seeing them interact with their father more than she ever had. There was genuine love and respect between them, which she knew wouldn't exist if he were sharp or harsh with them in any way.

Their first stop was at the dress shop. But Mr. Barrington took David with him to order some clothes for the both of them for the wedding, and Eleanore kept Iris with her so that they could do the same. Eleanore sensed some awe and curiosity from the dressmaker over the situation, but her only comment was, "Congratulations on your engagement, Miss. I understand he's a fine man."

"Thank you," Eleanore said. "He is, indeed."

While Eleanore answered this woman's questions regarding her wardrobe, she was relieved to find that Mr. Barrington had requested the majority of her clothes be suitable for comfortable everyday use and traveling. But an evening gown was included, and Eleanore looked at some drawings and patterns to determine what she wanted in a wedding gown. Iris was consulted on the gown, and Eleanore took her suggestion for the very long train and the veil that hung nearly to the floor. Iris also gave her opinions on the dress to be ordered for herself for the event. They were nearly finished when Mr. Barrington and David returned. They made a few other stops, then had lunch together at a pub where Mr. Barrington declared he ate occasionally. After lunch they went to the bookshop, and David and Iris were thrilled to be able to each pick out two new books. As they stepped through the door, Eleanore paused habitually to close her eyes and breathe deeply.

"Smelling books again?" her fiancé asked.

"Indeed," she said, and they exchanged a smile.

"Get whatever you like," he said, then followed after Iris to supervise her.

Eleanore noticed that Mr. Harvey was busy in the back with a customer. She looked at the books available through a whole new light. *Get whatever you like.* Could it be so easy? Suddenly an endless budget for the purchasing of books if she chose? But such a limitless possibility almost made the choices more difficult. There were so many wonderful books, and whatever she might get would have to be transported to America. She was settling on a novel she'd read more than once and would love to read again, when she heard Mr. Harvey say from the other side of the shop, "Good day, Mr. Barrington. And how are you this fine afternoon?"

"Well, and you?"

"Very well, thank you. I see you've brought the children along this time. And I've been hearing rumors about you."

Then men both chuckled comfortably, and Eleanore realized they had an established rapport. Had Mr. Barrington's love of books brought him frequently to this place that was one of her favorites?

"Have you now?" Mr. Barrington asked lightly. "Do tell."

"I've heard you're moving to America, which of course breaks my heart to think of your leaving—mostly because I envy you. But I've also heard that you're getting married again. And I'm glad to hear of it. If it's true, then I must offer my congratulations."

"Yes, it's true," Eleanore heard her fiancé say, but she wondered if Mr. Harvey had heard the most ludicrous aspect of the gossip. "And I thank you for your well wishes."

When Mr. Barrington went to gather up the children and see if they'd found what they wanted, Eleanore found Mr. Harvey beside her. "Why hello, Ellie," he said. "I missed you coming in."

She asked him about his family, wanting to keep the conversation away from herself. They chatted a few minutes, then he took notice of the book she was holding. "Will you be wanting to borrow this or—"

"No, thank you. I'll be keeping it."

"But I thought all of your book money was being saved for passage to America," he said.

"That's been taken care of," Mr. Barrington said from behind, startling her. He took the book from her and asked, "Is this all?"

"Yes, thank you."

He looked at the cover and smiled. "Jane Austen?"

She wanted to comment on the need to fulfill her romantic notions, but Mr. Harvey was standing beside her, looking as dumbfounded as the servants had at breakfast. Instead she said, "You should try it, sir."

"Thank you, no," he said and handed her book along with a few others to Mr. Harvey. "This should be all today." And in exactly the same tone, "I believe you know Miss Layne, soon to be Mrs. Barrington."

"Indeed I do," Mr. Harvey said, seeming pleased. She felt mildly embarrassed when he added, "You'll not find a finer young woman than little Ellie."

While Mr. Harvey was adding up their purchases, Mr. Barrington spoke to her in a quiet voice. "You were saving for passage to America?" She looked up at him, attempting to gauge if he was teasing her or whether he was genuinely offended. She honestly couldn't tell. "You were planning to leave us and said nothing?"

"It would have taken years," she said. "But as you mentioned, it's now been taken care of."

On their way home in the carriage, David leaned his head out the window, and Iris fell asleep on her father's lap. Eleanore took advantage of a quiet moment to say, "Thank you, Mr. Barrington . . . for everything. Your generosity leaves me humbled."

He took in her comment with wonder, then he spoke with an intensity that surprised her as much as the words did. "All that I have is yours, Miss Layne. I will give you anything you ask of me."

Except your love, she thought. He'd made that very clear. Still, she had to admit, "You have already been more than generous. I have everything I could ever hope for."

Again she had supper with him that evening, and when she went up to her room she found a beautiful new dress on her bed. Lizzie came in a minute later to see if she liked it, which of course she did. It was a deep mauve trimmed with crocheted ivory lace. While she was holding it in front of herself, gazing into the mirror, Lizzie told her it had been delivered earlier this evening since Mr. Barrington had requested that one of her new dresses be ready before Sunday.

"Good heavens, tomorrow *is* Sunday."

"Yes, it is," Lizzie said, then she teased Eleanore a bit and went off to bed.

Eleanore was grateful for exhaustion that allowed her to sleep in spite of something new to worry about. But attending church with Mr. Barrington didn't prove to be as difficult as she'd expected. The new dress did add to her confidence, and she liked the way he held her hand during the sermon. It wasn't that she felt any tenderness in the gesture, either from him or herself. But it gave her a comfortable sense of belonging and connection, something she realized only then that she'd missed since her mother's death. Although it wasn't official yet, she was part of a family.

With the banns officially posted regarding their marriage, many people stopped him after the meeting to offer congratulations and to meet his fiancée. Eleanore said little, preferring to just nod and smile politely when she was introduced. Some people were very kind, others slightly cool, and some just offered silent condescension while they hypocritically told James Barrington they were happy for him.

That evening he presented her with a gift. "It's not nearly so cumbersome and difficult to carry around as that other one," he said as she realized it was a Bible.

"Oh, it's lovely!" she said with sincere eagerness. "I've never imagined such a fine gift. Thank you."

"A pleasure," he said and smiled.

Before going to bed, she returned the family Bible to its place in the library and went back to her room to read from the pages of her very own. She was truly blessed.

Throughout the following days a new pattern was established in Eleanore's life. She always had supper with her fiancé, and occasionally breakfast. Her other meals she ate alone or sometimes with Lizzie or the children, preferring to avoid the other servants altogether. Occasionally Mr. Barrington took her riding. Some days he spent significant time with her and the children, often sharing lunch with them. On other days he would be gone for several hours, explaining that he would be hunting or working on arrangements for their journey. When they were together, he was always kind and gracious and impeccably proper. Sometimes they would chat pleasantly, and other times they had nothing to say. But she quickly grew accustomed to being with him in silence and found that it wasn't uncomfortable. In every possible way she couldn't deny that they seemed well suited for each other, and she was grateful. Even if love wasn't part of the deal.

Chapter Seven
TWO WORLDS

James Barrington sat alone in his bedroom, struggling to stay immersed in a book while his mind wandered through sporadic memories that he preferred to avoid. The laughter of children from outside was a pleasant distraction, and he moved to the window, looking down into the gardens below where he could see David and Iris soaking in the rare appearance of the sun while playing some silly game on the lawn with Miss Layne. He marveled that she could interact with them so easily on their level, then turn around and exhibit the maturity and wisdom of a woman far beyond her years. He watched as the three of them ran around each other, apparently engaged in some varied version of tag. Then Iris jumped unexpectedly into Miss Layne's arms with such force that the two of them rolled back onto the lawn with laughter. James laughed just observing them.

Impulsively he tossed his book to the bed and hurried down the stairs, eager to join them. Surely there could be nothing more pleasurable than simply playing tag with his family. Coming onto the lawn, he felt inexplicably grateful for this woman God had sent into his life to make it possible for him and his children to actually feel like a family again. Or perhaps for the first time. Miss Layne brought a simple normalcy to their family structure that he'd only longed for in the past. He wished he knew how to tell her what that meant to him, but he felt certain that with time she would know. For now, he simply asked if he could join them. Within minutes they were all laughing together. He loved to hear his children laugh even more than he appreciated his own laughter, something that had become so rare in his life. The peace he'd felt over his recent decisions deepened inside of him. He'd never felt so blessed.

* * *

As Eleanore began discussing plans for the wedding with Mrs. Bixby, a definite problem occurred to her. She knew she needed to discuss it with Mr. Barrington before proceeding any further. Watching for him from an upstairs window, she waited for him to come in from riding, then she hurried to find him in the stable while the children were with Lizzie.

Eleanore entered the stable just as he was removing the horse's saddle, and it occurred to her that there were servants available to do it for him, but he chose to do it himself. He took up a brush and started grooming the horse.

"Hello," she said, and he looked up, smiling.

"Hello, Miss Layne. And how are you?"

"I'm well. And you?"

"Very well, thank you."

"May I talk to you?" she asked.

"Of course," he said but kept brushing the horse. Having him not completely focused on her didn't feel quite so intimidating. Maybe this was better.

"About the wedding," she began. "I'm not certain what to do."

"Anything you want. Do you prefer simple? Extravagant?"

"Personally I prefer quiet and simple. As long as the wedding takes place in a church, nothing else matters. But I believe the festivities afterward are important, not so much for myself, but more so to give the opportunity for others to participate in the celebration."

He paused to look at her as if the idea had never occurred to him. "That makes perfect sense," he said. "And the problem would be?"

"The problem is, that while you and I have lived under the same roof for several years, we come from two different worlds. Those who would want to be involved in the celebration of my marriage will not mix well with those who will come for the celebration of yours. In spite of the obvious purpose and importance of festivities following the ceremony, I wonder if it might not be better to just forgo them rather than create a situation that will be uncomfortable for everyone involved."

James put the currycomb down and leaned a forearm on the horse's back while he took a long gaze at his fiancée. Her insight continued to catch him off guard. He was prone to thinking that he didn't care what people thought about this marriage, and their discomfort was none of his concern. But Eleanore thought more deeply than that. And she was right. Whether he cared what people thought or not, there would undeniably be tension present if they attempted to mix people from all rungs of the social ladder. But in his opinion, omitting that part of the celebration was not an option. He wanted to show her off, and he wanted to celebrate this great event in their lives. He wanted the opportunity to help her become more accustomed to being the center of attention, and he wanted her to have the opportunity to associate with the class she had married into. But apparently it was equally important for him to be given the same opportunity. The solution was obvious. "We will simply need to have *two* parties. And then our marriage will officially become the best of both our worlds."

Eleanore was surprised by his suggestion—but pleasantly so. Two parties hadn't even occurred to her. But it was an obvious answer. Money wasn't an issue. And Mrs. Bixby seemed eager to do anything, and she would require the same of the staff.

"Is that acceptable to you, Miss Layne?"

"It should be fine," she said.

"I believe Mrs. Bixby will have a sense of what manner of celebration would be more suited to each group of people. And you and I shall have a marvelous time at *both* parties." He smiled. "Perhaps this will be an excellent opportunity for you and I to see how well we might mesh into each other's worlds."

"Just in time to leave the country and embark into a new world altogether?"

"Precisely," he said and smiled again.

"Thank you for your time, Mr. Barrington," she said and left the stable. She went straight to find Mrs. Bixby, who was clearly thrilled with the idea of separate wedding celebrations.

Over the next several days, the wedding plans came neatly together. Eleanore gained a new perspective of the value of having a qualified staff. She could offer her opinion, which had suddenly become of great value, but the complications and details were efficiently taken care of by those who had the knowledge and experience to do so. Mrs. Bixby made it easier for her to find her place as the future Mrs. Barrington. They could communicate comfortably, even as equals and friends, and she would then pass orders along to the rest of the staff, which prevented Eleanore from having to do so.

As the wedding date drew closer, Eleanore felt anxious to move beyond it and get on with their lives. She longed to leave this household behind and embark on her dream to travel to America. She wanted to be free of the underlying tension of knowing the servants were gossiping about her. And she'd come to hate the social distinctions that made her marriage to James Barrington the object of criticism and disapproval—even if no one dared say it to his face. He was considered to have lowered himself by taking a wife who was servant status. While Mr. Barrington apparently didn't care what anyone thought, and Eleanore was doing her best to ignore the occasional whispers and odd glances—both from the community and within the household—she looked forward to the day when they would be married and gone from here.

On the other hand, the very idea of being his wife left her frightened and uncertain. There were aspects of marriage she didn't even want to think about, simply because she had absolutely no idea what to expect. She wondered if she should be doing something to be better prepared, or at least more knowledgeable on what might be expected of a wife. She considered whom she might talk to about her concerns, but there was no one within her social realm that she felt comfortable enough with to embark on such a conversation, except for Lizzie, who had never been married. Eleanore brought it up anyway, but Lizzie had nothing to tell her that she hadn't already heard through gossip—and it wasn't very comforting. But Eleanore had made her decision, and she needed to stand by it, no matter what her fears might be. So she pushed her concerns aside, praying that when the time came she would be able to adjust and accept her place as Mr. Barrington's wife in every regard.

* * *

James wandered with practiced slowness through the darkened hallways of his home, carrying a lamp that barely put off enough light to show him the way. Everyone in the household was asleep, but he knew that even attempting such a thing himself would be futile. As the date for his marriage drew close, his hopes for the future collided with regrets of the past. Thoughts and memories tortured him, most especially in the darkest hours of the night. He longed to be away from here, to start a new life and never look back. And he could only pray that the experiences of this place that he loathed would remain behind. But for now they hovered relentlessly. His childhood. His youth. His marriage. And his wife's death. Since the day of Caroline's burial, he'd barely mentioned her and had kept thoughts of her forced beyond his conscious mind. What they'd shared in life had become ugly and tainted. And her death had sealed the hideousness of it into a place where he had chosen not to look. But now as he anticipated taking a new wife, he felt compelled to finally put the old one to rest.

James hesitated for several minutes outside Caroline's bedroom door. He'd not been in this room since she'd died with her hand in his, and prior to the horrid events of that day, he'd not set foot in her bedroom since she'd given birth to Iris. Upon Caroline's death, Mrs. Bixby had suggested leaving his wife's things as they were until he might feel ready to face their sorting. He'd felt indifferent but had told her that would be fine, thinking perhaps the children might find some solace there. He'd heard rumors that the servants considered his wanting her room to remain untouched, beyond dusting, as some kind of heartbroken devotion to the grief he felt over her death. There was certainly grief tied into the tangible remnants of her life, but it was rooted in events that had transpired long before her death.

James took a deep breath and opened the door. He turned up the wick on the lamp to illuminate the room as he walked its circumference, recalling memories that were better left locked away. Even the sweet and tender moments they'd shared here had become tainted by his learning the truth. He touched the pillow where her head had rested when she'd died. He opened the wardrobe and pondered the endless row of lavish, expensive gowns. He'd spent a fair amount of his inheritance keeping her properly dressed. Thankfully his inheritance had been sufficient not to feel the crunch. With methodical purpose he closed the wardrobe and turned his back to it, then he quietly examined the paraphernalia spread over her dressing table. The absence of dust was the only indication that the maids had been in the room. The items there looked as natural as if Caroline might have used them just today. He opened the elaborate jewelry box and examined its opulent contents. Oh, how she had loved her precious stones! Memories stung him as he fingered each piece, remembering how he'd bestowed expensive gifts so generously upon her, always declaring his undying love. And then to find out she'd been wearing them for another man—bestowing upon her clandestine lover all that was most precious to her husband.

James slammed the box closed and focused instead on the bottles of perfumes, lotions, creams, and bath salts. He questioned his own wisdom when he opened the bottle of perfume that was her favorite, and he immediately smelled the Caroline he had loved and then grown to hate. Still, he closed his eyes and lingered over the scent, feeling the memories long enough to let them go, rather than trying to avoid them. He put the perfume away and picked up a blue scarf; she'd likely worn it the day she'd died. He fingered it, then pressed it to his face, amazed to find that it still held the subtle fragrance of the perfume he'd just been smelling. He gently put the scarf back where he'd found it, and muttered into the empty room, "Good-bye, Caroline. You stole my heart from the woman who deserves it. I pray that one day she'll forgive you."

He almost left the room, then went back and picked up the jewelry box, finding some satisfaction in the thought of selling its contents and buying something of value—like a piece of land in America. Not that he couldn't afford it otherwise; it was the principle that intrigued him.

James put the jewelry box safely away in his own room and once again tried to sleep, but he was soon wandering the halls again, while echoes of the scenes those halls had witnessed haunted him. He eventually found himself in the library for no particular reason. He set the lamp down and ambled around the room, pondering the history, the marvelous things he'd learned from the pages of these books during his life. He stopped at the family Bible, touching its binding but feeling hesitant to even take it down, considering his state of mind. He felt tired but not sleepy, and he made himself comfortable in the center of the couch, putting his bare feet on the low table. While his mind wandered, he had no concern for time. He could nap tomorrow if he wanted to, even though he likely *wouldn't* want to. He was startled when the door came open, but Miss Layne looked horrified.

"Forgive me, sir," she said, backing out of the room. "I didn't know you were here and—"

"Miss Layne," he said, and she hesitated. "You are not a servant in this household. You are my fiancée. You don't need to apologize for being in the same room with me."

Eleanore looked down, not knowing what to say, wanting only to escape, wishing she hadn't come here. In all the years she'd been sneaking into the library at night, she'd only encountered him twice before. The memory of those encounters caught her off guard. And why did he have to be here now? Now, when her feelings about this pending marriage were her greatest source of concern.

Preferring escape to any other option, she said, "I'll just leave you to—"

"Miss Layne," he interrupted her again. "Why don't you just get what you came for?"

She entered the room, tying her wrapper more tightly around her nightgown, grateful she'd chosen to wear the extra covering. It wasn't uncommon for her to go wandering in her nightgown when she was alone. But her hair was hanging wild, and she felt immensely conspicuous. As she reached for the large Bible, she felt the need to explain, "I love the one you gave me, but . . . there's something about this one that . . . draws me to it." He looked intrigued but said nothing. She added, "I hope you don't mind if I—"

"I told you a long time ago that it was fine," he said. As she took the Bible down, he added, "Are you searching for peace and understanding, Miss Layne?"

She evaded the question. "I'll leave you to whatever you might have been pondering so deeply."

She moved toward the door, and he said, "Just keep it with your things for now. Should I decide I need it, I'll know where to find it. But I'm not likely to miss it."

Eleanore turned toward him, sensing something deep in his words. But she wondered if he would expound or leave it at that. When it came to sharing his deepest thoughts and feelings, would he still consider her as one of the servants in his household, or see her as the woman he was going to marry? His personal confessions to this point had been brief and cryptic. But she almost preferred to keep emotional distance between them and didn't know whether to feel comforted or terrified when he added, "Sit down, Miss Layne. Talk to me."

She took a deep breath, trying not to feel unnerved as she placed the Bible on the table and sat on the same couch, wishing there was more distance between them. She folded her hands in her lap, then, after a grueling silence, she said, "What would you like to talk about, sir?"

"You look absolutely terrified, Miss Layne."

"I am wearing my nightclothes, sir. I would prefer to—"

"So you are. And pathetically modest they are, too. You look positively spinsterish. Once we're married we must get you something a little less . . . prudish."

Eleanore couldn't even consider the implication, especially not in that moment. She hurried to change the subject. "Is there any particular reason you mentioned that you're not likely going to miss having the Bible in your library? Or were you just making clever conversation while you sit here in the middle of the night, looking as if you've just been informed of a death in the family?"

James felt unnerved at having his emotions read so easily, and even more so that she would confront him with them so boldly. He stuck to the original topic. "So tell me," he said, "do you really think it's possible to find peace and understanding from its pages?"

She turned to look at him, surprised by the sincerity in his eyes that contradicted a subtle bite to his voice. "I do," she said and turned away. He made no further comment, so she added, "Is there something particular you're attempting to seek peace over, Mr. Barrington? Is that too personal a question for the state of our relationship?"

She stole a glance to find him watching her contemplatively. He looked so relaxed, while she felt so rigid and awkward. Following more silence he said, "Let's talk in hypothetical terms, Miss Layne. Do you think that repentance and forgiveness are possible for a person who has willfully cheated and lied?"

She wondered if he meant himself and had to ask, "Are you trying to confess something, Mr. Barrington?"

He looked mildly alarmed. "I'm not speaking of myself, if that's what you mean. For all my shortcomings, I've always striven to be honest and trustworthy in every aspect of my life. My sins are more difficult to define—and to find peace with."

"Is the purpose of this conversation an attempt to define your sins, then?"

She saw hesitancy in his eyes before he said, "Should I feel guilt for feeling no remorse or sorrow over something that *should* have caused me grief?" She felt confused until he added, "Should I be ashamed to admit that I'm glad she's dead?" Eleanore was struck deeply by his question in light of everything she knew about Caroline Barrington. Before she could comment, he added, "On the other hand, I can't deny my concern for her eternal welfare. I cared for her. She's the mother of my children. But some are of the opinion that she will undoubtedly rot in hell for her choices. While her choices brought me a great deal of grief, hellfire and brimstone seem rather harsh. She had a difficult upbringing; her mother was promiscuous. How can I possibly judge Caroline's heart or motives? If a person makes bad choices in this life, are they irrevocably doomed in the next life? *Is* there truly a next life? If so, how can we possibly know? I truly believe in God, and I believe there is more to this existence than what we can see; however, I wonder sometimes if eternal life is something human beings have created in their fantasies to give hope to an otherwise hopeless existence. Or if there is life after this, is there only hope for those who live sinless lives? Is there any chance of redemption beyond death for those who make less than admirable choices? What do you think, Miss Layne?"

Eleanore found no words to answer except for the memory of verses from her most precious book that she'd read over and over. She looked away from him as she spoke. "'And now if Christ had not come into the world, speaking of things to come as though they had already come, there could have been no redemption. And if Christ had not risen from the dead, or have broken the bands of death that the grave should have no victory, and that death should have no sting, there could have been no resurrection. But there is a resurrection, therefore the grave hath no victory, and the sting of death is swallowed up in Christ. He is the light and the life of the world; yea, a light that is endless, that can never be darkened; yea, and also a life which is endless, that there can be no more death.'"

James felt stunned, not only by the message of the words, but by the way she'd spoken them so easily—and with such gentle conviction. "Apparently you know the Bible very well," he said.

Eleanore resisted the desire to tell him that these words were not from the Bible. She simply said, "There are certain passages of scripture that have profound meaning for me. Knowing them well enough to bring them to mind *does* give me peace and understanding. I suppose losing my parents has made me appreciate the message here, but . . . I think that we as human beings often overlook the fact that what Christ did for us compensates for our weaknesses, our grief. I believe that we will each be judged by the desires of our hearts in proportion to the level of understanding we have of such matters in this life." She shrugged. "At least that's how I see it. I believe that's what is truly meant by redemption."

Eleanore turned to look at him, surprised by his stunned expression. When he didn't speak she said, "You yourself called me a Christian woman. Surely you can't be so surprised to hear me talk of such things."

James wondered how to explain that his surprise was really a case of his marveling at her level of conviction, and a certain insight—however simple—that he'd never considered before. He just couldn't find any words and was relieved when she went on to say, "In answer to your questions, Mr. Barrington, I believe that what Christ did has already paid the price for your difficult feelings and for whatever Caroline did to hurt you and the children. You need to simply give that burden to Him and let go." She looked away. "And for what it's worth, I'm glad she's dead too. I don't think it's right to hold ill feelings toward another, no matter how badly they might hurt us. We've been commanded to forgive regardless. But that doesn't make it a sin to feel relief that you don't have to contend any further with the difficulties she brought into your life. When I think of how she treated you—and the children—I'm relieved too."

James felt even more stunned as her words crept into every part of his soul, spreading peace and hope that soothed his every concern. Everything she'd said made perfect sense; it was exactly what he'd needed to hear. And he instinctively believed that what she'd said was true. He just felt too choked up to be able to admit it without making a fool of himself.

Eleanore turned to look at him, wordlessly questioning his silence. The way he stared at her was almost unnerving, but not enough to keep her from staring back. Something intangible but undeniable connected between them in that moment. No words were needed to know that he agreed with her, that he shared her convictions and beliefs. And the discord in his eyes had been replaced with peace.

While James still felt too overcome to speak, he couldn't

resist lifting a hand to touch her face, as if doing so might prove that she was only human and not some angel sent to guide him to heaven. As it occurred to him that they would be married in a few days, he couldn't resist easing just a little closer, inhaling her aroma as he found himself closer to her than he'd ever been. Then he realized she didn't have one. There was a complete absence of any fragrance, and he wondered why. He'd learned years ago that he was a scent-oriented man. As a child he'd played with his mother's perfume bottles, and he'd loved to hover in the kitchen and play with the bottles of spices and herbs used for cooking. During his travels he'd been keenly fascinated with the smell of different cultures, different countries, different weather. He loved the smell of leather, of horses, of rain. And through many years of socializing he'd become aware of the fact that human beings put off certain aromas, mostly enhanced by particular types of perfumes, bathing salts, shampoos, or shaving lotions. His children smelled like the soap they were bathed in, except when they'd been outside for long hours in the sun. Then the smell of the outdoors, mingled with their own sweat, would come back into the house with them. Caroline had preferred certain fragrances of bath products, and she had a favorite perfume. It was the combination that he'd come to recognize as her scent. But Miss Layne had no aroma about her at all. He focused instead on the simple sensation of pressing his face to that of a woman, deeply grateful that he would no longer have to be alone.

Eleanore felt her breath catch as his fingers came to her face, but she managed to conceal how his touch affected her until he eased closer and pressed his stubbled cheek to her temple. The sensation stirred vague memories of her father. But not since his death had she been anywhere close enough to a man to be aware of the unique texture of a masculine face that had gone many hours without shaving. She became aware of a vague aroma hovering around him and wondered over its source. Shaving lotion, perhaps. At the realization that he would soon be her husband, she became unexpectedly breathless. She didn't consider herself attracted to him by any means. But the reality of being a wife to him was reinforced by the feel of his face against hers and the movement of his fingers on her cheek. Then she felt him press a lingering kiss just in front of her ear, and her heart raced to catch up with her breathing. He put his other hand into her hair, while she could only wonder over his motives, too stunned to respond, too affected to move.

James pressed her hair to his face and again found no fragrance. He watched it slide over his fingers and kissed her cheek once more before he eased back, well aware of her strained breathing. He wondered if her reaction was due to some positive response to his closeness. Or was she simply terrified of him? He drew back to look into her eyes and couldn't tell. She quickly looked away, then came to her feet.

"I'll see you tomorrow, Mr. Barrington," she said and rushed from the room, leaving the Bible on the table. James heaved a deep sigh and sat there for several minutes, allowing their encounter—and her profound healing words—to soak into him. Then he picked up the Bible and read from its pages until he was too tired to do anything more than lumber up to his room and sleep.

The following morning James awoke with thoughts of Miss Layne's words in regard to his present struggles. He realized that he needed to speak to her, to tell her what he'd been unable to say last night. But he arrived at her room to find her already gone with the children, since he'd slept late. Peering into her empty room, once he'd knocked and gotten no response, he couldn't resist the urge to go in, leaving the door open. He slowly walked the perimeter of the room, as he'd done recently in Caroline's room. The contrast was startling. He was stunned by how very little his fiancée owned beyond the clothing he had purchased for her. There were books here and there, and little else. The absence of aroma surrounding Miss Layne was evidenced by the absence of anything in the room that had any fragrance. There were no bottles of bath salts or perfumes. Only odorless soap and shampoo. On her dresser there was only a hairbrush and a handful of dark hair ribbons. And a tiny glass bottle that was empty. He picked it up and opened the lid, inhaling a fragrance that pleasantly startled his senses without seeming at all familiar. He glanced at the bottom of the bottle where a fading label read, *Rose Oil and Vanilla.* Then he inhaled the fragrance again, curious over her ownership of an empty perfume bottle.

"What are you doing?" Eleanore asked, and he turned, startled to see her standing in the doorway.

Forcing any guilt out of his voice and expression, he simply said, "I came to talk with you, but you'd already left. Forgive me. I was just curious as to what kind of perfume you wear."

Eleanore told herself he was going to be her husband in a couple of days and his standing in her bedroom in broad daylight was not inappropriate, nor was it a violation of her privacy. It took a moment for her to separate this experience from the way last night's encounter with him had left her disconcerted and restless without understanding why. Deliberately focusing only on this moment, she simply responded to his remark. "I don't wear perfume, Mr. Barrington. Perfume is a luxury rarely available for women of my social class."

"And this would be?" He held up the little bottle, and she took it from him, holding it to her nose before she took the lid from his other hand and replaced it.

"It was my mother's," she said, setting it back where it belonged. "Beyond her wedding ring, it was the only gift my father had ever been able to give her that had any monetary value. She used it very sparingly, only for special occasions. There was only a drop left when she died. But the bottle holds the fragrance. I can open it, and the scent brings my mother back to me."

James listened to her tender nostalgia and added another point of commonality to an already lengthy list. She too was a scent-oriented person. Recalling how she had mentioned her pleasure in smelling books only added confirming evidence of this.

"What did you need to talk to me about?" she asked.

It took James a long moment to remember. "I just wanted to . . . thank you. What you said last night . . . I needed to hear. Your words have made a difference, and I wanted you to know that I'm grateful."

She smiled. "You're feeling better, then?"

"I am, thank you."

"Also . . ." He recalled how quickly she had left the room and felt the need to clear the air between them. "If I said . . . or did . . . anything that upset you . . . I'm sorry."

Eleanore looked into his eyes for only a moment, then had to look away. His behavior had been completely appropriate for a man engaged to be married. Her difficulty in contending with how it had affected her was not his problem. She simply said, "No, of course not. There's nothing to apologize for." She drew courage to look at him again. "Was there anything else?"

"No . . . thank you," he said and hurried from the room. He felt the sudden need to buy her a gift. With any luck he could find exactly what he wanted without having to order it.

Eleanore watched him leave and drew a deep breath, wondering why encountering him in her bedroom had left her so unsettled. Then she reminded herself that in a few more days she would be sharing *his* bedroom. He'd already mentioned that once they were married all of her things would be moved into his room; that the reasons he and Caroline had kept separate bedrooms were irrelevant to the relationship they would share. Her nervousness over certain aspects of that relationship was so intense that she had to push thoughts of it aside and remember her purpose for coming to her room. She grabbed her shawl and went back downstairs to meet Lizzie and the children for a walk in the gardens.

* * *

In the late afternoon, Eleanore was reading with the children when Jennifer came to tell her that Mr. Barrington wanted to see her in his office. Leaving the children in Jennifer's care, Eleanore hurried downstairs, wondering why the comfortable relationship she'd gained with him now felt uncomfortable. Something had changed last night when he'd touched her cheek and kissed her face. But she didn't understand why. Feeling no attraction for him, she could only believe that it had awakened her to the reality that being his wife would mean sharing a physical relationship that she felt completely unprepared to face.

Approaching his office door, she pushed her anxious thoughts away and forced herself into the frame of mind established by their relationship beyond this one difficult aspect. She knocked, and he called for her to come in.

"Hello, my dear," he said, looking up from his desk with a smile.

"Hello," she said, closing the door.

"I have something for you." He stood and moved around the desk, picking up a small box as he did. "I hope it's not too presumptuous. I can exchange it if you don't like it."

Eleanore took the box, startled by the gesture. "It's not necessary for you to buy me gifts."

"I know," he said and nodded, encouraging her to open it.

Eleanore lifted the lid to see a beautiful crystal bottle, and their prior conversation about perfume came back to her. When she just stared at it, he chuckled and lifted the bottle out of the bed of tissue where it lay. He tipped the bottom of the bottle to her view so she could read the label. She gasped and looked up at him. He smiled and said, "Now you can smell like your mother *all* the time. Unless you would prefer to wear a different fragrance. That can be arranged."

"No," she said, surprised to feel tears threaten as he opened the lid and held it to her nose. "It's perfect. I never imagined anything so lovely." As he replaced the lid, she realized it was one of those that sprayed the perfume. She watched him hold out her arm and spray the scent on her sleeve, then he walked behind her and sprayed a fine mist on the back of her neck, making her laugh softly. "Oh, it smells heavenly," she said.

"Yes, it does," he agreed, facing her again. He leaned closer and inhaled.

Impulsively she hugged him, then wondered what she'd been thinking when he returned her embrace and she found herself in his arms. Her desire to let go quickly was thwarted when he subtly tightened his arms around her. She realized how tall he was when the top of her head brushed his lower cheek, then he pressed a kiss into her hair.

James loved holding her near, and he loved the aroma hovering around her that in his mind had already come to define her. He sensed a subtle resistance in her embrace and let her go, wondering again if she were afraid of him. Or perhaps repulsed. The thought left him troubled. He'd readily admitted that he would never love her. And he would never expect—or even want—her to love him. But he couldn't deny a certain attraction to her, and the anticipation of being a husband to her was undeniable. He had hoped, at the very least, that she might feel the same way. But he reminded himself that he was much older than she, and this was a marriage of convenience. He would be a fool to indulge in expectations that would only leave him disappointed.

James ignored her apparent aversion to his closeness and stepped back, putting the bottle of perfume into her hand. "And I want you to use it generously," he said. "We can always buy more."

She smiled and looked up at him in a way that counteracted

anything negative he might have felt. "Thank you. It's wonderful."

"A pleasure," he said, then steered the conversation to the pending wedding, if only to be assured that everything was in order. He asked if she would like to take a honeymoon, which had never come up before. He'd been so focused on getting married and preparing to leave for America that he'd overlooked something very important.

"Wouldn't it delay our leaving the country?" she asked.

"Yes, but . . . that's all right. There's no hurry. We have plenty of warm months ahead in which to travel."

"No," Eleanore said, unnerved at the very idea of going away, completely alone with him, "but thank you for asking. Going to America will be more than enough of a vacation, to be sure."

"Of course," he said, but he wondered if she had any idea of the importance of a honeymoon in allowing two people the time to become comfortable with being married. He wondered if he should just initiate their getting away, whether she wanted to or not. He felt certain that spending time alone together, without the surroundings of everyday life, would be good for both of them. It would help them past some of the awkwardness that was inevitably present in a new marriage, especially when it had been arranged as this one had. But she had already insisted otherwise. And whatever her reasons might be for feeling apprehensive at the thought of being alone with him, he prayed that this adjustment would not be too difficult for her. He only wanted her to be happy.

Chapter Eight
THE LADY OF THE HOUSE

Eleanore stood at the office window, looking out over the gardens, willing away her inner trembling while her fiancé agreed to forgo a honeymoon and focus instead on preparing for their journey to America.

Their conversation was interrupted by a knock at the door. At Mr. Barrington's request, a maid entered and said timidly, "There is a lady here to see you, sir. She is—"

Her sentence was cut short when a portly woman entered like a gust of hot wind. She reeked of aristocracy, dressed far too finely to ever be comfortable, heavy with jewelry and stinking of too much perfume, a stark contrast to the light mist of subtle fragrance Eleanore was now wearing. The maid discreetly left the room. Mr. Barrington's astonishment over the visitor was evident as he turned to face her sour expression.

"Please tell me it isn't true, James," she said, oblivious to Eleanore on the other side of the room and behind her.

"How are you, my lady?" he asked with subtle sarcasm. "How good of you to call. Although your etiquette in such matters leaves me in wonder."

"I've no time for etiquette when it comes to addressing such nonsense as has come to my ears this very morning. Please tell me that you, of all people, would not stoop to doing something so ludicrous."

Eleanore's heart quickened with dread. She knew what this was about, and wondered if he'd apologize to this woman for lowering his standards in marriage so dramatically. He tossed Eleanore a subtle glance, and she caught the slightest hint of regret before he faced his visitor and said firmly, "I can hardly contend the charges if I don't know what's upset you so badly."

"You can't seriously . . . be marrying . . . the *governess.*" She spoke it with a hushed voice and a rancid tongue, as if she were reluctantly repeating profanity.

James Barrington drew back his shoulders and stated firmly, "I am marrying a good woman with many fine qualities."

"But certainly no lady."

"*That* is a matter of opinion. Her social standing is of little relevance to me. I have every reason to believe she will make a fine wife and mother. And she—"

"Do you have any idea what this will do to your reputation, James?"

"My reputation has absolutely no value to me, whatsoever," he said, and the woman gasped as if he'd spoken treason. "And since the new Mrs. Barrington and I will soon be moving to America, such nonsense as this will no longer be a concern." While keeping his eyes sharply poised on his aghast visitor, he held out his hand toward Eleanore, saying quietly, "Miss Layne."

The woman gasped again and turned abruptly. But her embarrassment in realizing they weren't alone was quickly swallowed up by disgust as Eleanore stepped forward and put her hand into Mr. Barrington's. She felt him gently squeeze her hand as if to silently offer some kind of assurance to counteract the difficulty of the moment. The woman gazed at their clasped hands, then at his face, horrified. Eleanore expected some kind of introductions to be made, but he simply said, "Thank you for your visit. I ask that you leave now. Perhaps I will see you at the wedding." Eleanore suspected he had purposely avoided introducing the woman, intending some level of insult; he might as well have said, *There is no need for my fiancée to know this woman's name because she deserves no acknowledgment.*

Once the door had slammed he turned to Eleanore and said, "I'm sorry for that. She's a friend of my mother's; took it upon herself following my mother's death to see that I did not shame my family. I've never liked her. With any luck I'll never have to see her again." He pressed his lips to Eleanore's hand. "Now, where were we?"

"I believe we were finished," she said, not wanting to have the topic of a honeymoon come up again. "Perhaps I should check on the children."

"I'll see you at supper?" he asked as she took her gift and opened the door.

"Of course." She smiled at him. "And thank you again . . . for the gift. It's lovely."

"A pleasure," he said once more and watched her leave.

James looked at the closed door for a long moment before he reached into the pocket of his waistcoat and pulled out a piece of black hair ribbon he'd stolen from Miss Layne's room. Before giving her the perfume, he had sprayed the fragrance on the ribbon. Now he held it beneath his nose and breathed in her aroma, a scent that had quickly come to represent the essence of hope and security in his life that he'd long believed he would never feel again.

Forcing himself back to the moment, he tucked the ribbon in his pocket and addressed himself to the papers on his desk. There was much to set in order before he could put this life completely behind him and leave here to begin a new one. But he was counting the days. America . . . with the new Mrs. Barrington at his side. What could be better than that?

* * *

Eleanore woke on her wedding day, immediately consumed with an overt nervousness that dampened her anticipation. She wanted the next twenty-four hours to be over so that she could stop dreading those aspects of being a wife that she could not comprehend. She forced her mind to prayer, reminding herself that marriage was a sacred union, sanctioned by God, and He would surely sustain her through whatever that might entail. Following a lengthy prayer she felt drawn to the Bible, surprised to have it fall open to the story of Leah. She'd not even attempted to find it since the last time it had fallen open to the words of Leah, right after she'd accepted Mr. Barrington's proposal.

Eleanore felt frustrated by how little was actually written about Leah, at least in regard to her marriage to Jacob. But one fact stood out strongly to Eleanore. Leah had been arranged into a marriage with a man who did not love her. Tears came to Eleanore's eyes as she felt a deep compassion for Leah's heartache. And perhaps that was what troubled Eleanore most of all. Perhaps she wouldn't be so nervous and concerned about sharing an intimate relationship with her husband if she could believe that he loved her. But he didn't, and he never would. And perhaps such a notion was hypocritical in some way, because she certainly didn't love him. But the mutual respect they shared was firm and comfortable—and no small thing. She reminded herself to count her blessings, and to stop this self-pity that would surely accomplish nothing. She was about to become Mrs. James Barrington, and she was determined to face her new life with courage and dignity and appreciate the great blessing this man and his children were to her.

The wedding was perfectly beautiful, and beautifully perfect. David not only looked handsome in his wedding attire, but he looked so proud and dignified, like a miniature of his father. Clearly his duty in being responsible for the ring meant a great deal to him, and there was no questioning that he was happy about this marriage. Iris was equally pleased about her father marrying the governess, and she also took her duties as bridesmaid very seriously. The lovely new dress that had been made specifically for the wedding enhanced her delicate features. But Eleanore was most preoccupied with their father and the fact that she was truly becoming his wife.

The kiss they shared to seal their vows had an air of reverence, but she still found it startling. Perhaps it was because he'd never kissed her before. Perhaps it was due to the reality that he was now her husband. Perhaps it was the way something tingled deep inside of her when their lips met. And following the kiss, he looked into her eyes, as if he might be searching for something.

Throughout the wedding festivities he didn't allow her to leave his side. The celebration with those of his class was held right after the ceremony, and Eleanore preferred it that way. She wanted to have it over with. She watched her husband speak kindly and graciously to many people, and he introduced her to people he knew as if she were the most important thing to him, as if they shared a deep love for each other.

Later in the day as they socialized with the people of her own class, Eleanore felt far more comfortable. But she was surprised to realize that her husband was also completely at ease. He interacted with the servants of his household and the tenant farmers of his estate comfortably and with no difficulty whatsoever. She finally had to comment, "It seems you blend into my world much better than I blend into yours."

He looked surprised, but smiled. "Nonsense," he said and kissed her cheek, "you were brilliant." He kissed her other cheek. "You still are." He looked into her eyes while he kissed her hand, and she read silent meaning in his eyes, provoking a nervousness so intense that she almost felt sick. But she did well at covering it and forced herself to enjoy the moment.

The day came to a close along with the wedding festivities. When Eleanore realized her husband was guiding her out of the room and up the stairs, her heart pounded hard enough to kill her while she wondered what to expect now. He said nothing as they walked together, then he carried her over the threshold of his bedroom. He set her down, and she avoided his eyes. She was relieved when he said, "I need to take care of something. I'll give you some time alone. I won't be long." She said nothing. He left the room and closed the door behind him.

Eleanore breathed in her solitude, wishing it might last longer than a few moments. She was grateful for some time alone until she realized that she could never unfasten the back of the wedding gown on her own. Was her husband meant to help her with that? The thought increased her trembling. Her nervousness over the matter left her almost lightheaded. A knock at the door made her realize how jumpy she'd become. Certain her husband wouldn't be knocking at his own bedroom, she opened the door, glad to see Lizzie, but puzzled over the box she was holding.

"Let me help you take your hair down," she said with a compassionate smile and set the box on the bed.

"What's that?" Eleanore asked with trepidation.

"Mr. Barrington sent it and asked that I help you change."

Eleanore appreciated Lizzie's presence, as well as her help. But she felt decidedly unnerved as she opened the box and lifted out a white lace nightgown while Lizzie took pins out of her hair.

"Oh, it's lovely!" Lizzie exclaimed.

"It looks . . . scandalous."

"Not at all! Just because it's not one of those prudish things you're used to wearing doesn't make it scandalous. It's appropriate and suitable for a new bride. This is your wedding night. There is nothing to be afraid of."

"Forgive me, Lizzie," Eleanore said, "but it's difficult for me to consider you an expert on that count."

"I may not be married," Lizzie said, not sounding at all affronted, "but I've lived long enough to know what's right and normal." She took hold of Eleanore's shoulders and added gently, "This is the greatest opportunity that life can give a woman, Ellie—to share herself with a good man and bring children into this world. You mustn't be afraid." She hugged Eleanore tightly. "All will be well; you'll see."

Eleanore wished that she could feel convinced. While she agreed with what Lizzie had said, she still didn't feel any more prepared. Once her hair was down and brushed through, Lizzie helped her out of the elaborate wedding gown, just as she'd helped her into it this morning. Lizzie finally left Eleanore alone with one more tight hug and an apparent lack of concern. Wearing the new nightgown, Eleanore looked at herself in the long mirror. She had to admit it wasn't *scandalous*. In truth, she felt beautiful. But would James Barrington see her that way? The thought increased her trembling. Then he came into the room and it took every bit of will power she possessed to keep her anxiety concealed. His feet were bare. The jacket he'd worn was absent; his waistcoat unbuttoned. Except for the marked contrast of his countenance, his appearance reminded her of the night she'd seen him in the library, the night his wife had died. *Good heavens*, Eleanore thought, *now I am his wife!* What would she have thought then if she could have seen this day?

Eleanore met his eyes with courage only a moment before he scooped her into his arms and put a knee on the bed to place her there in the center. The breathlessness of being swept off her feet increased tenfold when he stretched out beside her, leaning on his elbow, his head in his hand. For all of Eleanore's effort to remain calm and keep her anxiety from showing, she knew she'd failed when his brow creased with concern. He touched her face and said, "You look positively terrified."

Eleanore turned away. She couldn't even look at him. She felt him take her hand. "You're trembling, Mrs. Barrington. Is the prospect of your wedding night so upsetting?"

"Forgive me, sir," she said with a quaver in her voice that only made the problem all the more evident.

"Forgive you? For what?"

She closed her eyes and forced out the confession. "For being positively terrified."

His silence confirmed his surprise. "There is nothing to forgive, madam; I only wish to understand it. Are you afraid of *me?*"

She answered carefully. "You have never given me any cause to be afraid of you, sir. I simply have no idea what to expect."

He sounded astonished. "None?"

"No, sir."

"Surely . . . someone has . . . told you . . . *something.*"

She kept her eyes closed and her face turned away. "My mother died when I was fifteen. She was a forthright and loving woman, and I'm certain she would have informed me had she anticipated dying long before I was wed. The only other woman with whom I've ever been comfortable enough to discuss such things has never been married, and her mother was apparently too embarrassed to speak of it. She would only scold her children for asking questions about such things. She had nothing to tell me, except . . . what I had already heard . . . only through the gossip of others, and that is practically nothing."

"Which is what?" he asked.

Eleanore turned to look at him then, if only to be assured that he was serious. He truly expected her to answer that question. She quickly took back her gaze. "How can I speak of it, sir?" she asked, turning warm just to think of it.

"You can speak of it because we are husband and wife, and we will not be ashamed to discuss in an appropriate way what rightfully takes place between us. It is the very nature of God-given life and not to be shunned or taken lightly." In a voice even more gentle he said, "Please tell me what you know. If it is practically nothing, then it shouldn't be so difficult to say."

Eleanore forced the air out of her lungs, fearing she might faint if she didn't remain conscious of breathing. She convinced herself that she could say what needed to be said. He was right. They were husband and wife. She didn't have to look at him; she just had to say it. But another moment's thought made her realize she couldn't. She just couldn't. She cleared her throat carefully, but her voice squeaked as she admitted, "I can't."

Eleanore heard him sigh loudly and knew that he'd lain back on the bed. She turned to her side, facing the other way, fighting to hold back a sudden rush of hot tears. She'd ruined their wedding night by her ignorance. Why hadn't she overcome her timidity enough to ask more questions of the women she worked with? Or at the very least, had the discipline to conceal her anxiety and simply allow this event to take place without drawing attention to her naiveté?

James settled his head back into the pillow and pushed a hand through his hair. He used the silence to consider the source of his wife's concerns and prayed to be guided in alleviating them. How could he communicate to her his feelings on the matter? His beliefs were a result of many years of contemplation and analysis—and much of it the result of the bad examples and experiences in his life that he was determined to counteract and make better, given this second chance. His parents' marriage had been a disaster, and he had been privy to some things he would have preferred not to have overheard. Having known all of his grandparents, it hadn't been difficult to see that his parents had simply mimicked all they had grown up observing. But their lack of happiness and ill treatment of each other had troubled him to the point of nearly making him obsessed with the desire to study the marriage relationship and do everything right that they had done wrong. He'd traveled the world and moved among many cultures. He'd observed the public interactions of the people in his social encounters, holding an uncommon fascination with how spouses interacted. He'd studied the scriptures arduously regarding all matters of life, but the marriage relationship had fascinated him most of all. He'd longed to understand its purpose and meaning in God's eyes. He'd prayed to have his mind and spirit opened to comprehension. He'd spoken frankly with his peers, who had varying degrees of success or failure in their marriages. He had purposely waited some years to be married initially, wanting to feel prepared and knowledgeable. While he'd admitted it aloud to no one, he'd accepted that creating the perfect marriage had become his highest priority in life. He'd stopped questioning why he would be so obsessed with such a thing and had simply pressed forward with the intent to prove that all he'd learned would allow him the opportunity to be part of a family structure where fulfillment and happiness existed. Unlike his own childhood, he wanted his children to grow up secure and confident in seeing the appropriate behavior between their parents that would in turn create good marriages in future generations. He considered it his personal responsibility to stop the patterns that caused such attitudes in marriage and family; he felt sure those patterns were not God's intention when he had created man and woman and commanded them to multiply and replenish the earth.

James had married Caroline with the belief that she was a woman capable of joining forces with him in his quest. But he had quickly come to realize that he'd ignored hints and clues during their engagement that had gradually led to disaster. She had proven to him that creating a good marriage and raising children well took two people who were in mutual agreement. After all he had studied and learned, he had—for reasons he still had trouble understanding—been drawn to the very kind of woman he'd been determined to avoid. Her true nature had manifested itself eventually, and the results had been disastrous. He had failed in what mattered most to him, but in spite of his scarred heart and broken pride, he had struggled, at the very least, to be a good father, to somehow compensate his children for their mother's bad behavior. Upon Caroline's death, he had initially believed he would never marry again. He wasn't certain he could ever trust again, or ever find a woman who would meet every requirement that Caroline had lacked. And then she had appeared, right before his eyes, leaving him continually stunned with the evidence of her integrity, her forthright communication, her appropriate guidance and undeniable love for his children. And he knew that God had given him a second chance, an opportunity to prove himself capable of doing that which meant most to him. He'd considered her naiveté and innocence a blessing in the respect that he could gently guide and teach her by example all that he had so carefully learned. The fact that she had proven incapable of being manipulated against her will was equally important. It was not his intent or desire to indoctrinate or coerce a woman into doing things according to his dictate. But he had seen in Eleanore Layne an instinctive compatibility to his own feelings and beliefs, and in his heart he had known she was the one. He knew it still. But he'd never stopped to consider that her naiveté might cross over into this aspect of marriage that was at least as important as any other. While intimacy could never replace the value of integrity, communication, or mutual respect, a marriage without it was no marriage at all. That too he had learned from experience. He knew from bitter experience how betrayal related to this aspect of marriage was the deepest betrayal of all. That in itself had proven to him the immeasurable value of this aspect of marriage. If dishonoring it was so devastating, if going without it created such a void, then surely honoring it and giving it proper priority according to God's purpose would make intimacy in marriage as glorious as anything in this life could be. But faced with this unexpected reaction from his sweet wife, he felt completely unprepared to address what he had assumed had already been addressed. Then it occurred to him that he *was* prepared. He had just told her that they would not be ashamed to discuss in an appropriate way what rightfully would take place between them. He took pride in his ability to effectively communicate anything that needed to be said, convinced that thoughts and feelings unspoken were at the root of unfathomable damage in relationships. Surely he could say what needed to be said in a way that would alleviate her fears rather than compound them. Hearing unmistakable evidence that she was crying, he prayed again and resigned himself to doing whatever it took to alleviate her fears and appropriately educate her regarding the intimate relationship between a man and a woman. Considering her tender emotions, he shuddered to think of the women pushed blindly into marriage, innocent and unsuspecting, victims of the embarrassment and shame that some people attached to this aspect of the relationship, and of the men who were calloused or indifferent, or even cruel. But he knew that such attitudes were not God's way, and in spite of whatever his own shortcomings might be, in his heart he wanted most of all to live his life as God would have him live it. And right now that meant taking very seriously this stewardship he had taken upon himself to care for and honor this woman.

"Come," he said and touched her shoulder to turn her toward him. "There's no need for tears."

Eleanore felt doubly mortified that he'd realized she was crying. But she turned to look into his gentle eyes and saw no sign of impatience or aggravation.

"There will be no hiding your tears from me, my dear," he said. "Your tears are my responsibility now." She felt both confused and touched by such a statement, but couldn't deny the comfort she felt in the way he wiped her cheeks dry with his fingers. "If you don't know what to expect, then we must talk about it before this marriage goes any further."

Eleanore wondered how she could ever bear such a conversation, but she should have known that if anyone could tactfully approach such a topic, it would be James Barrington. With delicate frankness he explained the function of a man and a woman and exactly what would take place between them. He said it so easily that she was left wondering what all the embarrassment was about. And he only teased her once about blushing. Eleanore said nothing. She only watched her husband and listened, while ideas settled into her that she'd never considered before. Three times he referred to God's purpose in creating men and women in the way that He had, and he spoke of things from the Bible, referring to Adam and Eve, how God had brought them together and they *were not ashamed*. He quoted a scripture that she remembered reading more than once. *Wherefore they are no more twain, but one flesh. What therefore God hath joined together, let not man put asunder.*

Her husband's candid explanation of physical function gave way to a spiritual perspective of the cycle of human life, and the purpose of the marriage relationship in that cycle. And he expressed his opinion that the closeness and pleasure that were a part of the experience were surely every bit as important to marriage as the ability to create life. Hearing him put it that way, her heart warmed, and her fear vanished. *Together, they had the ability to create life.*

James finished what he needed to say and silently thanked God for having that behind them. He felt certain his words had somehow been guided. He'd watched his wife's expression merge from fear into astonishment, then soften into intrigue and acceptance. Still, he could well imagine that his explanations could feel overwhelming and even frightening without having time to allow them to settle. He felt he had to say, "We can wait . . . if you prefer. If you need some time to . . . think about what you've just learned, and feel more prepared, I certainly understand."

He could see her considering the option, but she said, "You don't want to wait."

He was committed to honesty. "No, I do not. But neither do I want you afraid and loathing it. This is meant to be an experience shared with tenderness and affection, not pleasure for me and some dreadful duty for you. In my opinion, the consummation of a marriage is equally important to the vows, so long as one comes after the other in the proper order. You spoke your vows with conviction and confidence, of your own free will. Did you not?"

"Yes, of course."

"I would not expect anything less of you now. If you're not ready, we will wait. I should not have just assumed that you knew what to expect." Still she said nothing. He asked, "Are you still afraid?"

"Yes . . . no; I mean . . . nervous, perhaps. But . . . if we wait, that will only be longer for me to feel nervous." She drew a deep breath and let it out slowly. "I don't want to wait."

James pondered his relief for only a moment before he touched one side of her face and kissed the other. He let his fingers wander through her hair, exploring it free from the restraint of pins and ribbons. Methodically and with patience he savored minutes of touching only her hands, her hair, her face, while he sensed her relaxing.

Eleanore was reminded of those few moments in the library as the brush of stubble on his face made contact with her own sensitive skin. He kissed her cheek, her temple, her eyelids, while his nearness became more alluring than frightening. She became so caught up in his gentle, passive affection that she was barely aware of crossing boundaries that had frightened her. What happened between them was more brief than she'd expected, and when it was over she had trouble deciding if she felt traumatized or awed. Both, apparently. But he whispered to her that with time they would become more comfortable with each other, implying that she had only just begun to comprehend this aspect of their marriage. She felt deeply relieved when he relaxed with the intent to sleep but didn't let go of her. Instinctively she wanted to hold him close, to cling to the experience they had just shared. And she felt deeply grateful to know that she would never have to let him go; he would always be a part of her life.

James urged the side of her face to his chest and wrapped her in his arms, relaxing more deeply than he had in years. This was the moment he'd been waiting for, longing for. The pleasure of intimacy was undeniable, and he'd certainly missed it during these years of celibacy. But it was this calm contentment he'd truly craved. This was what he'd missed most when his marriage with Caroline had crumbled. This was what he'd envisioned months ago, the first time he'd allowed himself to entertain the idea of asking this sweet woman to marry him. He'd wanted this moment when he could hold her close and luxuriate in the sustenance of human contact. But he'd always known that a moment such as this would have no value without the commitment of marriage behind it. Men who sought pleasure outside of marriage would surely always come away empty, returning in search of something they would never find. This moment was perfect only in knowing that she was his, and he was hers, and they would be together for a lifetime. Trust and respect and commitment were vital to creating such a moment as this. And he treasured it deeply, absorbed it fully, longed for it to never end. He fought sleep, not wanting to let go of the tranquility surrounding them. Then he reminded himself that this was only the beginning. She would be here tomorrow, and next month, and next year, and forever. Because she was that kind of woman.

Eleanore found the night to be dreamlike. Unaccustomed to sleeping so close to someone, she often woke up when either of them would shift positions, but he always drew her back into his arms as they got comfortable again and drifted off. She woke up feeling briefly disoriented, then her eyes adjusted to the morning light, and her mind accepted the fact that she was in her husband's bed. She turned to find him watching her, and he smiled. She returned his smile and resisted feeling embarrassed. After all they had talked about last night, and what they had shared, there was no room for shame or embarrassment in their relationship.

"Good morning, Mrs. Barrington," he said and leaned over to press a kiss to her brow. "Did you sleep well?"

"Yes, and you?"

"Oh, yes," he said and touched her face. His voice became tender. "It's so nice . . . not to be alone."

Eleanore had to admit, "Yes, it is."

"And you are so beautiful," he added, taking her by surprise. "I consider myself greatly blessed to wake up every morning and see such beauty beside me."

"I dare say in thirty or forty years I may not look the same."

He chuckled. "You'll always be beautiful."

He eased closer and urged her into his arms, only to relax and go back to sleep. And she did the same. She woke to find him dressed and leaning over to kiss her brow. "I have some business to attend to, but I'll see you later. There's some breakfast for you." He nodded toward the table near the window. "I'll meet you in the nursery for lunch with the children."

James watched her smile, and she lifted a hand to touch his face. He felt deeply relieved to see no evidence of aversion to him. Apparently her fears had been the reason for her resistance prior to their marriage. And while he'd tried to convince himself that whether or not she was attracted to him didn't really matter in the grand scheme of life, seeing her look at him that way most definitely added to his happiness.

"I'll see you then," she said, and once again he kissed her brow before he left the room.

Eleanore remained in bed long enough to allow the last twenty-four hours to catch up with her. She was amazed to realize that what she had dreaded had now become a rich and tender memory. And she was especially pleased to note that whether or not James Barrington ever came to love her, his tender nature and his kind regard for her were pleasant blessings. She was grateful to have found a man who became more admirable in her eyes every day.

Eleanore ate her breakfast, then decided she'd like a long, hot bath. But her attempt to heat the water, as she was accustomed to doing, was met with strong protest. She was also scolded by one maid for having straightened the bed, and by another for taking her breakfast tray to the kitchen. Both told her she was now the lady of the house, as if she'd committed a crime in simply wanting to take care of herself. While her bath was being prepared in the separate bathing room adjacent to the bedroom she now shared with her husband, Eleanore sat on the floor, leaning back against the side of the bed, unable to keep from crying.

"Whatever is wrong?" she heard him say, and she gasped.

"Oh, you scared me!" she scolded and turned away, quickly drying her tears.

"I didn't mean to frighten you," he said, squatting beside her. "But what's wrong?"

"It's not important."

"You're crying," he said as if she might not know. "If something makes you cry, it must be important." He urged her to her feet and put his arms around her, but that only propelled her tears back to the surface. "What is it?" he murmured, stroking her hair while she cried against his chest.

"I make a horrible lady of the house. I don't know what you were thinking when you asked me to marry you."

He chuckled. "Questioning my judgment again?"

"Yes!" she insisted, sniffling; but she didn't let go of him. "If I try to take care of myself, they all scold me. If I let them do for me I feel so foolish and out of place. I'm like a fish trying to live in a tree."

James chuckled again at the analogy and just held her close while she cried. The volume of her tears made him wonder if all of her stress and worry leading up to the wedding was tied into the issue at hand. But he didn't feel at all impatient. He relished holding her close and loved the way she needed him.

When she finally calmed down, he said gently, "You mustn't be offended by the servants wanting to help you. It's their job. And very soon we will be leaving here, and no one will be helping you but Lizzie, and that will be only as much as you want her to."

She looked up at him. "How soon?"

"Nine days," he said, and she smiled. But he felt the need to clarify, "The journey will be long and not necessarily pleasant. And once we get to America, it could take some time to decide where we want to settle, and to get there. Everything will be much different than it is here, for all of us."

"Do you think I'm not up to it?" she asked, challenging him with her eyes.

He laughed softly and touched her face. "Oh, I'm not worried about that. I'm certain you could take on just about anything and conquer it. I am concerned about the children, however. I fear it's not going to be the exciting adventure they think it will be."

"We'll just have to redefine the meaning of *adventure,*" she said.

James couldn't resist saying, "Like . . . becoming the lady of the house is a great adventure?"

Eleanore sighed and put her head again to his chest. "I suppose," she said and felt him chuckle while he ran a hand through her hair. How could she not be grateful to be the woman with James Barrington's ring on her finger? Even if she knew he would never give her his heart.

* * *

Late that evening, Eleanore sat in the center of the bed, wrapped in the sheet as far as it was possible without disheveling the bed. As she waited for her husband, she had to wonder what had become of the peace she'd felt over this aspect of marriage. While he'd held her close, his tender explanations had left her feeling completely content and comfortable. But now she felt uneasy, without understanding why. She focused her mind on prayer, wanting to feel what God would have her feel. Surely He would help her know what was right, what was best. He knew her desire was to be a righteous woman, and she knew He had guided her into this marriage. But at the moment she felt almost dark with confusion.

Eleanore's heart pounded when her husband came into the room. Without dousing the lamp, he sat behind her on the bed and wrapped his arms around her. "And how are you this evening, Mrs. Barrington?" he asked close to her ear. She didn't answer before he kissed her neck and added, "Oh, my darling, you are so very . . ." He stopped when she flinched involuntarily. "What's wrong?" he asked. She wanted to say nothing but couldn't bring herself to lie. He moved to her side and touched her chin, lifting her face to his view. "What is it, my dear?" Still she didn't answer. "I thought we'd gotten past all of this." He brushed the back of his fingers over her face. "Are you still afraid?"

Eleanore quickly searched her feelings. "No."

"Uncomfortable?"

She admitted it readily. "Yes."

"This is something new and foreign in your life. Surely it takes some adjustment to become accustomed."

"I'm sure you're right."

"But it's more than that," he guessed with certainty. She looked away. "Talk to me, Mrs. Barrington. I'll not have unspoken matters between us." While she was searching for the right words and reminding herself that she *could* talk to him, trust him with her deepest feelings, he asked, "Are you uncomfortable with *me?*"

"No," she said, and it was easy to add, "more . . . what we're doing, I suppose. I feel like . . . we're doing something wrong; that it's perhaps . . . wicked . . . or sinful."

"Why?" His brow furrowed; the concern in his eyes went deep. "We are husband and wife."

Eleanore cleared her throat and forced herself to go on. "But . . . all my life . . . I've heard it spoken of as if it were to be abhorred, always in hushed whispers, as if just talking about it at all was a sin in itself. And now . . . suddenly . . . everything is supposed to be different?"

"Yes, my dear," he said. "It *is* different, because we are *married*. What even good people fail to clarify when such things are discussed is that the intimacy between a man and a woman is not in itself sinful, but only when it is misused outside of marriage. The intimacy is not wicked, my dear, so long as it is honored in the way that God intended." Again he touched her chin and looked into her eyes. "What we share is a God-given gift, Mrs. Barrington. And because we have honored Him by keeping it within our marriage, we have every right to find great joy in what we share."

Eleanore felt his words penetrate her heart, and a trembling in her spirit seemed to echo their truth, filling her with unmistakable warmth. And she knew her prayers had been answered. She knew that what he said was true. Her confusion fled, and only light and peace remained. Memorized words from her most precious book came to mind. . . . *Remember that every good gift cometh of Christ.*

Eleanore smiled and touched her husband's face. She loved the feel of stubble on his cheeks in the evening as much as she loved the feel of his freshly shaven skin early in the morning. He asked with typical tenderness, "You're feeling better now?"

"Yes, thank you," she said. "You're right. It may take some time to adjust . . . to such changes, but . . . it's right and good that we should be together this way."

He smiled and eased her into his arms, kissing her cheek, her throat, her shoulder. What followed proved to be the most exquisite experience of Eleanore's life. Free of the fear and inhibition she'd felt the previous night, something inside of her came to life that she'd never imagined. And yet she felt as if she'd only begun to comprehend—that it could take her a lifetime to fully understand the glory of being a woman, and how that glory could only be fully manifested by sharing her life with a good man who honored and revered her as this one did.

* * *

Once she'd adjusted to allowing the servants to do their jobs on her behalf, Eleanore was surprised at how quickly she had become comfortable with being James Barrington's wife. And they'd only been married five days. While she soaked in steaming, lavender-scented water, he sat nearby and talked over something he'd read in the newspaper concerning a political event in America. Then he stood, bent over to kiss her brow, and left the room. She never would have imagined at the time of his proposal that she could feel so at ease with him under such intimate circumstances, let alone so quickly. Thinking back to her encounters with him prior to their engagement, she tried to imagine how she might have felt to think of their relationship coming to this.

Eleanore found great joy in officially being a mother to David and Iris. They'd started calling her Mama the very day of the wedding, and Eleanore loved hearing them say it in reference to herself. Their time together was much the same as it had always been, but now she felt a personal investment in their lives. They shared the same name; they were family.

Later that day, trunks were brought to their rooms and, with the help of Lizzie and Higgins, they slowly became filled with all that would accompany them to America. Eleanore was grateful for Lizzie's help, especially in packing for the children. While Eleanore's belongings were minimal, the children had far too many clothes and toys to take with them. David was more eager and willing to leave certain things behind and choose only his favorites, or things that were more practical for the life they would be living in America. But Iris was extremely sentimental and wanted to take everything. Eleanore prayed for guidance in handling the situation, not wanting this move to be any more traumatic for Iris than it might already prove to be. It occurred to her, laying in bed that night while her husband slept close beside her, that she needed to appeal to Iris's giving nature. The following morning she casually told David and Iris how she'd heard of some children who only had two sets of clothes and one toy each, because their families were so poor. She read some scriptures from the Bible about what Jesus said about giving to others, then she changed the subject. Later in the day, while they were once again faced with trying to pack Iris's belongings, Eleanore simply said, "My goodness, you surely have a lot of clothes and toys. When I was a little girl I never would have imagined so much."

"Did you only have one toy?" Iris asked.

"I had two or three, but not nearly so many as you have."

Iris was thoughtful, then suggested that they could give some of her things to children who didn't have so much. Eleanore told her it was a brilliant idea, and very generous. Dividing her belongings became much easier after that.

When Eleanore's things were packed, with the exception of the bare necessities she would need until they left, her husband commented while looking at her two open trunks. "An entire trunk of books, Mrs. Barrington? How many books does one woman need?"

"It's up to you, sir," she said. "Given the choice between the books and the wardrobe, I would prefer the books. You decide. You may grow weary of seeing me in the same dress every day, however."

"Very well," he said with mild severity, but later that day she learned that he had *two* trunks of books. She called him a scoundrel, and he laughed.

Chapter Nine

THE RUNAWAY

The day before they were scheduled to leave, Eleanore woke to the sound of thunder and heavy rain. After she'd shared a breakfast with her husband in their bedroom, she chose a simple burgundy dress from her new wardrobe and got dressed. While she was sitting at the dressing table in the bedroom, pinning up her braided hair, her husband sat on the edge of the bed to pull on his boots while he told her what time they would be leaving, and of their need to stay one night at an inn on their way to Liverpool, where he had passage booked on a sailing vessel.

"And how long will it take to sail to America?" she asked. "Do you know?"

"About six weeks," he said, and she turned to meet his eyes, feeling some concern over keeping the children entertained that long.

"It's a good thing we're taking all those books," she said.

"Actually, most of our belongings will be in the cargo hold, and we won't have access to them."

"Then I need to repack the bags we're keeping with us," she said. "Especially the children's. If we can—"

A knock at the door interrupted. "Come," he called, and David entered the room timidly.

"What is it, son?" James asked, sensing a melancholy mood in the child. He sidled up next to his father on the edge of the bed but said nothing. "You must tell me what's wrong," James urged and saw his wife turn toward them, her concern evident. "Are you afraid to go to America?"

"No."

"Are you sad to leave here?"

"Maybe a little. But not really."

"Then what's wrong, darling?" Eleanore asked, wondering if he might be more apt to speak openly with her absent.

She was considering a gracious departure when he said quietly to his father, "May I go in Mother's room? Iris wants to go in there too . . . before we leave."

James felt his heart quicken as he recalled his own need to go into Caroline's room and say good-bye to her. He put his arm around David and said, "Of course you can. And if you need to cry while you're in there, that's all right. Do you want me to come with you?" David shook his head vehemently and hurried out of the room.

A moment later he was startled to hear his wife say, "He'll be all right."

"I'm certain he will," James said and came to his feet. He put his hands on her shoulders while she was putting a pin into her hair. He pressed a kiss to her neck and murmured, "Tomorrow we start a new life, and we can put the old one away—forever."

Eleanore met his eyes in the mirror and put a hand over his where it rested on her shoulder. She couldn't even remember what it had been like not to have him at the center of her life. Or perhaps she could remember, but she couldn't imagine. He made it so easy to be his wife.

"I'll see you at lunch," he said and again kissed her neck before he left the room.

An hour later, Eleanore was rechecking the things she'd packed for the children when she heard David shouting, then glass breaking. She'd peeked into Caroline's room for the third time not ten minutes ago to find both children sitting on their mother's bed, talking quietly. She ran into the hallway only to see David run out of his mother's room and down the stairs, shouting, "Leave me alone!"

Hearing Iris crying, Eleanore hurried to see if she was all right before she went after David. He'd not run away in a long while, but she felt confident she could find him. Peering around the door of Caroline's room, Eleanore gasped to see a horrible mess on the floor. Broken bottles of bath salts and perfumes were scattered among a number of Caroline's belongings. Iris was screaming, holding tightly to a blue scarf. Eleanore rushed to take the child in her arms and remove her from the room. In the nursery, the child calmed down and managed to tell Eleanore that David had gotten angry while talking about things their mother had said and done that were hurtful. She left the child in Lizzie's care, then put on a heavy cloak to go out and look for David. After checking the usual spots, she became alarmed and went back in the house to find her husband.

"What is it?" he demanded, hurrying from behind his desk when she came breathlessly into the office, dripping water on the floor.

"David's gone," she said. "I thought I could find him . . . in the usual places . . . but he's not there." She started to cry. "The rain is cold today. I fear he—"

"I'll find him," he said and rushed past her. "Get some dry clothes on."

Eleanore changed her clothes, then paced and wrung her hands for more than an hour before her husband finally returned, carrying David into the house. The child was shivering violently, and Eleanore felt as panicked as Mr. Barrington sounded when he ordered the servants to do his bidding. "Get a doctor here, immediately. I need some hot tea, and warmed blankets, and towels. And the fires in his room stoked. Now!"

He carried the boy up the stairs with Eleanore close on his heels. "How did you find him?" she asked tearfully.

"A lot of praying," was his only answer. He led the way to

David's room where they worked together to get him out of his wet clothes and into a heated blanket that was provided.

Eleanore watched her husband as he sat on the floor near the fire, cradling his son against him, more upset than she'd ever seen him. When the obvious occurred to her, she said, "You need to get some dry clothes on." She urged the child to her own lap. "You can't help him get warm if you're freezing. Hurry."

He rushed from the room and was back in five minutes, holding his son while he prayed aloud that the boy would come through all right. By the time the doctor arrived David had warmed up, but he didn't look at all well. He was declared to have a fever, and it was made clear that until the child was well, he could not be traveling. The doctor gave them instructions and promised to check back in the morning. Eleanore sat with David while her husband went downstairs to arrange to have word sent to cancel their travel plans. Of course, the price for the passage could not likely be refunded at this point. But he considered that irrelevant. He made it clear that he wasn't taking any chances with his son's health. Eleanore couldn't help thinking how long it would have taken her to save passage just for herself, and how easy it would be for her husband to pay twice for six people and hardly bat an eye over it.

Eleanore was sitting at David's side, holding his hand in hers while he slept, when her husband returned to the room to tell her that everything had been postponed.

"Tell me what happened," he said, sitting on the opposite side of the bed.

Eleanore repeated all she knew. He hung his head and made an angry noise.

"You must forgive her," she said, and his head shot up, his eyes turned angry.

"I am trying, Mrs. Barrington, truly. But when her behavior is *still* hurting my children and she's been more than a year in the grave, I have trouble contending with that."

"I understand, sir," she said. "But harboring anger toward

her will not help your children heal."

He sighed. "Our children, you mean," he said more gently.

"Of course." She smiled at him, then turned her attention to David, pressing a damp cloth to his face.

James watched her and tried to figure how Eleanore Barrington had gotten the best of whatever Caroline had gotten the worst of. He marveled that they could be so completely different. She was so easy to be with, and she had taken to marriage and being the lady of the house far more graciously than even he had anticipated.

Caught up as he was in thoughts of his sweet wife, he was surprised to hear her say, "He looks like you."

James felt his heart quicken, certain she was seeing things. He forced a light enough voice to say, "Surely you jest. He looks nothing like me."

"Oh, but he does," she said and touched the child's face. "I've clearly seen it, right from the start. I see you in Iris as well, but not so strongly as I see you in David. Of course they have their mother's coloring, but sometimes when he assumes a certain expression he's almost like a miniature of you."

Eleanore heard a strange sound and looked up from her attention to David to see Mr. Barrington leaning over, his hands planted on the low windowsill, apparently upset. She rushed to his side and found him heaving for breath. "What is it?" she asked gently. "What's wrong?" He only shook his head. "Are you ill?" she asked, and he shook his head again. "Did I say something to upset you?" she asked. He made no comment, didn't move beyond his continued effort to catch his breath. Eleanore tried to recall what she'd said, wondering if there was a connection. Then her heart quickened. She put a hand on his shoulder, and another over his arm. "Talk to me," she urged.

He looked up at her, and she saw a vague glimmer of tears in his eyes. "Are you sure?" he whispered. "Do they really look like me?"

"Of course I'm sure," she said firmly. He closed his eyes

and pressed a hand over the center of his chest while a noise came out of his mouth that was some combination of sobbing and laughter.

Eleanore couldn't believe it. All this time, had he truly believed they were not his children? Recounting the evidences of his love and concern for David and Iris, for as long as she'd been working with them, she couldn't comprehend that such devotion could accompany his belief that the children had been fathered through his wife's affair.

"Talk to me," she said again.

He turned around and leaned against the windowsill, breathing more easily but with a hand still over his chest. "I can't believe it," he muttered, and his voice quivered. "When she . . . was pregnant with Iris . . . I found out about . . . her involvement. She admitted then that it had been going on between them almost from the start. She said that . . . she didn't know if the children were mine, but they were more likely . . . his."

"And yet you love them as much as any father could."

He looked at her, surprised. "And why wouldn't I? They have no control over the circumstances of their birth. They were born into *my* marriage, with *my* name. Do you consider yourself any less capable of loving David and Iris, or being a mother to them, even though you share no blood with them?"

"No," she said.

"Then you understand," he said and moved back to David's side to find him still feverish.

James sat beside him far into the night, pondering what he'd just learned through his wife's observance. He was most surprised to realize that it didn't change how he felt about his children. But it warmed something inside of himself.

Throughout the next two days, David's condition only worsened. The doctor said he didn't know if it was contagious or not, but they chose to keep Iris and all the servants at a distance. James found a new connection to his wife—and a deeper admiration—as they shared the bedside vigil of his son. Their son. She had taken to mothering so easily that he could almost wonder if she had been meant to raise them, even though another woman had brought them into the world. He observed with growing awe her reluctance to leave David's side. She slept on the bed beside the child, keeping a hand against his face as if to monitor his fever. And she knelt beside his bed through lengthy sessions of silent prayer. Caroline would have declared that she couldn't watch the child suffer, leaving him in the care of servants while she went about her life as if nothing were wrong.

David drifted in and out of fevered sleep, showing no appetite and declaring that his entire body ached. The doctor had come each day, reporting that there was nothing to be done except to attempt to keep the fever down. On the third day the doctor announced, "I believe it would be in his best interest to bleed him. Perhaps that way we can get rid of the infection as much as possible."

While James's heart quickened with dread, he saw his wife's expression become panicked.

"No!" she said, crossing the room to stand beside him. With a hand on his arm she said firmly to the doctor, "If there is infection in his blood, no matter how much blood you take, the infection will still be there. It will only make him weaker."

"Mrs. Barrington," the doctor said with controlled patience, "you clearly have no understanding of such medical procedures and—"

"Please . . . no," Eleanore said, looking up at her husband. She could never explain the intensity of her feelings on the matter. She softly implored, "I truly believe it will do more harm than good."

She waited, heart pounding, while she expected her husband to gently reprimand her for going against the doctor's judgment. He looked hard into her eyes as if he might find her reasoning there, then he turned to the doctor and said, "Thank you for the suggestion, Doctor, but our son will be keeping his blood."

"Mr. Barrington," the doctor countered, none too kindly, "surely you can see that—"

"You heard Mrs. Barrington," he interrupted. "Let me remind you that I am paying you to care for my son, and it's up to me whether or not to take your advice. If that is a problem for you, I'm certain I can find another doctor."

The doctor heaved a disgusted sigh, picked up his bag, and snarled, "I'll check on him tomorrow. God willing, he'll still be alive."

Stark silence resonated through the room in the doctor's absence. Eleanore again met her husband's eyes, wondering if he might reprimand her now that they were alone—or at least express some doubt in her conviction. But he simply said, "How do you know, Mrs. Barrington? How do you make such a decision with so much confidence?"

"I just . . . know. The same way I knew it was right to marry you."

He looked startled by the comparison. "You just . . . know?"

She took a deep breath and ventured to give him the whole answer, praying that he would accept it. "The scriptures tell us that . . . *By the power of the Holy Ghost ye may know the truth of all things.* They also say that . . . *The word of the Lord came . . . by the power of the Holy Ghost.*" She sighed and looked away. "I've been praying very hard that we would know what to do for him. I can only say when the doctor said what he did, something inside of me protested strongly. Call it instinct. Call it whatever you like. I believe it was God answering my prayers." She looked again at her husband. "I don't know whether or not David will survive this, but I firmly believe that what the doctor suggested would only make matters worse, and make it harder for him to recover."

For a long moment he contemplated in silence before he

said, "I pray you're right, Mrs. Barrington. And I pray that God will see fit to allow him to stay with us. I'm not certain how I could go on without him."

He moved to David's bedside and touched the boy's face. Eleanore moved to the other side of the bed and went to her knees, praying in silence, pleading with God to make David whole and well, and to calm his father's troubled heart. She looked up a few minutes later to find her husband across the bed, on his knees as well, his hands clasped, his head pressed against them. She bowed her head again and continued to pray.

After a grueling, sleepless night, David's fever broke in the early morning hours, and by afternoon he was asking for something to eat. After he'd eaten some broth and was sleeping peacefully, Eleanore found her husband standing beside her, and then he was holding her tightly. "Thank you," he murmured close to her ear.

James saw the puzzlement in her eyes. She was so oblivious to her own charitable nature. He smiled and touched her face. "For staying with him, for standing by me. For your insight, your faith. What I ever did without you I cannot imagine."

Eleanore felt so deeply warmed she could barely manage to utter, "A pleasure, sir."

He looked firmly into her eyes, saying, "My sweet wife, all that I have is yours. Tell me anything you want and I'll give it to you. Anything that is in my power to give. Anything . . . for the asking."

Eleanore recalled him saying the same when he'd proposed marriage. But she was startled now by the conviction in his eyes. Did he believe that bestowing lavish gifts on her would somehow make her happier?

"You're very generous, sir," she said, "but I already have more than I could ever hope for, or want."

He looked disappointed but said, "When you think of something . . . anything . . . you only have to ask."

"Thank you," she said.

He kissed her cheek, her neck, her shoulder, then kissed her cheek again. "You are truly precious, Mrs. Barrington," he said and left the room.

During the following days David regained his strength quickly, although they watched him closely and didn't allow him to overdo and tire himself. His parents agreed that they wanted him strong and well for the journey ahead.

David was thrilled when his father announced the family would be taking an excursion into town to eat lunch at the pub and do a little shopping. He specifically said the children could each pick out a new book and buy some candy for the journey. Travel plans had been arranged once again, and they would be leaving in less than a week.

Eleanore was pleased with the prospect of an outing, and even more pleased to have their departure date on the calendar. She was beginning to hate this house. For all her efforts, she still felt uncomfortable interacting with the servants. Mrs. Bixby and Miss Gibbs were kind, and she felt as if nothing had changed with them; or perhaps more accurately she felt that they respected the reasons for the change and were happy for her. Of course, she felt completely comfortable with Lizzie and Higgins, and she was grateful to know they were coming along. Of all the servants, she would have missed them most. But when it came to the rest of the staff, she would consider it a blessing never to have to see them again. Some of them seemed ridiculously in awe of her, as if her marriage had transformed her into some kind of goddess. But the majority carried an attitude of barely polite snideness toward her. It was too subtle to reprimand, but evident nonetheless. And Eleanore wanted to be away from them. She longed for the new life that her husband spoke of regularly. A new home. Land. And most enticing of all to him, freedom from ridiculous social barriers. Eleanore certainly placed a high priority on that as well. But what she longed for most was to find this new religion, to go to a country where such a thing as a new religion was even possible. She had continued to read every day in her most precious book, while its precepts and her conviction regarding them only deepened with time.

During the carriage ride into town, Eleanore pondered the forthcoming changes in their lives and felt far more excited than afraid, even though certain aspects were a little frightening. She had no idea what to expect. She was startled to remember the last time she'd felt afraid due to her own ignorance. Her wedding night. That seemed so insignificant now—thanks to her good husband, who was continually kind and gentle, and, thankfully, skilled at communicating sensitive matters. Watching him across from her in the carriage, with Iris on his lap, Eleanore reasoned that she had no cause to fear the unknown as long as he was beside her. And she knew he always would be. He was that kind of man.

As they stepped out of the carriage, Mr. Barrington said, "There's something I need to take care of; I will only be a few minutes. Once you're finished at the bookshop, go ahead to the pub—where we've eaten before—and I'll meet you there." He kissed her brow. "If you get there before I do, order for me whatever you get for yourself."

"We'll see you there," she said and took the children's hands. "Come along," she said and guided them into the shop. She let the children each pick out one new book with the specific purpose of helping to keep them entertained during the forthcoming journey. It was good to see Mr. Harvey, and they chatted comfortably while the children browsed. She told him how their journey had been delayed due to David's illness, but that he was doing well now and they would be leaving in a few days. He said with some tenderness that he was going to miss her, but he smiled when he told her that marriage suited her.

"Does it?" she asked, surprised by the comment.

"It does indeed, Mrs. Barrington. I've never seen you so . . .

content."

Eleanore just smiled and passed off the comment by checking on the children. Once their purchase was completed, Eleanore defied decorum and gave Mr. Harvey a quick hug, thanking him for his friendship through the years.

Eleanore took the children to the pub, disappointed not to find her husband already there. She sat at a table that had some distance from the sparse crowd. Iris sat beside her and David sat across from her. Eleanore was startled when Iris jumped from her chair and shrieked with excitement, "Wucy!" As she ran across the room, Eleanore recognized Lucy, the former nanny, who was apparently working here now, since she was wearing an apron and holding an empty tray. Iris wrapped her arms around Lucy's legs, taking the woman off guard. But Lucy laughed and squatted down to speak kindly to Iris, who then took hold of Lucy's hand and urged her to where they were sitting. "I found Wucy!" Iris said, clearly unaware that her absence in the household had any negative feelings attached.

"Hello, Lucy," Eleanore said kindly, finding no need or reason to hold ill feelings toward this woman. She noticed that David was avidly engaged in reading his book.

"Hello, Eleanore," Lucy said, equally kind. "How are you faring?"

"Well, and you?" Eleanore asked.

"Very well, thank you," she said and seemed to mean it.

"You're working here, then?"

"Yes," she said, "and I rather enjoy it. Although I usually do the evening shift."

"That's good," Eleanore said.

"I like being around so many different people," Lucy said, seeming genuinely content.

"Perhaps you were ready for a change then," Eleanore said.

"I believe I was."

Lucy told them what was on the menu that day and asked

what they would like to eat. Eleanore chose the shepherd's pie, and the children heartily agreed.

"Enough for four," Eleanore said before Lucy moved away. "Mr. Barrington will be joining us."

Lucy looked surprised but didn't comment before she went to the kitchen. A minute later Eleanore saw her husband come in. He caught her eye and smiled, crossing the room to join them. He bent over the table and kissed her brow before he took his seat across from her.

"Show me what you've got," he said to the children, and they eagerly showed him their new books.

While he was looking at them, Iris said, "We saw Wucy!"

"Did you?" he asked and glanced skeptically at Eleanore. She just shrugged and nodded as Lucy approached the table with their food. "So you did," he said quietly, and she sensed his disdain, however subtle.

"Hello, Mr. Barrington," Lucy said, surprising Eleanore with an attitude that seemed to say they'd once been well acquainted on a social level. Apparently she'd forgotten that their last encounter had been his dismissing her from his service due to her blatant dishonesty. Eleanore's surprise turned to mild astonishment when Lucy gave him a coy smile and added, "And how are you faring, sir?" Eleanore couldn't believe it. She was *flirting* with him! Eleanore watched her husband closely, wondering what his perception might be of Lucy's behavior.

"I'm very well," he said with a kind but indifferent smile while she placed their meal on the table. "And you?"

"Very well, thank you. I—"

"Have you told Lucy the big news?" James asked his wife, interrupting whatever Lucy might have felt the need to say.

James saw a sparkle in Mrs. Barrington's eyes as she said, "No, we hadn't gotten to that yet."

Iris piped in to say, "We be going to Amewica!"

"Truly?" Lucy asked, her surprise evident. James noted the

subtle, dubious glance she tossed toward his wife as she added, "All of you?"

"Of course," James said. "Which brings us to the *really* big news." He took Mrs. Barrington's hand where it rested on the table. "You wouldn't expect me to go to America and leave my wife behind, would you?"

Eleanore couldn't help but treasure the shock on Lucy's face. "Wife?" she echoed in a voice that squeaked. "You're getting *married?*"

"Already married," Mr. Barrington said and pressed Eleanore's fingers to his lips.

Lucy muttered some halfhearted congratulations and hurried away. Eleanore wanted to comment to her husband on this interesting interchange, but not in front of the children. "Later," he said as if he'd read her mind, and they proceeded to eat. They didn't see Lucy again before they left the pub.

Once outside, the children ran ahead to look in the window of the candy shop. Eleanore put her hand over Mr. Barrington's arm and said, "She was horrified, you know. She and a thousand other people are certain you must have lost your mind."

"Whatever are you talking about?"

"Lucy. She can't believe you would lower yourself to marry a servant girl."

He let out a good-natured chuckle. "That may be the opinion of some, but not Lucy. She's horrified, yes. But only because she's jealous."

Then Eleanore remembered her previous impression. "She was flirting with you."

"Yes," he said as if it were nothing, "she always did. I ignored it because I'd believed she was a fine nanny, and her behavior was too subtle to be out of line. When I realized her blatant lack of integrity, it was a relief to let her go. But she was far from the only woman in the household to flirt with me."

"Who?" Eleanore asked, then wished she hadn't sounded so

alarmed.

He chuckled at her response. "Several; I don't know. It doesn't matter. They're all a bunch of simpering fools. They see only money and position."

Eleanore glanced at her husband as they walked slowly. "I think it might be more than that." His brow furrowed with a dubious scowl. "Perhaps they see a fine man who treats a woman well."

He made a cynical noise. "I can assure you that anyone serving in my household had no evidence of my treating Caroline well for many years. They may not have had evidence to the contrary—except for you of course, sneaking into the library at night." His mouth twitched upward for only a second before his voice became severe. "But the servants' belief that my marriage was good could be nothing more than the absence of seeing anything bad—which means they were either blind, or they chose not to see the obvious." He shrugged. "It's money and position."

In spite of his heedless attitude concerning the way others viewed him, Eleanore couldn't help wondering if, somewhere inside, he had to be troubled over having his value as a man being measured by his finances. She tightened her hand over his arm and said, "For what it may be worth, that's not why I married you."

He glanced at her and chuckled. "No, you just wanted a ticket to America. It comes down to the same thing."

Eleanore stopped walking and held to his arm so that he would face her. "No, it's not," she insisted.

"Mrs. Barrington," he said in a voice too soft to draw any attention from others passing by, "I made it unmistakably clear when I proposed to you that I was offering passage to America and a lifetime of financial security for you and our children. I have no delusions over the practicality of the arrangement."

"And I will not deny that those aspects of *the arrangement* were certainly enticing. But I had worked with your children for more than a year, Mr. Barrington. I'd seen much evidence of the kind of man that you are. I can assure you that no amount of money would have lured me to accept such a proposal from a man if he were difficult or unkind. I married you because I knew you were a fine man, a man with integrity and ethics." She saw more than heard him take a deep breath. "And I've been married to you long enough to know that you *do* treat your wife well."

He smiled and touched her face. "You are a good wife and mother. It's easy to treat you well. I do no more for you than you would do for me."

Eleanore returned his smile and touched his face in return. He pressed a lingering kiss to her cheek, which brought her back to the realization that they were standing on the high street. "We mustn't," she said. "People. The children." A quick glance told her they were impatiently waiting, and watching.

He kissed her cheek again and murmured close to her ear. "I don't care what people think, and it's good for the children to see evidence that their parents . . ." He stopped abruptly, and she heard him take a sharp breath before he looked into her eyes, showing only a vague hint of some kind of guilt. Or was it regret?

Eleanore felt tempted to ignore it, but his lack of subtlety made the issue too pressing to avoid. "You were going to say it, weren't you." His eyes showed the tiniest spark of embarrassment before they turned down. "You were going to say that it's good for the children to see that their parents love each other. But you can't say it because it's not true." He met her eyes firmly, but she couldn't read his reaction to her accusation. "So . . . is your affection for me some kind of . . . acting . . . for the benefit of the children? Or perhaps a declaration to the rest of the world that you will do as you please? Or is it—"

"Mrs. Barrington," he said in a voice that was more calm

than she'd expected, "is the attitude behind my affection for you any different in private than it is in public?"

She had to say, "No." Beyond the fact that he'd never done anything in front of others that could ever be construed as inappropriate, there was no difference.

"Then you have your answer." He blew out a long breath and added, "It's good for the children to see evidence that their parents care for each other. It gives them security and a good example to follow when they become adults."

He started walking again. Eleanore made no further comment.

Once the children had picked out some candy, they were headed home. Eleanore felt some mild tension between her and her husband until he sat close beside her in the carriage and kissed her hand. Then he smiled and touched her face. How could she not feel the evidence of his caring and kindness? The display of his affection was far more than she'd ever hoped for. She needed to learn to be content.

While her thoughts were focused on the counting of her blessings, he held up a small package that she realized had been left on the carriage seat. "Was this your errand before lunch?" she asked as he handed it to her.

"Yes," he said with a gentle smirk. "We don't want to run out before we find a place to purchase its equivalent in America."

Eleanore opened the package to find more of the perfume he'd gotten for her. She laughed softly and thanked him. She couldn't deny that she enjoyed this indulgence. Each time she sprayed the perfume on herself, she would smile with memories of her mother. And then she'd smile again to think of her husband's insight and thoughtfulness in giving her such a gift. He'd told her to use it generously, and she had, enjoying every moment the fragrance touched her senses.

Eleanore was surprised to see her husband take the bottle out of its packaging. He sprayed the perfume on her arms and the back of her neck, then he sprayed some on Iris, making her giggle. He set the bottle back in its box, hugged his little daughter and said, "You smell beautiful, little lady."

"Wike Mama," she said proudly, smiling at Eleanore.

"Yes." He took Eleanore's hand and gave her a warm glance. "Like Mama."

Chapter Ten

THE DISPUTE

That evening while she was brushing out her hair, Eleanore's mind wandered back over the incident with Lucy and everything her husband had said afterward. And something incongruous struck her.

"Mr. Barrington?" she said and turned toward him. He was sitting in bed, reading a book on American politics. He made a noise to indicate he'd heard her, and she added, "Wasn't Lucy the nanny before Mrs. Barrington's death?"

He set the book down and gave her a searching gaze, as if he might find the motive in the question. "The former Mrs. Barrington, you mean?" His lips twitched with subtle humor. "Let's keep them straight, shall we?"

She smiled in return, and asked, "Wasn't she?"

"Yes," he said. "She'd worked with the children for a couple of years before you became the governess."

"Then I must have misunderstood you earlier."

"How so?"

"You said she had *always* flirted with you."

He picked up his book again, as if that might deflect the focus of the conversation. "No, that's what I meant."

Eleanore turned more fully in her chair. "Even while you were married?"

"Yes, my dear," he said and turned a page.

"Other women in the household too?"

"Yes," he said, his tone bored.

"Then . . ." she was so astonished she could hardly put the idea to words, "it wasn't money and position they wanted; it wasn't even marriage. They wanted . . ." She couldn't say it.

He looked at her over the top of his book. "Ludicrous, isn't it?" he asked.

"It's appalling!"

"Yes, it is." He set the book down again. "Allow me to explain something to you, Mrs. Barrington. Men in my position are reputed for being promiscuous. Not all of them are, but the majority, perhaps. Marriages are arranged, and men consider themselves unhappy so they go seeking for affection elsewhere. It's not terribly uncommon for serving girls to become involved with their employer."

Eleanore forced back an audible gasp, already embarrassed over her own naiveté. She simply asked, "Why?"

"I don't know all the reasons. Perhaps they're hoping for favoritism, gifts, money. Perhaps it's just about the attention from a man in a higher social class. Whatever it is, it's despicable. If people would stay in the beds they married into, the world would have fewer problems." Vehemence came with that last sentence, and she knew his personal pain over that concept was still close to his heart.

"So," she asked as a matter of principle, "what do you propose people do . . . who are unhappy in arranged marriages?"

His glance was sharp, perhaps suspicious. Did he think she was claiming to be unhappy? He said firmly, "They should keep their focus and attention on the marriage and allow it the time and attention needed to grow into something good."

"I agree," she said, realizing she loved such stimulating conversation with him, "but what happens when only one marriage partner is committed to such an attitude? Clearly, for all your efforts, the *former* Mrs. Barrington did not honor her marriage." She saw him bristle, however slightly. "You must have been terribly unhappy . . . and lonely . . . throughout those years."

"I was, yes."

"Yet you never sought affection elsewhere?"

"Never!"

"Even though servant girls were flirting with you."

She'd meant it as a compliment to his integrity, but he sounded mildly angry when he said, "Their lack of morals was not a problem in my life, Mrs. Barrington, because I knew my own morals very well. I still do. I know who I am, and I know the lines I would never cross." His voice softened, along with his eyes. "But I believe that biding my time and holding my ground paid off. I've been very blessed."

Eleanore realized he was referring to her, and something quivered inside her. She set the brush down and moved to the edge of the bed. He set his book on the bedside table and took her hand. "Now I am no longer lonely." He touched her face. "And I'm certainly not unhappy." He kissed her face. "In fact, I don't believe I've ever been happier."

"Why did you choose me?" she asked in a whisper, pressing her hand into his hair while he kissed her throat.

He paused to look into her eyes, and that faint smile of his vaguely touched his lips. "I just knew you were the one." He tickled her just enough to get a giggle out of her before he guided her into the bed beside him and kissed her throat again. And again. She wondered by the way he'd expressed that if he was referring to her declarations on how the Holy Ghost had guided her own decisions. Acknowledging her own happiness, she couldn't deny the hand of God in bringing them together. How grateful she was to be the woman He had guided into James Barrington's life!

* * *

In spite of the journey drawing closer, Eleanore found her excitement over the matter being pushed away by other, more consuming thoughts. She'd become surprisingly obsessed with her husband. When they were not together she wondered what he was doing, and she found herself gravitating toward him more frequently during the course of a day. Just being in the same room with him felt exciting and often left her jittery. Occasionally she would think of the intimate relationship they shared, and her stomach would quiver, often provoking a temptation to laugh aloud at the joy she'd found in being his wife. She was grateful for his explanations of how such aspects of their relationship were right and good; otherwise, she'd have to wonder if she was somehow wicked for entertaining such thoughts of her husband. But he was, after all, her husband.

While they sat in the office together, going over a final list to be certain that everything was in order for their journey, Eleanore couldn't keep her eyes off of him. She wondered why, in all the time she'd worked for him before he'd proposed marriage, she'd had no comprehension of how incredibly handsome he was. He looked younger than his years, and thoroughly masculine. Looking back, however, she was grateful she'd never noticed, never given a thought to such attraction. The very idea of putting herself into the same category as the other servant girls who admired him for any number of reasons—most of which were not appropriate or ethical—was repulsive. But she was his wife now, and she wondered what sweet twist of fate had given her such a rich privilege. To be the woman who shared every aspect of his life seemed too huge a blessing to hold in her heart.

He caught her looking at him and smirked playfully, while a recently familiar sparkle danced in his eyes. "What are you staring at, Mrs. Barrington?"

"My husband," she said. "It's the common consensus among the household that he is considered handsome and virile."

"I hold no regard for the common consensus of the household," he said. "It's only your opinion that matters."

"Oh, I heartily agree," she said. "Although, the thought never crossed my mind until after I became your wife. I was more attracted to other aspects of your character."

He smiled as if that pleased him. He held out a hand, and she rose to take it. He urged her onto his lap. "Now, are you interested in my opinion?" he asked.

"Of course."

He pressed a kiss behind her ear, making her shiver and giggle. "I think you are the most beautiful woman I have ever laid eyes on." He kissed her throat and pressed the fabric of her dress aside to kiss her shoulder.

"I know better than to think a man like you would marry a woman based on beauty."

"You know me well," he said and kissed her shoulder again and again.

"But I have to say that . . ." She hesitated, caught up in the sensation of his lips against her skin.

"What?" he asked, lifting his head to look at her.

"I never thought I was beautiful; I never felt beautiful until . . ."

"Until?"

She touched his face and pushed her fingers into his hair. She loved the thick richness of his hair. "Until you made me feel beautiful." A concept occurred to her, and she put it into words. "It doesn't matter what I see when I look in the mirror. The way you treat me makes me *feel* beautiful."

"As you should!" he said and kissed her throat, urging her more tightly into his arms.

They were both startled when the door came open, and Eleanore felt decidedly embarrassed to be caught in such a passionate embrace.

"Oh!" Mrs. Bixby said, her eyes wide. "Forgive me, sir. I didn't think you were in here. I was just going to leave a note and—"

"It's all right, Mrs. Bixby," he said with easy nonchalance, while he made no effort to relinquish his hold on his wife.

The housekeeper left and closed the door. Eleanore groaned.

"Are you embarrassed?" he asked as if he found the idea amusing.

"Yes, I am," she said firmly.

"Why? She saw nothing inappropriate. We're married, and this is our home. She walked in on us without knocking. It's not as if we're necking in the kitchen, or something."

"You're a scoundrel," she said lightly and eased away from him.

He chuckled. "If I were, you wouldn't have married me."

"Perhaps," she said and looked out the window while he resumed going over their final list.

When he was finished, he stood beside her and gently pushed back the hair from her face that had strayed out of the pins that held it to the back of her head. "You *are* beautiful," he murmured. Their eyes met, and again she saw his sparkle. She couldn't resist the urge to be close to him and loved the way he put his arms around her. He kissed the side of her neck while his fingers caressed the back of it, passively evoking memories of all they'd shared, and giving her anticipation in the knowledge that they would yet share it again. She sighed and leaned herself against his chest, holding his upper arms in her hands, noting how her fingers couldn't reach nearly around them. She couldn't help being overcome with the feelings that had been coming to life inside of her, feelings she'd never anticipated. She sighed again, and he asked, "What are you thinking?"

She hesitated only a moment before admitting to the truth, perhaps with the hope that he could answer the question. He always had the answer, it seemed. "What is this I feel?" She kept the side of her face to his chest but lifted her fingers to his slightly stubbled cheek. She could measure the time of day according to the growth on his face. "What is it that makes me want to be near you, every minute of every day, as if I might become eternally lost without you?"

Eleanore wasn't surprised that he had the answer, but it wasn't what she'd expected to hear, and she didn't at all like the methodical way he spoke it. "This is physical attraction, my dear. It's what draws men and women together."

She looked up at him, imitating his emotionless tone as she asked, "And what *keeps* them together?"

"Commitment," he said.

Yes, he certainly had all the answers. But being committed to honesty she had to say, "What I feel is more than that." She hoped she wouldn't regret adding, "Perhaps it's love."

"No! It's not love."

She took a step back, then another. It was the first time he'd ever spoken harshly to her. She would have never expected such a reaction to come from speaking of love with her husband, in spite of his prior declarations on the matter. She saw him check his emotion. His voice softened, but his eyes remained firm, almost hard. "You're far too young and naive to have any comprehension of love, Mrs. Barrington. What you feel is infatuation. It's nothing more than romantic notions mixed together with physical attraction. And it has led many a fool into destroying their lives. It distorts facts and casts any regard to compatibility or common beliefs to the wind. Respect and commitment are required to keep a marriage strong."

"Then physical attraction is irrelevant? Is that what you're saying?"

"Not irrelevant, my dear. But it certainly needs to be kept in proper perspective. Clearly what we share in that regard is sweet and wondrous, and it certainly strengthens the bond between us. But it will likely fade with time. And then what would we have?"

She wanted to say love, but she hardly dared let the word slip out of her mouth again.

He went on to say, "If physical desire were the only requirement of love, my dear, then love would abound in every brothel in the world."

"I can't believe you said that. You make it sound as if what *we* share is nothing more than—"

"It *is* more, Mrs. Barrington," he said and took hold of her arm. "It's more because I gave you my name before I ever touched you. It's more because we have committed our lives to each other, because we will share every day working together to make a good life for our children."

"And yet you make it sound so . . . systematic, so methodical. You've clearly thought everything out in detail, but where does emotion fit in, Mr. Barrington? I thought you cared for me."

"I *do* care for you." He spoke close to her face, sounding mildly angry. "You are my lover and my friend. I am profoundly fond of you. I enjoy your company, and I respect you deeply. I am committed to your happiness for as long as there is breath in me. But I do not, and will not, *love* you. I made that inescapably clear right from the start. You cannot expect it of me, because it's not in me to give, and you will only end up feeling hurt and disappointed."

I'm already hurt and disappointed, she wanted to say, but he was right. Whether or not she was only attracted to and infatuated with her husband could perhaps be disputable. He could never know or dictate *her* feelings. But he'd not given her any room for disillusionment regarding his own. She had simply chosen to forget his declarations in light of his tender behavior toward her. She reminded herself to be grateful that he *was* a kind and tender husband, that they were friends as well as lovers. She needed to restrain herself and have some compassion for how deeply he'd been hurt. If he were using his broken heart as an excuse to be cruel to her, she could never tolerate it. But that was not the case by any means, and she needed to let go of her own selfish disillusionments and be appreciative of what she had. Their marriage was far more comfortable and pleasant than she had ever imagined it could be. She needed to keep perspective.

As if he'd read her mind, he said gently, "We must not let such things come between us, my dear." He touched her face, and then he kissed it. "Forgive my anger."

She looked into his eyes. He didn't ask her to forgive him for denying her his love, but she did anyway. How could she not when his sincerity and caring were so evident?

"Of course," she said, and once again put her arms around him, relieved to feel him return the embrace. "Forgive my naiveté and ignorance. I don't intend to be demanding or impertinent."

"And you're not."

An unexpected surge of emotion rushed out of her deepest self, threatening to burst from her eyes and throat. Grateful that she'd at least maintained her dignity during the conversation, she rushed from the room, saying, "I must check on the children."

James watched her leave before he heaved a sigh and cursed Caroline under his breath. He hated what she had done to him, but he didn't know how to undo it. He'd anticipated the conversation he'd just had with his wife, but he'd not predicted how horrible it made him feel. He'd come into this relationship determined to be a good husband to her in every respect, and to remain emotionally detached. Clearly, it was not going according to plan. He could never love her; he was a man with no heart to give. But his concern for her tore at him. Still, all he could do was show her every day that he was a man who kept his promises. He would see her cared for in every respect. He would devote himself to her, honor her, and treat her the way she deserved to be treated. But he could never love her.

* * *

Eleanore hurried to find a place where she could be completely alone. Ironically, she found herself in a secluded corner of the maze, a place where David had often gone to hide. She cried long and hard while the truth of everything her husband had said battled with her emotions. She concluded that she wasn't nearly so disappointed with his lack of love toward her as she was to have her own feelings labeled as infatuation. But maybe he was right. She *was* young and naive. Still, she felt so drawn to him, so desirous to be with him day and night. Then it occurred to her that she had one distinct advantage over many women who might find themselves caught up in physical attraction and infatuation. She was married to the man. She concluded that she should consider herself blessed to feel the way she did, whatever those feelings might entail. What if she felt repulsed by her husband? Or simply indifferent? She believed so strongly in the sanctity of marriage that she knew, regardless of her feelings of attraction or the lack of them, that she would remain committed to the relationship. But having one with the other gave her life a certain blissfulness that she would enjoy while it lasted. Perhaps what she felt *would* be fleeting. Only time would tell. But the commitment would always stand. With that firmly in place, she resolved to enjoy this sensation of being young and in love. Were she not married she would need to use a great deal of discipline while matters of . . . how had he put it? While matters of *compatibility and common beliefs* were weighed and measured. As it was, she thanked God for guiding her into the life of this good man. Or had He guided this man into *her* life? Both, perhaps. Strange how they'd lived under the same roof for so many years but had needed to be guided together. God worked in mysterious ways.

Having vented her emotions and come to a firm resolve, Eleanore returned to the house and found the children playing a game with Lizzie in the nursery. She joined in, and they were soon laughing together. The evidence of her blessings mounted as she considered that very soon she would be going to America, and all of her favorite people were going with her. How could she not be happy?

Late that evening Eleanore sat in bed, leaning comfortably against several pillows while she read from her most precious book. Excitement filled her to think that she would soon be going to America, although she felt certain that finding the people who shared her beliefs would not necessarily be easy once they arrived. Still, being on the same continent would increase her chances.

As her husband came into the room, her heart quickened as it always did at the sight of him, then it unexpectedly tightened as a new reality occurred to her. He was her husband. She could never go searching for anything without him. As of yet, she'd not even told him about the book in her hands. She'd not purposely tried to hide it from him, but she'd not necessarily given him ample opportunity to notice it either. To this day she'd discussed it with no one except Mr. Harvey, and that had been cursory. No one knew what this book meant to her; no one knew of her absolute knowledge of its truth. Normally, she might have discreetly slipped the book into the drawer of the bedside table, but tonight she kept it open on her lap while they chatted comfortably, as if the dispute that had come up earlier were nothing. He opened a window, commented on what a warm day it had been, then removed his waistcoat and shirt. He sat on the edge of the bed to pull off his boots, then he stretched out beside her, putting his head in her lap, apparently oblivious to sharing the space with a book, now closed with a ribbon left between the pages where she'd been reading.

"Are you nervous?" he asked.

"About what?"

He looked up at her and smiled. "Oh, nothing significant," he said with light sarcasm. "You're just . . . leaving everything you've ever known behind and traveling a few thousand miles to a place you've never been before to start a new life in a place that's reputed to be rugged and unrefined."

"Oh that," she said and laughed. "Why should I be nervous when I have you to take care of me?" He smiled and rubbed a gentle hand on her leg. "Besides, I'm *not* leaving behind everything I've ever known. What's most important is going with me. I'm taking you and the children and my very best friend."

"And a trunk full of books."

"Exactly," she said. "Are *you* nervous?"

"A bit, to be truthful."

"Why?" she asked, toying with his hair.

He sighed. "I just want everyone to stay safe and strong. There is so much that's unpredictable. I don't want this to become a hardship for you or the children, or for Lizzie or Higgins. I feel responsible for all of you. I *am* responsible."

"God will be with us, I'm sure. So long as we turn to Him, then whatever happens is surely His will."

He contemplated her words. "Where *do* you get such faith, Mrs. Barrington?"

She only shrugged, then she almost shivered as his eye was drawn to the book on her lap. Was it her imagination that something instinctive in him was drawn to it in answer to his question?

"What are you reading?" he asked and picked it up.

"I found it," she said, "a long time ago."

James's attention was diverted from the book to a sudden nervousness in his wife. He realized now that he'd seen her reading this a great deal, but he'd never bothered inquiring about it. Now, he simply asked, "Why are you concerned about my looking at this?"

Eleanore was startled by the question, but she knew this conversation was necessary. She not only needed to be honest, she needed to be *completely* honest. He was her husband. He needed to know what this meant to her.

"I haven't told *anyone* how important this book is to me. It is my most priceless possession."

James attempted to consider the depth of feeling behind such a statement—and the intensity in her eyes. "Beyond the Bible?" he asked, knowing how precious the scriptures were to her.

"Along *with* the Bible," she said with no hesitation. "The two go . . . together."

"Together?" he asked skeptically, but still he didn't open the book.

"They are both scripture."

"This is *scripture?*" he echoed, even more skeptical. "How can anything but the Bible be considered scripture?"

"I can answer that question, but it could take some time . . . and it's late."

Eleanore longed to discuss the principles she'd learned with him. But at the moment she was more concerned with him knowing the truth behind her motives. She didn't want him to think she'd been keeping secrets from him. She decided to start at the beginning.

"Before your first wife died, I was walking into town one day . . . in the rain . . . and there it was, lying in the mud. Thankfully the damage to the cover was minimal. The first time I opened it I just . . . felt something."

"Something?"

"Something . . . powerful. Something sweet. I turned right around and came home. I couldn't stop reading. I didn't want to eat or sleep. What I've learned from this book has affected me more than anything else in my life. And I know beyond any doubt that it's true."

James allowed everything she'd just said to sink in. *Scripture?* And she *knew* that it was true? He felt tempted to doubt her, but he'd never once questioned her instincts before. Could he doubt them now simply because what she was telling him sounded odd? He turned his attention to the book in his hand and sat up in the center of the bed. He thumbed through it and let the pages fall open. His eyes focused on the words, *Behold, my soul delighteth in proving unto my people the truth of the coming of Christ; for, for this end hath the law of Moses been given; and all things which have been given of God from the beginning of the world, unto man, are the typifying of him.*

That didn't sound so strange. In those words alone he could see what she meant about it going together with the Bible. "It's Christian," he said, feeling deep relief over that alone. He could tolerate his wife believing just about anything, as long as it was Christian.

"Yes," she said eagerly. "It's the translated record of an ancient people who left Jerusalem and went to the promised land. And they had prophets just like in the Old Testament, who prophesied of the coming of Christ. And after Christ was resurrected, He visited these people and taught them all of the same things He taught in the New Testament. That's what He meant in the Bible when He said there were other sheep. I've heard there is a new religion based on the principles of this book . . . in America."

Again James had to let her words settle in. Her passion and vehemence were touching, but perhaps a bit disconcerting. This was simply an aspect of his wife he'd never seen, or even considered. And then it struck him. Everything made perfect sense.

"This is why," he said, holding up the book. "This is why you want to go to America. To what? Find these people? Become part of a new religion?" She glanced down, but not before he saw the truth in her eyes.

Eleanore's heart pounded, and tears overtook her. What if he strongly opposed her desires? Would her greatest passion become an ongoing dispute between them? And if it did, what would she do? In her heart she knew the answer. She'd exchanged vows with this man. She knew that being with him was right. She could only pray that he would come to understand what this meant to her. The gentle tone of his voice was a relief when he lifted her chin and said, "Tell me."

"Yes," she said, "this is why." She sniffled, and he wiped at her tears. "I never had any desire to go anywhere until I found the book. And then it was all I could think of. I prayed for a way. I knew that saving for passage and enough money to meet my needs could take years, and then . . ." She sobbed and grabbed the handkerchief he offered her, holding it briefly over her mouth. "Then . . . you insisted that I become a governess to your children, and my salary was raised significantly. I had believed it was an answer to my prayers. It would still take years, but not nearly so many. And then . . ." She became too emotional to speak, but she found her husband's arms around her.

"And then you were given the opportunity of a lifetime." James felt her nod against his shoulder, while the words he'd said to her at that time came back with clarity. *If you prefer to keep the arrangement simple . . . I need a mother for my children, and you want to go to America. We are in a position to help each other.* He'd never imagined in that moment that her desire had a specific purpose, which brought him to one undeniable concern. He didn't want to, but he had to ask, "So tell me, Mrs. Barrington, when you get to America, which will be most important? Seeking out this new religion, or your family?"

Eleanore lifted her head abruptly, astonished by the question. "I could never leave you. *Never!* Not for anything. The vows we exchanged are most important, above all else. What value would any religion have without family?"

James felt inexplicably relieved. Whatever her religious beliefs might be, her priorities were where he needed them to be. He could support her in just about anything, as long as she remained by his side and did the same for him.

Eleanore pondered the implications of the question he'd asked her and had to say, "Did you think I would . . . what? Leave you once I safely arrived on American soil?" He didn't answer, and she said, "I would hope you know me better than that."

James weighed his words carefully. "You've never given me any reason not to trust you, Mrs. Barrington. But . . . I admit to being overly sensitive in regard to . . . trust in marriage. I just . . . need to know where I stand." He handed the book to her. "America is a huge country, my dear. How do you propose to go about finding a small religious group?"

"The book was printed in New York."

"We're not going to New York," he said, and she was both horrified and surprised. She'd heard him say more than once that New York was one of the country's major ports.

"But I thought . . . our passage was to—"

"Our original passage *was* to New York. This time I got what was available. We're going to Virginia. Since we have no idea yet where we're actually going to settle, I didn't believe it would make any difference. For what it's worth, Virginia just felt right. At least I believe that's where we need to start out."

Eleanore nodded, fighting to hide the depth of her disappointment. She knew that once they arrived, he intended to ask around and get information about different areas before deciding where they would travel. They had both agreed that God would guide them to the place that was right to raise their family. He wanted a significant piece of land and knew they had to travel west a ways to find any. But Eleanore had hoped that they would at least be in New York long enough for her to get some information.

James noted the resignation in his wife's expression that didn't hide the vivid sorrow in her eyes. He lifted her chin and wiped away a new stream of tears. "Once we're settled, we'll write and inquire according to the information you have. If this new religion is as wonderful as you claim, surely they can't be too difficult to find. Surely God will show us the way to go."

She nodded, showing a genuine smile before she embraced him and put her head to his shoulder. "You're really very good to me," she murmured.

He ran a hand through her hair and kissed the top of her head, inhaling the sweet mixture of her shampoo and the rose-scented perfume he'd given her. "Being good to you, my dear, is the easiest thing I've ever done." She tightened her arms around him, and he prayed that she wouldn't be too disappointed when this new religion could never be found. He couldn't imagine any such thing as *new* religion lasting for more than a moment.

Chapter Eleven

THE PROMISED LAND

Eleanore didn't shed a tear when they left the house where she had lived since her childhood. And she could feel only fond farewells of the countryside they passed as the carriage took her farther than she'd ever traveled in the whole of her life. Having her husband beside her, the children always near, and her dearest friend along, she could find no regrets. They all stayed that night at a country inn and were on their way before dawn the following morning.

They arrived in Liverpool late in the afternoon. Eleanore was even more stunned than the children to see the vastness of the ocean. Before nightfall they were settled into their cabins on the ship—cramped quarters that were, surprisingly, the best available for any price. They sailed with the evening tide, and Eleanore felt a deep thrill to sense the motion of the vessel that lulled her to sleep in her husband's arms.

Five weeks into the expected six-week journey, Eleanore mentioned to her husband that they'd been very blessed. The weather had been fair, and they were all healthy. No one in their little group had even struggled with the seasickness that many on board were contending with. The children had even done well with the restricted space. Their love of reading had been a huge blessing while Eleanore kept them lost in stories in order to avoid having them become impatient with no place to run and play. She was just writing in her journal that the journey had been without event when a knock came to the cabin door.

Her husband got up to answer it. The children remained asleep. It was Lizzie and Higgins together, which had become a common occurrence since they'd set out. Apparently the two of them had a great deal to talk about.

"Could we speak with the both of you, sir?" Higgins said.

"Of course," Mr. Barrington said, and they all stepped into the narrow hallway where they wouldn't disturb the children.

Eleanore wondered what this might be about, and then she saw Higgins take hold of Lizzie's hand. He cleared his throat, then laughed softly. "We're getting married in the morning, sir."

"Married?" Mr. Barrington chuckled. "Truly?"

"Yes, sir," Higgins said, looking at Lizzie with glowing eyes. "I hope that won't be a problem."

"No, of course not," Mr. Barrington said. "Congratulations."

"The captain will be performing the ceremony on deck, right after breakfast," Higgins went on. "Of course we want the both of you there, and the children."

"We'll be there," Eleanore heard her husband say while she hugged Lizzie tightly.

"Why didn't you tell me?" Eleanore asked her quietly while the men spoke between themselves.

Lizzie whispered, "I thought we were just friends, although we've grown very comfortable with each other. Then out of the blue, a couple of hours ago, he just . . . asked me. He told me that he's grown to love me. What could I say? He's a fine man."

"He is," Eleanore said, noting a definite sparkle in Lizzie's eyes. "I'm so happy for you." They hugged again.

Higgins took hold of Lizzie's hand, saying, "We'll see you in the morning then, sir, madam."

"Of course," they both said.

Eleanore felt her husband's hand on her shoulder as they watched them walk away. "Who would have guessed?" he said.

"Apparently they're quite in love," she said, and the glance he gave her was only mildly sharp.

"Perhaps," he said. "And it's certainly convenient. If one or the other of them were running off after romantic notions, it would certainly create challenges, now wouldn't it."

They went back into the cabin, and Eleanore finished writing in her journal, now that she had much more to write about. She was grateful to know that her husband would respect her privacy with her journals. She doubted he would appreciate reading her most honest emotions in regard to his opinions on love. She reminded herself once again to be grateful for all that she had.

The following morning, Eleanore couldn't keep from crying during the ceremony, mostly because she was happy for Lizzie to have finally found someone after so many years. But a little part of her felt sorry for herself, wishing that James Barrington might be willing to actually love his wife, and even declare it boldly. *Count your blessings,* Eleanore commanded herself and focused on Lizzie's joy. Her new husband looked happy as well.

The day after the wedding, Eleanore stayed close to her bed, not feeling at all well.

"What is it?" Mr. Barrington asked, checking her face for fever. It wasn't like her not to be up and dressed long before now.

"It's nothing to be worried about," she said, wishing she could have prevented tears from accompanying her explanation. "I'm not pregnant . . . again."

He sat on the edge of the bed and pushed her hair back from her face. "You mustn't worry," he said. "It's not been so terribly long. It will happen."

She forced a smile, and he kissed her brow. She could never explain how desperately she wanted to have his baby. But clearly the time had not yet come. And all she could do was wait.

The skies were overcast when the ship came into a port in Virginia with the morning tide. Eleanore waited on the pier with Lizzie and the children while the men went to secure accommodations. They weren't gone as long as Eleanore had expected, and a few hours after arriving in America, they were settled into a comfortable hotel, with all of their trunks being stored by a company that would transport them to a desired location when they figured out where that would be.

They stayed in Virginia only one night before they traveled by coach farther than they'd gone in England to get from their home to Liverpool. This place had an entirely different feel from the port in Virginia, but they found adequate accommodations and settled in until they could make a decision on where they were going, and acquire the necessary supplies to get there. For more than a week Mr. Barrington and Higgins went out each day, gradually gathering information and supplies for travel, while Eleanore and Lizzie cared for the children much as they had in England. They worked on lessons, played games, and went for walks. On the second day, Mr. Barrington brought home some maps and quietly studied them. Eleanore became intrigued, almost amused, with the way he talked to anyone congenial enough to talk and asked their advice on where to settle. He started keeping a list when there were too many places to remember. A few of these places came up multiple times. He also asked people their reasons for suggesting such a place, and he started writing those things down as well. On the fifth day, Eleanore found him looking at the maps, his expression sober and concerned. She sat down beside him and took his hand.

"This could be one of the most important decisions we ever make. We're not just talking about a place to live. We're talking about the community our children will be raised in, the influence of the people and the culture. I don't just want to find any piece of land. I want to stand on it and feel like I've come home."

"You said that God would guide us. Surely He understands your desires."

"I believe that," he said. "But . . . where do we even start? It's so overwhelming. And how do we know if it's really right? Or if we're drawn to a place for the right reasons?" He handed her the list of cities and areas. "What do *you* think, Mrs. Barrington?"

"What do you mean?"

"You've got good instincts; you've proven that over and over. I want to know what you think."

"I don't know," she said, handing back the list. "What if I choose wrong? Or what if I choose a place you wouldn't have chosen?"

"This should be a mutual decision, something we should both agree on—with confidence."

"Of course, but if either of us even makes a suggestion . . . will it influence the other?"

He sighed, then chuckled. "You're making this more difficult; you're supposed to make it easier."

Eleanore said, "Read me the list, and tell me what you know of the advantages of each place."

They spent nearly two hours going over cities and counties, states and territories. Eleanore found a couple of names standing out in her mind, but she felt hesitant to say them, not wanting the burden of this decision on her shoulders, or for her suggestion to influence him if he had different ideas. Then a thought occurred to her. "How about if we each write down three places, in order of preference, according to our . . . well . . . our instincts; according to what feels right. I believe God will guide us through our feelings. Then we'll trade papers. If we have a match in any of the three, we'll have a place to start. If not, we'll try it again."

He clearly liked that idea, but it took them both another twenty-four hours before they were willing to sit down and write the names of three locations. Eleanore didn't want to admit that intertwined in her prayers was a desire to find the people who shared her beliefs. She didn't know where they were, but God did. She felt tempted to locate these places of her choice more specifically on the map and consider their distance from New

York, where the book had been printed, but she didn't want to be influenced even by that. And she reminded herself that even if God guided her to a specific place, it might take time to reach her quest.

As she put the pen to paper, only one place stood out in her mind—so strongly that it almost felt like the pen refused to write down anything else. She wrote it next to number one, then resisted the urge to write the same city down two more times. Instead she wrote a couple of other names that clung less intently to her mind. They each folded their papers in half, then slid them across the table. He let go of his as he took hers.

"You go first," he said.

Eleanore took a deep breath and opened his paper, expecting to be disappointed or frustrated by this process. But tears quickly blurred her vision as what he'd written coincided eerily with her own feelings. Just seeing *Iowa City* written at the top in his hand left her suffused with warmth. She *knew* it was the right place.

James saw tears in her eyes and wondered over their source. Instead of asking, he just opened the paper she'd given him and took a sharp breath. If it hadn't been her handwriting, he might have thought he'd somehow ended up with his own. There it was, in black and white, in the same order that he'd written them. Iowa City. Illinois. Missouri. He took her hand across the table and said, "It looks like we're going to Iowa City." But he couldn't help wondering what significance there might be to the other two locations. Perhaps they would never know. Or perhaps they too would prove significant to their future. For now, however, he knew their destination, and fresh excitement filled him.

"Come here, Mrs. Barrington," he said as he stood and pulled her into his arms. He laughed and held her against him, lifting her off the ground. She laughed with him, and he set her down. "Do you think you're up to this?"

"I've told you before, I know you'll take care of me. I'm certain we'll all be fine."

Two days later they set out at dawn. James put the sleeping children into the back of one of the two covered wagons he'd purchased, which were loaded with supplies. He helped his wife onto the seat and sat beside her, taking the reins into his gloved hands.

"You know how to do this?" she asked with a humorous edge to her tone.

"No," he admitted, and she looked startled. "But Higgins gave me a quick lesson last night. He was once employed driving a carriage and four." James snapped the reins, and the team of two horses moved forward, following the wagon in front of them that Higgins was driving.

"Very good," Mrs. Barrington drawled with humor as they moved forward.

"The horses know what to do better than I." He chuckled. "Truthfully, I know nothing, Mrs. Barrington. I've been trying to keep it a secret until now. Face it, I was raised a useless man. But I'm willing to learn. Higgins will save us. He grew up on a farm and has been employed in a variety of occupations that will be helpful to a fool like me. You don't think I just brought him along for company, do you?"

Eleanore felt a deep pride in her husband, and a growing admiration. She put her hand on his arm and kissed his cheek. "Well," she said, "he does make fine company."

"Yes, he does," he said, and Eleanore focused on the way the scenery changed as the sun came up.

By noon she already hated it. A pillow solved the problem of the hard seat they were riding on, but the heat and the dust were not so easily dealt with. She told herself she was a woman who knew how to work hard, and she could survive this. She was determined not to complain, and instead put her focus on helping keep the children cheerful and distracted.

On the second day, she watched her husband take the reins in hand and felt a quiver in her stomach. Already this adventure had brought out something indefinable in him that stirred her. It was as if he'd been born to lead a different life than the one he'd been leading. Seeing a subtle sparkle in his eyes, and the easy way he took to such rugged living, she felt less prone to thinking of her own misery. As the horses moved forward she touched his face and found unexpected stubble.

"You didn't shave," she said.

"It's too much bother."

"So, is this the beginning of a beard then, Mr. Barrington?"

"We'll see," he said and kissed her hand.

Again Eleanore kept her focus on the children, proud of them for their lack of complaining. And she told them so. For variety they occasionally rode the horses, which were being controlled by their father. And sometimes they all walked beside the wagon for the sake of exercise. Eleanore often preferred walking to the bumpy ride. She and Lizzie often walked side by side, exchanging pleasant chatter that helped pass the time.

Within a few days they had all become adjusted to cooking over an open fire and keeping covered to avoid the bite of the sun and wind. Accustomed to the mostly cloudy skies of England, they were all amazed at the endless stretch of blue sky that allowed the sun free reign. The heat was unbelievable. Eleanore had never imagined that the human body could sweat so profusely. She lost track of the days and stopped trying to guess when they might arrive. She just put one foot in front of the other, always grateful for a good meal and a good night's sleep, certain it could be much worse.

The men calculated that they were more than three-quarters of the way to Iowa City when Eleanore woke up feeling ill. She scrambled out of her makeshift bed in the predawn light and ran barefoot into the tall grass where she heaved for several minutes, grateful her stomach had been mostly empty. She returned to find her husband just coming awake and said nothing to him, since she felt fine after breakfast. Then it happened again the next morning, accompanied by a horrid spell of light-headedness. Again she returned and found that no one had noticed her new early-morning routine. But when her husband was harnessing the horses, she stood beside him and said, "There's something I need to tell you." He stopped what he was doing and gave her his full attention. His expectant expression prompted her to just say it. "I think I'm pregnant."

She saw his lips show the hint of a smile, while his eyes showed concern. "Are you ill?" he asked.

"Just a little . . . early in the mornings. I'd honestly lost track, but . . . now I'm . . . relatively certain."

He sighed loudly and wrapped her in his arms, holding her tightly for a long moment before he looked into her eyes. "You must be very careful."

"I'll be fine," she insisted but saw worry in his eyes. Eleanore felt more preoccupied with the joyous prospect of having a baby—James Barrington's baby.

Throughout the remainder of the journey, Eleanore's joy became entirely swallowed up by her misery. She'd never been so sick in her life. The times when she actually threw up were a relief. Most of the time she just felt as if she were going to. The constant nausea was made worse by an exhaustion that threatened to devour her. The heat and the motion of the wagon aggravated her condition immensely. She was continually amazed at her husband's kindness and patience, and his repeated apologies for putting her into this situation.

"There's no need for that," she said, holding his hand while he sat beside her at the end of another long day. She sniggered at an unexpected thought.

"What's funny?" he asked with an edge, as if humor at the moment was entirely out of line.

"Just think, Mr. Barrington, if Lucy could see me now, she'd surely fly into a jealous rage." He reluctantly chuckled, then pressed his forehead to hers, and she added, "A thousand women would envy my position right now." He groaned with just a touch of humor as he remembered words he'd said the day he'd proposed.

"Oh, my dear," he murmured, "this is very poor timing, indeed."

"It will be all right," she insisted, but he didn't seem convinced. "I have no regrets," she added and touched his face, and for a moment she almost thought he looked like he might cry.

Throughout the following days he repeatedly suggested that they stop at some other settlement along the way and take up residence elsewhere; there was certainly plenty of civilization available, and more than enough land for sale. But Eleanore felt an urgency to get to their destination. She wanted the journey behind them. She insisted that they keep going. In her heart she knew it needed to be Iowa City, even if she didn't understand why.

A break in the monotony occurred when they arrived at the banks of the Mississippi River. Eleanore had never imagined a river could be so wide. It had a lazy elegance in the way it flowed that intrigued her. The wagons were ferried across the river for a price, an experience that was a gentle reprieve from the rough motion of the wagons. Eleanore stood at the edge of the ferry as it moved from east to west, and she felt calm and full of hope. The river seemed to represent a defined boundary between the life ahead of them and the life they were leaving behind. When they arrived at the west bank, she was glad to be that much closer to their destination, but hated the continuation of this experience that was so utterly miserable for her.

Lizzie took good care of Eleanore and watched out for the children while the men drove the teams. And Eleanore became mostly incapable of doing anything at all. She just lay in the back of the covered wagon while the motion of the journey only enhanced her sickness. But she was far too weak and exhausted to walk in the heat. Arriving in Iowa City was absolutely the greatest relief of her life. The day after their arrival, Eleanore found herself nestled in clean sheets, bathed and wearing a freshly laundered nightgown. The large open windows and huge trees outside them combined to usher a light breeze through the room that took the sting off the heat. Summer was easing toward autumn, and the temperatures were not quite so ghastly as they had been. Eleanore still felt horribly nauseous and exhausted to her core, but they had made it. They were here. Now her husband would seek out some property and buy it. And they would make their home near this place. He was hoping to find land with a home already in place, which would prevent them from having to find other accommodations while a house was built. Eleanore was past caring, as long as she had a bed that wasn't in motion.

Eleanore closed her eyes and inhaled the breeze. She was surprised to feel the bed move and opened her eyes to see her husband sitting beside her. He looked cleaner and better groomed than she'd seen him in weeks, but he still wore the beard he'd grown during the journey. It was now neatly trimmed and framed his face well. His cheeks were mostly clean shaven, and two narrow lines came down from the sides of his mustache to merge into the hair on his chin. She reached up to touch it at the same moment as he brushed her hair back off her face.

"My dear Mrs. Barrington," he said. "Are you all right?"

"I'm much better now, thank you," she said. "I'm sorry to have complained so much."

"You didn't complain," he said. "I thought you were very brave and dignified."

"I tried to be brave," she said with a little laugh, "but I made no effort toward dignified. I let go of being dignified the first time you found me throwing up in the grass." He only smiled, and she added, "But you took such good care of me."

"You're my wife." He put a hand over her belly. "This is our baby. And now I'm going to find a home where I pray you will never know misery again."

He kissed her brow, and again she touched his beard. "It looks very handsome, Mr. Barrington. I do believe I like it."

He left her to rest, and she woke to find Lizzie with her. The children were reading close by. When Iris saw that she was awake she crawled up on the bed and snuggled close to Eleanore, something she'd done a great deal of throughout the journey. Eleanore tightened her arm around the child and said to David, "What are you reading? Why don't you read it to me?" He seemed pleased and moved closer to the bed to read aloud.

Eight days after arriving in Iowa City, Eleanore was grateful to be feeling better. The absence of extreme heat, endless dust, and the motion of the journey helped immensely. And she had visited with a local doctor who gave her some suggestions for eating patterns, and instructions about certain types of food that might help the problem. His ideas worked wonders, and she was able to get up and get dressed, almost feeling like a normal person again, albeit very tired. But Eleanore noted that her husband was discouraged. He'd looked at a number of pieces of land and several houses, always taking Higgins along, but nothing suited him.

"Tell me we came to the right place, Mrs. Barrington," he said, pacing their hotel room. Lizzie and Higgins had taken the children for a walk.

"Do I need to remind you how we made this decision?" she asked, and he sighed loudly. "Surely the right place for us is out there. You'll know when you find it." She stood in front of him and laid her head on his shoulder, loving the feel of his arms coming around her. What had she ever done without him?

That night before going to bed, she urged him to pray with her, then he held her close while she slept. Three days later, following more disappointments, he bounded into the hotel room where she was just finishing the lunch Lizzie had brought her from downstairs.

"Good, you're up," he said. "There's something I want you to see. Are you up to it?"

"I believe so," she said, and he laughed.

They left the children with Lizzie and Higgins and went outside where he helped her into a small vehicle harnessed to a single horse. It had two wide seats, which she figured would comfortably seat six people. "Where did you get this?" she asked.

"I bought it," he said and urged the horse forward.

Eleanore inhaled the early autumn air, noting how much more smoothly the ride felt as opposed to the wagon that had gotten them here. He said practically nothing while they rode along, beyond occasionally asking if she was all right.

"The fresh air is nice," she said and meant it. "I'm actually feeling rather well at the moment."

He smiled, clearly pleased. But she sensed a deeper happiness. Had he found the place he wanted to call home? It seemed an obvious conclusion.

As they rode out of the city, Eleanore was struck by the beauty of the landscape. There were many trees and vast rolling hills. Apparently what the English called moors, the Americans called prairie. Whatever its name, it was beautiful.

They rode less than half an hour before he turned onto a lane that was more narrow, less used than the road they'd taken from the city. After going through a wooded area and over a bridge that crossed a large stream, a huge stretch of meadow opened up, and there in the distance, nestled among a cluster of massive trees, was a two-story white house, with a large, red barn nearby. Both were situated next to a lower portion of the stream they'd just crossed and against a long stretch of woods that almost formed a semicircle around them, a lovely contrast to the open ground that sloped gently toward the home.

James watched her discreetly for a reaction and wasn't disappointed by her smile. "Oh, it's lovely," she said and tightened her hand over his arm.

He pulled the buggy up in front of the house and helped her down, paying close attention to her eyes. Without a word, he motioned toward the house, and she lifted her skirts slightly to walk up the porch steps. She stood in front of the door but seemed more taken with the railed porch. It went to the edge of the house on the left, but on the right it circled around. She walked that direction to peek around the corner, and he followed, looking to where the porch ended at the back corner of the house. Willow furniture near a side door hinted at lounging on the porch on a warm evening. He followed her back to the front door where he turned the knob and opened the door.

"Is it all right?" she asked.

"Yes, of course. No one's lived here for months." They stepped into a long hall, and he closed the door, leaning against it. She took in the narrow staircase that rose from the hall, and the light-colored wood floor that stretched toward a door at the back of the house, directly opposite the front. Beyond that there was nothing to see but a series of closed doors.

She pressed a hand over the papered wall and looked up at the high ceiling while he explained, "A neighbor, Mr. Plummer, who lives about five minutes west of here, was put in charge of selling the property when the family left."

"Why did they leave?" she asked.

"He didn't know. They were acquainted, but he didn't know a lot about them. They had four or five children. They asked if he would try and sell the property for a percentage, but he's not had any luck."

"Perhaps God was saving it for us," she said, and his heart warmed at the evidence that they were of one mind.

"Perhaps," he said and opened the double door to his right, motioning her into a spacious parlor—fully furnished. The couches were covered with sheets. The rest of the furniture was thick with dust.

"They left everything behind?"

"Apparently," he said.

"I wonder why," she muttered, more to herself than aloud, and wandered the room. "Where did they go?" she asked her husband. Her intrigue with the former owners was touching.

"Somewhere in Illinois. Perhaps they needed to be with family, or perhaps he found work elsewhere."

"Perhaps," she said and pressed her fingers through the dust on a corner table.

"Obviously the house comes with all the furnishings that were left. If there's anything you don't like, it can be replaced. Some things are available locally; almost anything can be ordered."

"Oh, the furniture is lovely," she said and moved back into the hall toward the door opposite.

"No," he said, "we'll save that for last." They went down the hall and looked into a large dining room with a door that opened out onto the side porch. The kitchen was not very big, especially in contrast to the kitchens of the Barrington home in England. But it was more than adequate and fully equipped. There was even a set of china in one of the cupboards. A room at the back of the house had a large desk and a couch and little else. They went down into a spacious cellar under the house, where dusty bottles of fruit lined a set of shelves.

They went up to the top floor where there were five bedrooms and a bathing room with a large tub and a stove for heating water. The floor plan duplicated the main floor with a long hall down the center and huge windows at each end where the doors were placed downstairs. James told her, "Mr. Plummer said that by keeping the doors and windows open in the summer, it makes the heat almost tolerable. Apparently the house was built specifically to take the greatest advantage of the direction of the wind. He said the shade of the trees surrounding the house also helps, and their leaves fall off before winter, which allows more sunshine into the house."

"How delightful," she said and pressed her hands over the beautifully carved post of the bed in the largest bedroom. She glanced at him and smiled, then moved back into the hall, and he followed. She wandered slowly through each room, stopping to look out of each window, as if to ponder something profound while examining the view.

James then led her to the hall where he took hold of a small rope hanging from the ceiling. He pulled down on it, and a little door opened before a folding ladder came down. She gasped and smiled, then immediately started up the ladder as if her curiosity overrode any trepidation about ascending the narrow ladder in skirts. He stood beside her in the center of the attic where it was high enough to stand. The ceilings of the roof sloped out in every direction, with a gabled window at the front and back of the house where sunlight trickled in, illuminating the dust.

"Hot and stuffy," he said, "but quaint."

"Indeed," she said, as if her imagination were giving the attic many possible purposes. He could imagine her playing up here with the children when the temperatures were not so drastic.

Returning to the main floor, he led her out the back door and pointed to a small structure nearby, the opposite direction from the barn, well shaded by surrounding trees. "Apparently that's the summer kitchen. During the hot months all of the cooking is done there to keep the heat out of the house."

"How clever," she said.

"And in the winter, of course, cooking in the house aids in keeping it warm."

They wandered into a huge garden area, where vegetables had obviously been planted abundantly in neat rows. But it appeared as if they'd only been allowed to grow to a certain point, and then they'd been left to rot. Everything was dead now except the weeds.

"Look," he said and took hold of a shovel that had been left sticking in the ground, as if someone had left in the middle of working in the garden. He turned a shovelful of dirt and squatted down to take a handful, allowing it to sift through his fingers. "It's black," he said. "They say you can grow just about anything here; the soil is so rich and easy to work." He brushed the dirt off his hands and straightened his back, sticking the shovel again into the ground. She watched his face as he looked around himself and sighed. "Apparently they were working on clearing the land with the intention to plant some kind of grain. I like the rough look of it. I'm no farmer . . . but bringing this garden back to life next spring sounds appealing. Higgins can teach me what to do."

"Us, you mean," she said, and he smiled.

"Only if you want to," he said and took her hand, guiding her into the barn.

"It's huge," she said once they'd gone inside.

"We'll need to acquire some livestock besides the horses. Cows, chickens." He chuckled. "Pigs, maybe."

"Why?" she asked.

"We'll be producing much of our own food from now on, my dear. Of course, there's plenty to be bought in the city, and we'll need to stock up for winter. I'm told that sometimes the snow gets so deep that it's impossible to go anywhere for days. But as long as we have plenty of food and water, that doesn't sound so bad."

"And wood for the fires."

"Of course." He chuckled again and pointed at a huge supply of chopped wood stacked neatly against one wall of the barn, just inside the door. "And there are plenty of trees to keep us supplied."

"So, you're going to take up chopping firewood now, as well?"

"Yes, I am," he said proudly, then changed his tone. "As I was saying, we need to have our own cows and chickens so that we'll always have fresh milk and eggs. Mr. Plummer knows where I can purchase some."

"Does Mr. Plummer have a family?"

"Yes, a wife and four children. I don't know their ages."

They went back into the house where he took her to the room he'd wanted to save for last. Inside was only a small couch, covered in a sheet, and many empty bookshelves built into the walls. He wasn't disappointed by his wife's pleasurable gasp, then she laughed.

"Apparently they took their books with them," he said.

"I'm glad to know they had correct priorities." She laughed again and touched the empty shelves. He watched her while a clear image appeared in his mind of how she had looked in the library of the home they'd left behind. She'd been beautiful then. She was more beautiful now.

"So, what do you think, Mrs. Barrington? Should we buy it?"

Eleanore took in her husband's expression. She knew he could have purchased a home without consulting her, and she would have been fine with that. But she was touched by the evidence that he valued her judgment. She smiled at him and said, "You don't need my approval, Mr. Barrington."

"No, but . . . I want you to be comfortable . . . and content."

"Well . . . I think it's perfect. It's a beautiful home. It has everything we need."

"Do you think we can be happy here?"

"Oh, I've no doubt of that," she said. "What do *you* think?"

"Truthfully, it's so much like what I envisioned it's almost eerie. It feels like home to me."

"Then home it is," she said and laughed.

Chapter Twelve
LIFE IN AMERICA

"When can we move in?" Eleanore asked.

"The transaction can be taken care of this afternoon," he said, "and we can move in anytime after that. But we might want to stay in town and take a few days to clean it up first."

"That's probably wise," she said, "although I believe we could manage."

He wrapped his arms around her, and she held him close, loving the familiar way he pressed his lips into her hair. "You must be careful, my dear. There's much work to be done, and I don't want you overdoing."

"I'll be fine. The doctor told me what I can and can't do. Beyond controlling the nausea, he said I can carry on as usual, so long as I rest when I'm tired."

"Still," his concern was evident, "you must be careful."

"You mustn't worry," she said and stepped back into the hall, then onto the porch where they both paused to absorb the view and accept it as home. "When will our trunks arrive?" she asked.

"They already have," he said. "They left for Iowa before we did."

"How marvelous," she said, and James watched her touch the outside of the house as if in some kind of formal salutation. When she was apparently finished, he helped her into the buggy, and they crossed back over the bridge before turning in the opposite direction from which they'd come. They went to the Plummer home, which was similar in style to the one they'd just

looked at, but not so large. The land was more groomed, and
Mr. Plummer made his living by tending to the many crops that
grew on his property. Mr. Plummer walked out of the field
where he was working to meet them as they came up the lane.

"Mr. Barrington," he said, taking the handshake James
offered as he stepped out of the buggy, "I didn't expect to see
you again so soon."

Eleanore observed the pleasant exchange between her husband
and Mr. Plummer, who was shorter and less muscular than her
husband, with a bristly beard and a balding head. His eyes were
warm, his smile pleasant. Her husband made introductions, and
Mr. Plummer nodded cordially, saying, "A pleasure to meet you,
Mrs. Barrington."

"And you," she said, remaining seated in the buggy.

Mr. Plummer was pleased to hear that they'd decided to
purchase the Jensen home, as he called it. They agreed on a time
to meet in town to take care of the transaction, but he insisted
that they couldn't leave without meeting his family.

At the house they met Mrs. Plummer, who was near the same
height as her husband but not so thin. She had blonde hair and a
pleasing countenance. She was so thrilled to learn they were
getting new neighbors that she could hardly stop smiling. They
had sons aged ten and eighteen, and daughters fifteen and twelve.
Eleanore was disappointed that the children weren't candidates as
playmates for David and Iris, but she couldn't expect everything
to work out perfectly according to her every whim.

The four adults sat in the parlor and visited for quite some
time while Mr. Barrington asked questions and Mr. Plummer
answered them. When Eleanore began to find their conversation
tedious, she was relieved to hear Mrs. Plummer say directly to
her, "I'm so delighted to have you here. It's been dreadful since
Sally moved away."

"Sally?"

"Sally Jensen, who lived in the house you're buying."

"You were friends then?"

"We chatted here and there; it was just nice to know another woman was close by. Of course there are other folks around the area, but Sally was the closest. So, you came from England?"

"Yes."

"And you have children?"

"Two. David is seven, and Iris five."

Eleanore felt a little queasy and wanted to suggest to her husband that they go back to town so that she could get something to eat. She wished she'd thought to bring something along, knowing she couldn't go very long without eating. Just thinking of the distance back to town increased her nausea.

"Are you all right, honey?" Mrs. Plummer asked.

"Oh." Eleanore felt embarrassed, wondering if her distress was so obvious, "I'm just . . ."

While she was wondering how to explain without embarrassing herself further, Mr. Barrington asked, "Are you feeling ill, my dear?" She was grateful he'd noticed Mrs. Plummer's inquiry.

"A little, yes," she said, forcing a smile. "Perhaps we should go and—"

"Is she not well?" Mrs. Plummer asked, sounding almost panicked.

"She's expecting," Mr. Barrington explained, "and the journey was difficult."

"Oh, I see," Mrs. Plummer drawled with such compassion that Eleanore was reminded of how her mother might have responded to the news that Eleanore had hurt herself. "Will something to eat make you feel better then, Mrs. Barrington?" Before Eleanore could answer, the woman urged her to her feet. "We mustn't send a pregnant woman away with an empty stomach. Come along."

"You're very kind," Eleanore said as they crossed the hall and went into the kitchen. "I must confess that just a little something to hold me until suppertime would help immensely."

"I know that feeling well, honey. You mustn't be afraid to ask. I'm sure you'll return the favor eventually. That's what neighbors are for." She guided Eleanore into a chair and said, "I've got some biscuits left from breakfast. It's not much, but they always did the trick for me."

"Anything would be fine," she said, but what Mrs. Plummer put in front of her was not what she'd expected. This was more like bread than a sweet, but with a little butter it tasted rather good and quickly eased the nausea.

Eleanore ate three biscuits with butter and graciously accepted a napkin filled with three more to get her home. Mrs. Plummer also provided a tall glass of milk for Eleanore to drink and talked about herself and her family in an effort to become better acquainted. She and her husband had been married nearly twenty years and had endured many difficulties in order to settle this land and harvest a living from it. But she declared they'd come far and they were doing well now.

When Eleanore was done eating, Mrs. Plummer asked, "So how long have you and your husband been married?"

"Only a matter of months, actually. The children are from his first marriage. His first wife passed away; premature child-birth."

"Oh, how dreadful. Your good husband's been through some struggles of his own, then."

"Yes, he has," Eleanore said.

"And how did the two of you meet?" she asked as if she might hear a fairy tale. Mrs. Plummer was a romantic.

"I was working in his household, actually. After the former Mrs. Barrington died, I was promoted to caring for his children."

"How very sweet," she said, and Eleanore felt warmed by evidence of something she'd longed for. This woman had no negative perception of a serving girl marrying her employer.

"Oh, here you are," Mr. Plummer said, and they turned to see him in the doorway, with Mr. Barrington beside him.

Eleanore said to her husband, "Mrs. Plummer was gracious enough to give me something to eat, and I'm feeling much better now."

"I'm glad to hear it," he said, then to Mrs. Plummer, "Thank you so much for your generous hospitality. I'm certain we'll be seeing you again soon." He held out his hand, and Eleanore took it. "We should be going."

Before they left, the Plummers insisted they would have them over for Sunday dinner once they got settled in. When they were on the road, Eleanore commented, "They're so kind and gracious."

"Yes, they are," James said and moved the reins to one hand in order to put an arm around her, pressing a kiss to her temple. "It would seem we were guided to a good place to raise our family."

"Indeed."

Again he didn't head back toward the city, and she asked where they were going. He told her he'd asked Mr. Plummer if there was anyone in the area who might be looking for work. He wanted someone to come in during the days and help around the house so that Lizzie could focus more on helping with the children.

"That's really not necessary," she said. "I'm certain we can manage."

"I'm certain as well," he said. "But it takes a lot of work to manage a household, and we've got to get the house in order first. And I don't want you overdoing."

"Millions of women manage a household and survive pregnancy at the same time, Mr. Barrington."

"I know you're capable, Mrs. Barrington. But I'm going to hire someone, nevertheless."

The conversation ended, but Eleanore wasn't certain she liked this. Until they met Mrs. Leichty. She was barely thirty, with an average build and light brown hair, and she had lost her husband recently to death. This woman was struggling to get by and care for her twelve-year-old son, fearing she would have to sell her home and leave the area. She got tears in her eyes when Mr. Barrington offered her the job, then she praised God and told them that such an offer was surely an answer to many prayers.

"Would it be all right if I bring my boy when I come to work?" she asked. "He's a good lad; he'll not cause any trouble. He's become a bit clingy since we lost his father. I'm certain he could help me with my work."

"Of course," Mr. Barrington said. "Perhaps we can find something for him to do as well, for a fair wage."

"Oh, that would be grand!" Mrs. Leichty said.

An arrangement was agreed on, and she assured him she had her own transportation and could get to their home with no difficulty. And then she became very social, wanting to know more about them and expressing her pleasure at having new neighbors. She too said that she missed Sally Jensen, although like Mrs. Plummer, she hadn't known the woman terribly well. Eleanore came right out and asked if she knew why the Jensens had left, and she didn't. She only said they made the decision quickly and were gone almost overnight.

Leaving the Leichty home, Eleanore said to her husband, "You must have been inspired. You were clearly an answer to her prayers." He said nothing, and she gratefully ate the biscuits Mrs. Plummer had sent with her. Once they were gone and her stomach felt settled, she asked her husband, "Will you teach me to drive it?"

He looked pleasantly surprised. "Of course," he said. "But why?"

"Well . . . perhaps I'll want to visit Mrs. Plummer and chat over biscuits or something. If I can drive myself, I won't need to bother you or anyone else."

"So, you're on the path to becoming an independent woman then," he said with a little laugh.

"Not *too* independent," she said. "I wouldn't want to be as independent as Mrs. Leichty." He glanced toward her, and she hoped he heard in such a statement how much she relied on him, and how grateful she was to be sharing his life.

"No, we wouldn't want that," he said and eased the reins into her hands while he gave her simple instructions for guiding the horse. She picked it up quickly and drove all the way back into the city where they left the horse and buggy at a livery near the hotel where they were staying.

James left his wife taking a nap while he walked down the street to meet with Mr. Plummer and a local attorney, who would make the sale of the property legal and see that the Jensens received the money. He arrived before Mr. Plummer but found the attorney, a Mr. Norland, to be kind and helpful.

"Could you tell me," James said, "if Mr. Plummer knows the selling price of the property."

"I'm not certain, but I'm doubtful."

"Could you . . . do me a small favor and raise the price enough that Mr. Plummer will get a larger cut, and the Jensens will get the full asking price for the house?" Mr. Norland looked stunned, and James added, "I can afford it."

"I don't understand," Mr. Norland said. "You want to pay *more* for the property so that . . ."

"You *do* understand, Mr. Norland, but I want the matter to remain between the two of us. And I want some kind of documentation to be certain the Jensens get their money, wherever they may be. It's not that I don't trust you. I'm simply in the habit of being thorough in my transactions."

"Of course," Mr. Norland said, showing a slight smile. "I'll see to it."

Mr. Plummer arrived, and the three men shared a fair amount of laughter and congenial conversation while the paperwork was taken care of. After finishing some errands, James returned to the hotel with the deed in hand, feeling as if his every dream were coming true. He'd never imagined being so happy.

The following day he left his wife and the children at the hotel while the rest of them went to the house to start cleaning. Eleanore wasn't very happy about being left behind, but she admitted that she didn't feel well.

"Once there's a clean place for you to rest," he told her, "then you can come and help as much you feel up to it. Watch out for the children."

James took Higgins and Lizzie with him in one of the wagons, which was loaded with some things he'd purchased the previous afternoon. Lizzie was visibly excited when she saw the house; Higgins had been with him when he'd first found it. He left Higgins to show his wife around while he got started on the enormous task of removing the huge accumulation of dust in the house. Higgins and Lizzie would be staying in one of the upstairs bedrooms until next summer. James had told his loyal companion that they would then work together to build another smaller home on the property, so that the Higgins family could have their own place but still be a stone's throw away.

Mrs. Leichty and her son, Ralph, arrived right on time. Ralph was small for his age, with timid eyes, but it didn't take long for James to see that he was a hard worker and very polite. Mrs. Leichty proved ambitious and capable as she took it upon herself to remove all the bed linens to clean them. She mentioned that it couldn't all be done in one day since there wasn't enough clothesline to dry so much at once, but she made a good start. James and Higgins took the mattresses outside to beat the dust out of them and let them air out in the sun. By lunchtime they were all sweating from their efforts but enjoyed the food James had brought from town, along with cool water from the well near the house. Throughout the afternoon, James pondered every aspect of the present situation and marveled at how blessed he was. Beyond his wife not feeling well, he couldn't think of a single negative aspect to the life they'd found here and the arrangements that had been made. He found himself thanking God repeatedly as he went about his tasks. While hard work was clearly unfamiliar to him due to his upbringing, he found satisfaction in it. The journey to Iowa had given him some experience at being sticky with sweat and covered with dust.

The following day James brought his wife and children with him. Higgins drove the second wagon, and both were filled with the trunks that had come with them from England. The children shrieked with excitement when they saw the house, then they ran around like little savages, exploring and making plans. The men took the trunks into the house, leaving them in the library and the front hall until more cleaning was completed. The horses were unharnessed and put into the spacious corral near the barn. James filled the trough with water and watched all four of them wandering lazily as if to explore *their* new home.

He went into the house to find his wife in the parlor, a scarf tied tightly around her head, completely covering her hair. She was cleaning out the fireplace flue with a long-handled brush.

"What on earth are you doing?" he asked.

She glanced at him with mild disgust in her eyes, softened by a little smile. "Surely it's obvious," she said.

"Where on earth did you learn to do such things?" he asked.

She turned toward him again and straightened her back. "Surely you jest," she said, astonished. He felt baffled until she added, "I learned such things by working the whole of my life in *your* household, Mr. Barrington." Then he felt stupid.

"Of course," he said. "How quickly I've forgotten. Where was it we lived before?" He walked toward her. "I can't imagine life ever being different."

"Well, it was," she said matter-of-factly. He stopped her attempt to return to her chore by putting his arm around her waist from behind. "You were lord of the manor, and I was scrubbing pots in your kitchen, and polishing furniture."

"And cleaning out fireplaces?" he asked and kissed the back of her neck.

"I'd graduated from that years earlier. And *then* some poor fool put me in charge of his children. Next thing I know, I ended up here."

"Cleaning out a fireplace," he said with mock chagrin and kissed her again. She laughed softly, and he added, "If Lucy could see you now . . ." She laughed again, then made a pleasurable noise when he moved his lips to the side of her neck.

"I have work to do, Mr. Barrington."

"It can wait," he said and continued kissing her throat, over and over.

"We have no privacy here, sir," she said, as if he might not know.

"How dreadful," he said, letting out a sigh of exaggerated disappointment, which made her laugh again. She turned toward him and touched one side of his face while she kissed the other. Then she stepped back, wearing a smirk, and he realized her hand was covered in soot. He touched his face and found soot there. "Wretched woman!" he snarled with a laugh.

She stepped back and said, "Now everyone will know you've been consorting with a servant girl."

"I only consort with one woman," he said, "and that is my wife . . ." he tipped his head, "who just happens to know how to clean out a fireplace. But," he added more seriously, "I think you should let someone else do this. And you should rest."

"Fine," she said and put the brush into his hand, "everyone else is busy. If you don't know how, I'd be glad to teach you."

He chuckled and said, "I think I can manage. Thank you, Mrs. Barrington."

She just smiled and laid down on one of the couches, which was still covered with a sheet that would protect it from her sooty clothing. He watched her get comfortable, then proceeded to clean out the fireplace.

* * *

A few weeks after the purchase of the property, James woke up to the realization that they were comfortably settled into their new home. The process had been exhausting, and his wife had struggled daily with not feeling well. But now all had been properly cleaned and put in order, and a routine had been established. Many neighbors had come with gifts and a warm welcome. There were cows and chickens in the barn. The pantry and cellar were filled with ample food supplies. And the books had been unpacked and shelved alphabetically by author according to his wife's request—which put Jane Austen's works nearly first on the shelf.

James turned to look at her, sleeping beside him, and wondered why he would be so blessed. She worked hard, didn't complain even though she clearly felt ill and exhausted much of the time, and she took such good care of him and his children that he wondered how any woman could be so fine. And she was going to have his baby. Life could be no better than this.

While she was coming awake, James said softly, "Good morning, Mrs. Barrington."

"Good morning," she murmured, her eyes still closed.

"Tell me what you want, my dear; anything, and I'll get it for you." She opened her eyes, silently questioning him. "Anything," he repeated, "from anywhere in the world. You name it. I'll find a way to order it and get it here." He kissed her cheek. "Tell me what you want and I'll get it for you if it's in my power to do so."

She looked puzzled as she said, "I have everything I could ever want, Mr. Barrington. But thank you." She closed her eyes again, saying a moment later, "Actually, I just thought of something."

"What?" he asked eagerly. "Anything!"

"You can either get me something to eat in a big hurry or hand me the basin so I can throw up." He chuckled, and she added, "You *did* say anything."

"So I did," he said and hurried to the kitchen.

Later that day James sat at the desk in the room that had been designated as his office, going over his financial figures. The door came open, and he looked up to see his wife dressed to go out, pulling dainty leather gloves onto her hands.

"I'm going into town," she said.

"What for?" he asked, wondering why he felt alarmed.

"I forgot to tell you, but . . . do you remember Mrs. King, the woman I met at the hotel, who is friends with the woman who owns the—"

"Yes, I remember."

"She's part of a ladies' club and invited me to join them. It's only once a week for a few hours. Higgins has harnessed the buggy for me." She kissed his cheek. "I'll be home before supper."

James looked at the door long after she'd closed it, wondering why he felt uneasy. He reasoned that he simply wasn't accustomed to having her go very far without him, and he was concerned for her health. But surely she would be fine. He said a little prayer that she would be safe and returned to his work. She came home a few hours later, full of excited chatter over the friends she had made and how she'd enjoyed visiting with such a diversity of women. He basked in listening to every detail. Apparently America suited his wife rather well.

* * *

Eleanore was thrilled to be able to attend church every Sunday, even though it wasn't the religion she longed to be a part of. But it was a Christian service, the closest to where they lived, and the one the Plummers attended, although she learned that there were several different religious denominations in the area. Apparently people chose which church they wanted to attend. Eleanore asked her husband if they could attend different churches and compare, secretly hoping that one of them might be teaching from the book she loved so dearly. He readily agreed, and she felt sure he knew her motives, even if he didn't comment. Higgins and Lizzie were intrigued with the idea and agreed to join them wherever they might be attending church.

In regard to her quest, Eleanore asked her husband if he would help her inquire over the whereabouts of this new religion that held her interest. "I don't know where to start," she admitted, "but I must try."

"Of course," he said. "Perhaps we could write to the city where the book was printed."

"Write to whom?" she asked.

He shrugged. "The postmaster, perhaps. He should know what's going on in town, and where to direct a request for information."

"That's a marvelous idea. Would you help me, then?"

"You write a letter, and I'll see that it gets posted."

"Thank you," she said and kissed his cheek.

That very evening she wrote a letter with a simple request for information regarding a religious group who based their beliefs on this particular book that had been printed in that city. And the next day she went into town with her husband, and it was mailed. She prayed that the reply would be swift and fruitful, then she tried not to think about it.

The following Sunday they attended church again with the Plummers, mostly because they'd invited them all over for dinner afterward. It was a lovely meal, and Eleanore enjoyed getting to know the entire family. Even though the Plummer children were much older than David and Iris, a couple of them instigated some games outside, and they all had a marvelous time. Eleanore enjoyed visiting with Mrs. Plummer and Lizzie while the men went to another room in the house to do the same.

On the way home, Higgins drove the buggy, and Eleanore rested her head on her husband's shoulder. She counted her blessings and soaked in the evening air, trying not to think of matters that were better left avoided. She really liked Mr. and Mrs. Plummer, but she found it difficult to be around them when they were so obviously in love with each other. She'd become accustomed to the tenderness between Lizzie and Higgins, and she'd learned to ignore certain implications in contrast to her own marriage. But how could she ignore the way Mr. Plummer told his wife that he loved her? And the way they spoke to each other using their given names? Eleanore had never spoken her husband's given name aloud, and he had never spoken hers. In fact, the Plummers had seemed a bit uncomfortable with his formality, but they were apparently willing to respect it. They were kind people, and Eleanore really liked them. But they had something she envied. She considered just asking her husband if they could let go of being so formal with each other, but she sensed that his reasons for it tied into that part of himself he kept bottled up. Still, her life was good, and she had only to count her blessings to realize her complaints were comparatively petty and insignificant.

They had settled into their life in America quickly and comfortably. Eleanore liked Mrs. Leichty and her son, and had fast become accustomed to having them around for several hours a day, six days a week. The woman eagerly did anything that was asked of her, and had proven to be an excellent cook. Young Ralph was also eager to help, and he was a good boy. In spite of his being older than David, they enjoyed playing together between Ralph's assigned chores. His mother had specifically requested that her son be given assignments, with consequences if he didn't accomplish them, just as it was for David and Iris. She confided to Eleanore that she hoped the time they were able to spend with Mr. Barrington and Higgins would help compensate for the loss of the boy's father, and give Ralph some men in his life that he could look up to.

On the first evening when they'd prepared to sit at the dining table for supper, Eleanore noticed that her husband took one glance at the table, then went back into the kitchen. Curious, she'd followed. He found Lizzie and Mrs. Leichty there and asked firmly, "Why is the table only set for four?" The two women exchanged a confused glance, and he added, "There are eight of us here, and more than ample room for everyone to sit around the table."

"But . . . sir," Lizzie said, "we work for you. We're dependent upon you for our earnings, and it's not proper to—"

"We're not in England anymore, Lizzie. Yes, you work for me, but that doesn't mean we can't all eat at the same table and be friends as well. We ate together on the journey well enough; I'm certain we can manage. Please set more dishes out and have the children wash up."

"Yes, Mr. Barrington," Lizzie said, tossing Eleanore a discreet, amazed glance.

The memory of this manifestation of her husband's goodness warmed Eleanore's heart, and she eased closer to him in the buggy, continuing to count her blessings.

By the time they got home it was raining. Instead of hurrying to the house, the children started playing outdoors in the rain. Eleanore and Lizzie ran to the porch and sat there to observe David and Iris immersing themselves in the deluge, while the men unharnessed the buggy and put it away. When they came out of the barn, Eleanore was surprised to see her husband join the children. The downpour had quickly created huge puddles. He picked up Iris and put her into one while they laughed together. Then he turned toward David, who laughed and ran when he realized his father's intention. After David had been tickled and thrown into a puddle, Eleanore saw her husband's eyes rest on her—with mischief in them. She pretended to be alarmed, and protested as she backed away. When he stepped onto the porch she ran the other way, into the rain. He chased her down and sat her in a puddle, laughing like she'd never heard. She yanked on his arm, and he lost his balance, falling into the puddle with her.

"This is quite some puddle," he said, still laughing.

"It's more like a pond." She practically had to shout to be heard above the continuing downpour.

"If you didn't want to get wet, why did you run into the rain?" he asked, helping her to her feet.

"Oh, I didn't mind getting wet," she said. "I just wanted you to work for it." He laughed again, and she added, "You laugh more than you used to."

He scooped her into his arms and walked toward the house. "It would seem America suits me, Mrs. Barrington," he said, and laughed again.

Chapter Thirteen
PRETENDING

As autumn deepened in Iowa, the temperatures became more comfortable than hot, and then the nights started getting chilly. Weeks passed while they attended different churches, and Eleanore kept praying for a letter from New York. Each day she read from her precious book, memorizing more and more from its pages while her conviction regarding it only deepened. The illness from her pregnancy grew less intense as she became aware of the baby growing inside of her, which required some changes to her wardrobe. She continued to attend the weekly ladies' club meetings, and enjoyed them for the most part. She also enjoyed visiting with neighbors in the area, and having company come over.

David and Iris thrived in their new surroundings, while their routine continued much as it had in England. They spent time each day working on their school lessons, reading together, and sharing the work as well as playtime. Eleanore appreciated the way their father would take them to the barn each morning and each evening to have them help him care for the animals. David learned to milk the cows, and Iris was assigned to gather the eggs, a task she became very proud of once she got over her fear of touching the chickens. The children also had chores assigned to them in the house, and Eleanore felt certain this was a much better life for them than having servants at every turn.

When the first snow fell, Eleanore couldn't deny that her life was good. There were only two things that caused her any dismay. The first was the passing of weeks with no word from New York. And the other was a growing confusion in regard to her feelings for her husband. He'd once told her that she was nothing more than physically attracted to him—infatuated, with no comprehension of love. But months had passed, and her fascination with him had not lessened; it had only grown in proportion to her high regard for his character. She admired him deeply, respected him beyond measure. She had observed the changes in him throughout the months of their marriage and found joy simply in seeing the happiness he had found in living this life. She liked the way he wore his beard, and how he'd let his hair grow more casually, as opposed to always being neatly in place as it had been in England. She liked the adjustments he'd made in his wardrobe to fit in with the people in their community. Were it not for a certain formality in his speech, it would be difficult to believe he'd been living as an English lord not so many months ago. She was mostly bothered that his formality was most noticeable with her. He'd taken to calling many people in the area with whom they'd become comfortable by their given names. But he continued to call her Mrs. Barrington. She wasn't certain why she held back in addressing the issue. Perhaps she feared having the conversation wander into matters of love. And she simply had no desire to hear him reiterate his declarations of how he could never love her. She feared if he had the nerve to say it now, she would boldly call him a hypocrite, and the tenderness between them would vanish. She preferred silence over the matter, even though the situation was a common source of confusion in both her mind and heart.

As always, Eleanore attempted to stay focused on the positive. James Barrington was a good man and a good husband. He treated her like a queen. And the full spectrum of all they shared as husband and wife was too wondrous to comprehend. She loved it when he held her close, as if she were the center of his world. She loved the way he would kiss her throat and face, and especially a certain place just behind her ear that would make her shiver or sometimes giggle. She loved the feel of his bearded face against her own. The very masculinity of the sensation stirred her. And she loved it best when he would look into her eyes, wordlessly claiming beyond any question that what they shared held no shame or guilt. Within the bonds of holy matrimony, it was sacred and beautiful, sanctioned by God and man. What they shared was echoed by the respect and commitment present in their relationship each and every day. He was not a perfect man; she'd been married to him long enough to be made fully aware of his weaknesses and shortcomings. But he was a good man with a good heart. He cared well for her as he'd promised he would. He was mindful of her needs, even her wants, and perhaps he was even reluctantly aware of her emotions. Were it not for the way he honored her in daily life, what they shared privately would surely lose its magic. For her, all aspects of their interaction as husband and wife were irrevocably woven together. His commitment and respect were priceless. She knew that many women were denied even that by men who were less than honorable. Each day she counted blessings that were too great to number, knowing that only *one* aspect of their relationship caused her any sorrow. For all the evidence she had of his dependence on her—his fondness, his caring—she knew he did not love her. But she could not deny her woman's heart, and it desperately longed for access to his.

Eleanore thought occasionally of Leah in the Bible, given deceptively in marriage to a man who did not love her. How Leah's heart must have ached! Had she loved Jacob? Had she longed for evidence that some tiny piece of his heart might be hers? Had she cherished the time they'd spent alone together, pretending that his heart and soul belonged to her? Or had she closed herself away from such thoughts and feelings in order to simply go on living and bearing his children? For Eleanore, pretending felt preferable. When they shared that most wondrous aspect of their marriage, it was easy to believe she was as precious to him as she was important. When he held her in his arms, it took no effort to imagine that mutual love existed. But inevitably, morning would come, and the routine of the day would settle between them. They ate together, and worked together, and together cared for the children. They conversed amiably and sometimes discussed topics in great depth. They understood and respected each other. They were one flesh and one mind, but she feared they would never be one heart. Perhaps one day she would grow tired of pretending and learn to close her heart away as he had done his. And perhaps in that way they *would* become one heart, or at least their hearts would be the same. Maybe their level of comfort and contentment with each other would deepen when she stopped hoping for that which was hopeless. But for now, she preferred to pretend—and to hope—that in spite of his bold declarations, love might eventually be part of the deal.

Snow continued to fall at regular intervals, and Eleanore was stunned by its depth, as were the other members of the household who had never imagined such quantities of snow. Occasionally Mrs. Leichty and Ralph didn't show up at all. It was understood that if the snow was too difficult to get through, they wouldn't come. And once in a while the two of them just stayed at the Barrington's rather than trying to get home in a storm.

Eleanore became focused on Christmas preparations, which became a marvelous distraction from her ongoing frustrations. Christmas was less than a week away when she came out of the kitchen to find Lizzie and Higgins in the hall, oblivious to her presence, consumed with a passionate kiss. Eleanore quickly stepped back into the kitchen to avoid embarrassing them. But the impression of what she'd seen was deep. She'd never seen anyone kiss like that, never imagined that such a kiss existed. She'd been married for many months and shared a passionate and intimate relationship with her husband. But beyond the kiss they'd shared to seal their marriage vows, his lips had never met hers. Never! It certainly wasn't the first time it had occurred to her, but getting a glimpse of how married people were supposed to kiss, she almost felt angry—cheated perhaps. He had made it clear that she could never have his heart, but why did he withhold his kiss?

When these feelings of anger became consuming, Eleanore went up to her bedroom and locked the door, going directly to her knees in prayer. She asked for understanding and forgiveness—for herself as well as her husband. And she asked for guidance, for a way to break past this barrier that troubled her in spite of all her efforts to avoid even thinking about it. She left the bedroom feeling more calm, knowing that she could not judge her husband's behavior. How could she focus only on the problems when all else he gave her was good? He asked her that evening if something was troubling her, but she forced a smile and assured him that all was well.

Lying in bed while he slept beside her, she prayed again for peace and guidance. She fell asleep praying and woke up with a memory in her mind. Something he'd said to her, numerous times. Was that the answer? Throughout the day she pondered the idea, and that afternoon she watched from the upstairs hall for him to come back from town. The window at the back of the house had a perfect view of the barn. When she saw him ride in, her heart quickened. She hurried down the stairs, grabbed her cloak, and trudged over the well-packed trail that led to the barn. She opened the door to find him removing the saddle. He glanced toward her and smiled before he led the horse to its stall.

"Hello, Mrs. Barrington," he said, removing the bit. "What brings you out here on such a cold day?"

"I wanted to talk with you . . . privately."

He looked surprised. "You have my undivided attention," he said, leaning a shoulder against one of the posts and folding his

"Forgive me," he murmured close to her lips, "for waiting so long."

"It was worth waiting for," Eleanore replied and kissed him. She met his eyes and saw him smile. She kissed him again, acquainting herself with simply being able to do so.

"Your hair's a mess," he chuckled, easing his hands out of it.

"It was worth that too," she said, snuggling the side of her face against his chest. He wrapped his arms around her and pressed a kiss into her hair. She couldn't count the times he'd held her this way, and she decided that being in his arms, with her ear against his chest, hearing the beat of his heart, was likely her favorite place in all the world. Wherever he might be, so as long as she could be with him, she would consider herself blessed.

"It's freezing out here, Mrs. Barrington," he said.

"I hadn't noticed," she said, and he chuckled before he let go of her to pick up his gloves.

They walked into the house holding hands and found the children in the kitchen helping Mrs. Leichty with a baking project. Eleanore sat down and just watched her husband while he washed his hands, then got into the middle of what they were doing. Every few minutes a fluttering of internal butterflies would catch her off guard as she considered the bridge they had just crossed. And then he glanced at her with a knowing smile, and she nearly melted into the floor. She loved him so much!

Eleanore left to help Lizzie with something upstairs, but not until after she redid her hair. While her thoughts remained with the kiss her husband had given her, she began to fear that it might never happen again. When she and Lizzie went down for supper, she found him supervising Iris while she set the table.

"Oh, there you are," he said when he saw her. Then to Lizzie, "Could you take over for a few minutes. I need to speak with my wife. I won't be long."

"Of course," Lizzie said.

Eleanore followed her husband to the library, wondering what he needed to talk to her about. The moment the door was closed he took her in his arms and pressed his lips to hers. He kissed her like a man in the desert suddenly given water. And she bathed in it. Everything he'd once told her about the glory and beauty of the marriage relationship settled deeper into her spirit. What they shared was wondrous and marvelous and beyond comprehension. She kept expecting their kiss to take them beyond boundaries they had long ago crossed together, but he only kissed her, as if that was all he needed in order to be thoroughly content. He finally eased his lips from hers and murmured close to her ear, "I think we're late for supper, Mrs. Barrington. This could look very suspicious."

"Not as suspicious as my hair looked earlier," she said, and he chuckled as he opened the door and they went back to the dining room.

That night when Eleanore climbed into bed and eased close to her husband, he met her with a long, savoring kiss. Gradually it merged into the experience she was more familiar with. The combination was exquisite. While she was drifting to sleep in his arms, she said, "I thought of something else I want."

"A new couch, perhaps?" he said. "That one in the office is hideous."

She giggled. "No, not a new couch. I want you to kiss me every morning and every night and whenever you leave, and when you come home, and other times in between . . . for as long as we both shall live."

"It's a lot to ask," he said with light sarcasm while tightening his arms around her, "but I think I can manage." And then he kissed her. "Good night, Mrs. Barrington."

"Good night," she said, and the next thing she was aware of was coming awake with a gasp. She quickly ascertained that she'd not disturbed her husband and forced herself to relax while she attempted to remember the content of her dream. She could remember nothing except for a feeling of fear, and James Barrington saying harshly, *"No! It's not love!"*

She reminded herself that it was only a dream, but throughout the following days she found the sensation of fear hovering near her. She'd come to terms with her feelings for him, but her reasons for keeping them to herself cemented more deeply with the fear of having him discount what she felt. She began to fear that he might see the truth in her eyes, and she found it difficult to look at him directly.

* * *

The arrival of Christmas brought with it much joy. Eleanore was stunned to realize how far they had come in a year. Last Christmas she had been the governess, celebrating with the other servants in the Barrington household, never dreaming of the twists her life would take. Now she could feel James Barrington's baby moving inside her, filling her with the joyous anticipation of becoming a mother. Last Christmas the children had given her a set of beautiful journals and pens, and she had helped the children make gifts for their father. This year she had the privilege of acquiring gifts for her husband and children and the others in her household, while the anticipation left her feeling like a child again. Not since her father had died had she found so much pleasure in the holiday and its preparations. Everyone worked together to make the house look more festive, and the extra baking projects in the kitchen filled the house with the warm and spicy fragrance of Christmas. And the greatest fun of all was assembling packages to deliver to the neighbors, sometimes anonymously.

Higgins went out with James on a bright day in search of an appropriate Christmas tree. They had to go quite far, since the majority of trees on their land were not evergreens. They came back with a beautiful specimen that was erected in the parlor.

Everyone, including Mrs. Leichty and Ralph, who also came to share their Christmas dinner, worked together to decorate it. Their celebrations turned out to be perfect. The occasional kiss she got from her husband added to Eleanore's contentment, while her love for him settled deeply into her spirit. She continued to fear that he might see the truth in her eyes and discredit her feelings. But she resolutely pushed such concerns aside and reveled in the magical celebration of Christ's birth, sharing her joy with these people she loved so dearly.

Because of her sacred book, Christmas took on deeper meaning for Eleanore. She continued to read from it daily and knew more than ever that what Christ had done was real; and she also knew that the scriptures in her possession that testified of these truths were real as well.

The new year arrived with more snow, and the baby continued to grow and move inside her more every day. David and Iris loved to put their hands on her belly and try to feel it, but she assured them the baby would have to get much bigger before they would be able to do so from the outside. Still, the children were excited for the new arrival and speculated a great deal on whether it would be a brother or a sister. Neither of them seemed to care which; they simply couldn't wait to know. Eleanore and her husband heartily agreed that the children were flourishing in their new environment. David especially seemed to have come beyond the confusion and grief that had troubled him prior to the move.

Eleanore cherished the way her husband loved to rest with his hand against her belly, as if he could feel the same closeness to their baby that she could feel by carrying it inside of her. He told her often that he envied such closeness. Sometimes he put his ear to her belly, or kissed it and whispered tender messages to their child.

On a particularly cold morning, Eleanore was talking over trivial household matters with her husband while he got dressed to go out and feed the animals. While he was speaking, he motioned toward his waistcoat that was draped over the chair at her side, and she tossed it to him. He stopped mid-sentence when a piece of black ribbon fell on the rug. She glanced at the ribbon, then his face, wondering why she saw something bordering on guilt in his eyes. He quickly laughed the tension away as she bent to retrieve it. She might have thought he'd picked up a ribbon that had fallen from her hair and just tucked it in his pocket to return to her, except that it was far too worn. She would have thrown out such a ribbon long before it became this shabby. And holding it in her hand she was struck with the distinct fragrance of her own perfume.

"That's mine," he said, grabbing it from her. He chuckled uncomfortably and added, "I stole it from you . . . before we were married."

"It smells like . . ."

"Your perfume, yes. I keep it sprayed with your scent so I can smell you wherever I go." He said it as if he'd told her he was going into town to pick up the mail, while a bittersweet combination of joy and sorrow swelled inside of her. How many men would be so tender and sentimental? Yet, for all his sentiment, she knew his heart was still beyond her reach.

He quickly kissed her cheek and put his waistcoat on as he headed out the door, saying over his shoulder, "I'll see you at breakfast."

Before they were married? He'd been carrying her perfumed ribbon in his pocket, without her knowing, since before they were married? She wanted to run after him and make him look at her and insist that he admit to the truth. But in her head she could hear him declaring hotly, *No! It's not love!* Instead she shoved down her flailing emotions and got ready for the day.

That evening Eleanore was reading near the fire when her husband entered the room and bent to kiss her in greeting. She closed her eyes to receive the kiss, touching his face at the same time. The moment their lips parted, she looked away as had become her habit. But this time he took her chin and forced her to look at him. "What is it?" he asked, and she silently cursed his perception. "I sense that something is troubling you; it has been for some time. Are you all right?"

"Of course I am." She forced a nonchalant laugh. "Tell me again about your plans for the yard when spring comes."

James tried to force away his uneasy feelings as he sat down across from her, and they talked of trivial things for nearly an hour. They went up to bed, and she quickly fell asleep beside him while he considered the possibilities for her behavior. She avoided looking him in the eye, and when she did he saw something bordering on guilt there. Then something twisted in his heart. Memories mingled with fear, and he could hardly breathe. Surely there was some other explanation. She would never do to him what Caroline had done. She *wouldn't!* But as night settled more deeply around him, his tortured emotions began to distort the facts. And while a part of him knew that was the case, something deeper, more raw, more scared, began to see the logic. He could almost hear a voice whispering in his mind, telling him that no matter how much he gave to any woman, she could never be trusted, never be loyal. A silent argument ensued in his brain. Eleanore *could* be trusted! But even if she couldn't, she'd had no opportunity to become involved with someone else. Then the knife twisted again. Once a week. She went into town. Alone.

"Heaven help me," he muttered into the darkness and tried to pray away the fear and lack of reason, but it refused to relent. In his deepest self he began to wonder if his instincts were drawing him to accept something he'd been blind to. He finally got out of bed and went downstairs where he could pace and fret without disturbing his wife's sleep.

* * *

Eleanore woke sometime during the night and found her husband gone. She couldn't recall it ever happening before. She got up and lit a lamp. The room was freezing, so she stoked the fire, then she took up the lamp and set out in search of him. He wasn't in the children's rooms, so she went down the stairs. The library was dark and void of human life. She saw a light under the door of the office and carefully opened the door. She found him sleeping on the couch; he had left a lamp burning on the desk. The room was warm. It hadn't been very long since he'd stoked the fire. She wondered over the source of his restlessness but left him to sleep and went back upstairs, hating the coldness of the bed without him there.

The following morning she didn't see him until breakfast. He barely acknowledged her as they were seated, but with everyone else in the room, she didn't comment. When the meal was finished, she followed him when he left the room.

"Where are *you* going?" he asked in the hall, stopping to look at her over his shoulder.

"Wherever you're going," she said. He turned to face her fully. "And I will be your shadow, Mr. Barrington, until you tell me what's wrong."

He looked hard into her eyes, and she glanced away as she said, "I woke up and you were gone. I found you sleeping on that ugly couch, and this morning you're not yourself. I need to know what's wrong."

James didn't feel prepared to face this moment, even though he knew it needed to be faced. But perhaps this was best. Perhaps it was time to stop pretending and bring the truth into the open. He motioned toward the library with his hand and followed her into the room. She closed the door and leaned against it. He sat down, and she sat to face him. He felt sick to his stomach. *Why?* Why would she do this to him? He couldn't deny that he'd stubbornly withheld his heart from her. Was that why she'd gone seeking affection elsewhere? Had he truly done something to deserve this?

Eleanore watched her husband and felt frightened. "Please . . . talk to me," she said, wondering what could have gone wrong to upset him so completely. He cleared his throat and leaned his elbow on the arm of the couch. He glanced at her, then looked away, resting his chin on his fingers. "We always agreed to be completely honest with each other."

"Yes, of course," she said.

He turned to look at her with a penetrating intimidation in his eyes that she hadn't seen since prior to their marriage. Her heart beat painfully hard. This had to do with *her*. But *what?*

"So, I need you to be completely honest with me, Mrs. Barrington, and tell me what secret it is you're keeping from your husband."

Eleanore opened her mouth to speak, but no sound came out. Her heart pounded harder, and she looked quickly away. Was he so perceptive? Clearly, yes. And what was she supposed to do about it? While she was pondering how to answer—or get out of it—he added firmly, "I need to know the reasons, madam, for the guilt I see in your eyes, for the way you won't look at me . . . as you used to." Eleanore's astonishment deepened as she turned slowly to meet his gaze. The implication settled in fiercely, and compassion for him made her only option clearly evident. She *did* have to be completely honest with him. No matter how unequal the ground it put them on, no matter how exposed or vulnerable it left her, she could never leave him to wonder even slightly if she had broken trust with him for any reason. She just had to say it, but she could never tell him how deeply it touched her to see, even more than the anger in his eyes, the fear. In spite of his refusal to open his heart, her loyalty was deeply important to him.

"I'm waiting," he said with a subtle harshness that she knew was an attempt to mask whatever his fears might have conjured concerning her behavior. She lowered her eyes, and he added, "Please look at me while you tell me the truth, and I beg you not to make any attempt to cover the truth, because no truth can go unknown forever. And whatever it is you're hiding has already gone on too long."

Eleanore caught his eyes and held them, telling herself she could do this. But she felt so unprepared. She tried to keep in mind that she could have no expectations over his response, now or from this moment on. His anticipation faded visibly to impatience, and she cleared her throat. "I . . . um . . ." She cleared her throat again. "Forgive me. You caught me off guard. I . . . don't know how to say this."

James swallowed and felt his fists clench unwillingly. His stomach tightened further. She looked downright terrified. "It's not what you're thinking," she said.

"How do you know what I'm thinking?" he asked, sounding more defensive than he'd intended.

"You're thinking of Caroline . . . how she betrayed you. I would never do any such thing. I would never do *anything* behind your back. I have no reason to."

James wanted to feel relief. She seemed sincere. But what other explanation could there be? "Then why?" he asked.

"What you have interpreted as guilt in my eyes, Mr. Barrington, is more accurately my personal struggle to come to terms with my own thoughts and feelings. If I've had any hesitance to look you in the eye, it was only the fear that you might guess my feelings, and perhaps make light of them. No, let me correct that. I don't believe you would make light of them, but you might discredit them, perhaps try to convince me that I'm too young or naive to even understand such feelings. So I chose to keep them to myself."

James listened to her words and felt the truth in them, but he still felt baffled. When she seemed reluctant to go on, he asked, "What is it, my dear? Are you unhappy here? Do you regret your decision to be my wife? To leave England? To—"

"No," she interrupted firmly. "I regret nothing. I love it here. I never imagined that I could be so happy."

"It's not happiness I've seen in your eyes, my dear. Tell me what thoughts and feelings could possibly warrant such obvious discomfort."

He wondered if this had something to do with the religion she was seeking; but still he couldn't imagine what. She made a nosie that sounded like a chuckle attempting to stifle a sob. His relief in knowing she'd been faithful to him was submerged in absolute bewilderment—and a different kind of anxiety.

"Perhaps it's better this way," she said. "I didn't want to tell you, but perhaps it's best you know. You're right. There should be no secrets between us. We should always be completely honest with each other. We should stop pretending. But please know that what I have to say does not alter my understanding of your stipulations when you proposed marriage to me. I have no expectations, sir. I only know how I feel."

Eleanore ran out of preamble and knew she just had to say it, but she couldn't bring herself to utter such words with the formality they were both so accustomed to. She wondered if he would be more upset by her confession—or by the use of his name. But she just had to say it.

James watched her draw courage. His heart quickened anew in proportion to an ongoing effort to guess what could possibly explain all that she'd said. And then the words came out of her mouth. "I love you, James."

His chest tightened. He could make no sound when he couldn't even draw air. He didn't have to wonder for even a moment over her sincerity. Her behavior made as perfect sense as her explanations. And he couldn't discredit her feelings. She'd remained by his side and proven her love for him over and over. Her confession was as magical as it was terrifying. The irony of his former suspicions made him a little queasy. He finally exhaled harshly, which brought him to an awareness of the audible pounding of his heart. What could he possibly say? She'd told him she had no expectations, that she didn't antici-pate any change from his prior stipulations. She was making it clear that she knew where he stood. But did *he?*

Eleanore watched him take in her declaration with stunned surprise. But he looked more afraid than pleased. Not wanting to bring any further attention to the matter, or make him even more uncomfortable than he already was, she hurried to add, "There. I've said it. You asked for the truth. Now you know. There's no reason for us to ever discuss it again."

James watched her stand up and leave the room. She closed the door behind her. The clicking of the latch startled him to an awareness of her absence. How could she tell him something like that and just leave him alone like this? He wanted to run after her, take her in his arms and demand that she tell him more. How long had she felt this way? What had made her realize it? And most of all, what could possibly drive such a remarkable young woman to actually *love* a man like him?

For more than an hour he pondered this discovery, attempting to resolve his recent thought processes with the history he shared with this woman he'd married. Still, he had trouble believing it. *She loved him.* He'd believed for many months that she'd grown to care for him, as he did for her. But *love?*

Eleanore left the library and went quickly up to her room, needing only to be alone. She cried long and hard, grateful that no one found her there—especially her husband. *James.* She'd spoken his name aloud, spilled her deepest confessions. She wandered the room while her emotions quieted into fear. She didn't want anything to change between them.

More than an hour after she'd exposed her heart to him, she heard him come into the room. She held her breath and remained looking out the window, hoping that he would ignore their prior conversation. But there was purpose in the way he put his hands on her shoulders and squeezed gently. She closed her eyes and took a slow breath. He put his lips behind her ear and whispered, "Have you lost your mind, Mrs. Barrington?"

"No, my dear," she said. "Only my heart. I will never try to talk you out of your feelings, or your reasons for them. I simply ask the same in return."

"That sounds completely fair and equitable," he said, "but it's not, is it?"

"I have no comprehension of what your heart has suffered. You have given me a good life, as you promised. I have no cause to complain. I have everything I could ever ask for."

"Not everything," he said and sounded sad. He sighed, and she sensed his regret, but even that warmed her. "You must forgive my cold heart. You deserve better. I just don't know how to give it."

Eleanore turned to look into his eyes and wanted to point out that he gave pieces of himself to her each and every day. His heart was not nearly so cold as he believed, but if he felt more comfortable in defining his love for her on different terms, that was more than all right with her. She touched his face and whispered, "It doesn't matter. You asked, so I told you. Enough said." She lifted her lips to his and relished his immediate response.

James took her fully into his arms and kissed her in a way that felt hypocritical following declarations of his cold heart. He could admit that he needed her, he wanted her near him day in and day out. He depended on her and found his greatest fulfillment in his own ability to make her happy and meet her needs. But in the deepest part of himself, he simply couldn't accept that it was in him to truly love her. Still, he'd been honest with her as she had with him, and her acceptance was as it had always been. However, there was something more that he needed to say. He drew back and said, "You must forgive me . . . for doubting you . . . for assuming that you would . . . betray me. You're nothing like her. You've never given me any reason to doubt you, and I'm sorry for assuming . . ."

"It's all right," she murmured and smiled.

He wrapped her tightly in his arms and admitted, "I was so afraid. I need you . . . Eleanore."

Tears crept into her eyes to hear her name pass through his lips. She tightened her hold on him. "I need you too," she admitted.

"Say it again," he whispered. "Say my name."

She looked into his eyes and touched his face. "James," she whispered intently. "I need you, James."

He smiled with wonder in his eyes and bent to kiss her. Eleanore silently thanked God for making her the happiest woman on earth.

Chapter Fourteen

SHATTERED PRIDE

That night James couldn't sleep. While his sweet wife slumbered deeply near his side, the words kept repeating in his mind. *I love you, James.* He wanted to hear her say it again, perhaps with the belief that it might fully sink in. And oh, to hear her say his name! Why did such a simple thing have such profound meaning for him? Caroline had only spoken his given name with contempt once the truth had come out, and before then her use of it had only been attached to the lie she'd been living. His parents had never been so informal with each other; at least not that he'd ever heard. But then he'd never heard—or seen—any evidence that there was any tenderness or caring between them at all, and certainly not *love*.

He finally slept, having reconciled the fact that she knew where he stood, and he knew the same of her. Everything could go on the way it had. Their life together was close to perfect, and he was grateful.

* * *

Eleanore became concerned, as did everyone else in the house, when Lizzie showed signs of illness. Then the doctor came and declared that she was pregnant. Lizzie and her husband were both as pleased as they were shocked.

"I thought I was too old," Lizzie admitted. "Apparently not."

"Apparently not," Eleanore said, hugging her tightly. "Who would have dreamed that we would be having babies together?"

"Your mother must be smiling down upon us from heaven."

"Indeed she must," Eleanore said, liking the idea.

Mrs. Leichty's value in the household rose immensely with Lizzie not feeling well and Eleanore reaching a stage in her pregnancy where she began contending with many aches and pains. And she still had nearly three months to go. But Eleanore and Lizzie had both been blessed with caring and considerate husbands, and the men went to great trouble to make certain all was well.

Winter had not yet shown any sign of relenting when Eleanore woke up on a bright, cold morning, feeling ill and achy, especially in her lower back. She was disappointed to find James already gone, but looking at the clock, she realized how late she'd slept. He likely hadn't wanted to disturb her.

For a long while she battled between her urge to stay close to the bed and her desire to get dressed and go downstairs, to be with James and the children—whatever they might be doing. Her stomach rumbled with hunger, but she felt no desire to eat. The ache in her back abruptly turned to pain, and a startled cry came out of her mouth. Hearing her own reaction frightened her, but she wondered what to do. Only seconds later there was a knock at the door.

"Come in," she called, and Mrs. Leichty peered into the room.

"Are you all right?" she asked. "I was in Iris's room changing the sheets and thought I heard you cry out."

Eleanore considered her intervention nothing short of a miracle when the pain came again. "No, I'm not all right. Something hurts." She recalled the story of Caroline Barrington's dying. She'd not reported the problem initially and had ended up bleeding to death. "Perhaps we should send for the doctor," she said firmly, "and I think I . . ." She hesitated at a sudden wet sensation, then began to gasp, barely able to breathe.

"What is it?" Mrs. Leichty took hold of her shoulders.

"I think I'm bleeding."

The woman's eyes widened fearfully, but she didn't hesitate a moment to throw back the bedcovers and check. "It's not blood," she said with a loud sigh, "but your water's broken."

"What does that mean?" Eleanore demanded.

"The baby's coming, dear."

"But it's too soon!" she protested as if she could stop it.

"I'll send for the doctor," Mrs. Leichty said on her way out of the room. "You stay down flat and I'll be right back."

Eleanore prayed frantically while fear and pain manifested themselves in an ongoing flow of tears. She couldn't lose this baby. She just couldn't!

* * *

James was shoveling fresh snow off the path to the barn when the back door came open and a flustered Mrs. Leichty announced, "Mrs. Barrington needs you, sir." Higgins then rushed out the door and past both of them, putting on his coat while he ran to the barn. Mrs. Leichty added, "Mr. Higgins is going for the doctor. Lizzie is with the children."

James felt his heart leap into his throat. He threw down the shovel and ran past Mrs. Leichty, taking the stairs three at a time, pulling off his coat and gloves as he went. He tossed them carelessly in the hall and hurried into the bedroom. His stomach tightened to see Eleanore crying, and clearly in pain.

"What's wrong?" he demanded.

Her answer was forthright, but her voice quivered. "My water broke, and I'm having pains."

James cursed under his breath and fought away a surge of disturbing memories. He sat on the edge of the bed and bent over to wrap her in his arms. She clung to him and cried harder.

Mrs. Leichty entered the room. He glanced toward her and spoke in a calm voice that he hoped would keep Eleanore from feeling his own panic. "Tell me what to do." He was grateful to know she was a mother, that she had to have some minimal knowledge of such matters. Surely she could offer some words of comfort.

"Once the water has broken, the baby must be delivered, whether it's ready or not." He looked at her sharply, not liking the answer at all, nor the way Eleanore's distress increased. "Until the doctor arrives there's nothing to be done but wait and try to keep her comfortable."

"I'll be right back," he whispered to Eleanore and went into the hall, motioning for Mrs. Leichty to follow him. He closed the door and spoke in a low voice. "Mrs. Leichty, I have no idea of your level of expertise on such matters, but Mrs. Barrington needs some hope, not—"

"Sir," she interrupted, "allow me to explain my level of expertise. Ralph is my only child, but I was pregnant six times." Her gaze became intense, her eyes reflective of a depth of pain that stopped the blood flowing in his veins when she added, "Trust me when I tell you that once the water has broken, there's no stopping this. Telling her now that the baby will stay in her long enough to live and be healthy would only be giving her *false* hope, which is doubly cruel. Trust me."

James closed his eyes, wondering how many times Mrs. Leichty had been given false hope. His heart sank as his own hope tumbled out of him. He took hold of the wall for support and hung his head. "Forgive me," he murmured.

"I know this is difficult, Mr. Barrington, but all we can do is help her get through this."

He nodded, and Mrs. Leichty opened the door, going back into the room. He took a deep breath, forced back a burning behind his eyes, and followed. He listened through a fog while Mrs. Leichty spoke to Eleanore in a gentle tone. "The doctor is coming. I'm going to heat water and get some things prepared that he'll need. Your husband is going to be here with you." She touched Eleanore's face. "Now, you mustn't worry. I know it's hard, but I've been through it and I've survived. So will you. You're a strong woman, and you're going to make it through this. Do you understand?"

Eleanore bit her lip, and her chin quivered. She nodded stoutly, then turned her tear-filled eyes to James as Mrs. Leichty left the room. He was afraid to speak for fear that the knot in his throat would manifest itself in childish sobbing. He scooted a chair close to the bed and sat there, taking her hand, but she immediately said, "No, come closer. I need you to hold me."

James quickly examined his options, knowing the doctor was on his way. He pulled off his boots and moved to the center of the bed, leaning against the headboard where he took her in his arms.

"It's going to be all right, Eleanore," he said, his voice trembling with lack of conviction. She just held to him more tightly, and they waited while the pain came and went, her reactions proportionate to their intensity. James fought to keep his mind from wandering to the night Caroline had died. But how could he not consider the similarities? The evidence of Eleanore's ongoing pain threatened to eat him alive.

James felt some relief when the doctor arrived. He asked questions while he washed his hands, then he set to work with calm efficiency. He gently and firmly told them she was losing the baby, and the experience of getting through it would be painful and difficult, but there was no reason to believe she wouldn't come through just fine. James felt prone to believe him until he heard him comment quietly to Mrs. Leichty, who was assisting him, "She's bleeding." He then asked her to help him with something that James didn't understand.

"I'll be back," James muttered to Eleanore and couldn't get out of the room fast enough. He felt as if the walls would come down and crush him; even the smells in the room were horridly familiar, bringing it all back. Once the door was closed, he heaved for breath and sank to his knees. "Please, God . . . no! Don't take her from me like this! I beg you!" His heaving turned to sobs that he fought to keep silent. He was grateful to know the children were downstairs with Lizzie and Higgins, and that Mrs. Leichty was occupied with assisting the doctor. Unleashed torrents of emotion surged out of him as the memories fed his fear. He'd grown bitter toward Caroline, but watching her die was one of the worst experiences of his life, even though he'd not been let into the room until the trauma was over and she'd been nearly gone. He couldn't go through that again. He couldn't! Especially not with Eleanore, not like this. He *needed* her. Everyone who knew her needed her. He thought of the children losing her and groaned. Then he felt a hand on his shoulder.

"She's going to be all right," Mrs. Leichty said gently.

"But . . . she's bleeding," he muttered, beyond caring that he'd been caught crying like a baby.

"The doctor is not concerned. It's not enough to be a problem."

He wiped a hand over his face and felt her hand tighten on his shoulder. "May I ask what's got you so upset?"

"Um . . ." He cleared his throat and sniffled. "My first wife died in premature labor."

"Oh my," she said with a tone of surprised understanding.

"She . . . uh . . . was bleeding; they couldn't stop it."

"I'm so sorry, Mr. Barrington. But . . . truly . . . there is no indication that her life is in danger." He looked up at her to check the sincerity in her expression. She added firmly, "She needs you."

At that very moment, he heard Eleanore cry out in pain. He wiped his face with his shirtsleeves and hurried back into the room, resuming his place on the bed at her side. While her pain continued to escalate, both physically and emotionally, James felt his entire life fall neatly into perspective. More than three hours after the doctor's arrival, she finally gave birth to a dead baby. The doctor told them it was a boy, but Eleanore buried her face against

James's chest and wept, declaring that she couldn't look. James closed his eyes and held her, sharing her sentiment completely. But Mrs. Leichty said gently, "If I might offer a suggestion . . . I know it's hard, but given my own experience, I believe it's easier to let go if you *do* hold the child."

Eleanore looked up to see Mrs. Leichty holding a tiny, motionless bundle wrapped in a little white blanket. Without waiting for further permission, she eased the baby into Eleanore's arms, saying with tenderness, "Perhaps you need a moment to say good-bye."

Eleanore felt her husband's arms tighten around her and felt a kiss in her hair. As the baby came into view, she heard James whimper at the same time as she moaned softly. But her anguish was soothed for a moment when she admitted firmly, "He looks like you."

James couldn't see the resemblance, but he did find some abstract comfort in simply seeing that it *was* a baby—*their* baby. The grief burning inside him felt more valid with the evidence that human life had been lost. Still, the perfect serenity in the baby's countenance left a peaceful impression.

Eleanore was reluctant to let go of the baby, but did so when Mrs. Leichty assured her that they would give him a proper burial. James held him for a long minute, then turned him over to this sweet woman. Once she left the room, Eleanore clung to James, and together they cried until the doctor said that she needed some medical attention; the birthing process was not entirely completed.

When the ordeal was finally over and Eleanore was left to rest, James sat in a chair near the bed, fighting a new assault of tears. The doctor had told him he'd check back later to see how she was doing. Alone with the silence, he watched her sleeping and recounted the nightmare they'd just endured together, surely more hellish for her than for him. He resented the grief burning in his chest and throat and wondered how it was possible to grieve for the death of a child that had never breathed. But he was. He couldn't deny it. The loss felt horrid and senseless. He considered how Eleanore might cope with that loss, and he groaned, pressing his hands brutally into his hair. That, combined with the physical strain she had just endured, threatened to break his heart in two. She didn't deserve this. She was precious and fine and completely without guile. She had given everything to him without question. He wanted to be able to help her through this. But how could he comfort her when he felt so close to crumbling himself?

James was startled by a light knock at the door, and he was relieved when it didn't rouse Eleanore from her sleep. He moved quietly to the door so as not to disturb her. While he'd expected one of the women, he wasn't disappointed to see Higgins.

"Is she all right?" he asked.

"She will be," he said, stepping into the hall so they wouldn't wake her.

"I'm so sorry about the baby," Higgins said with the compassion of a true friend.

James looked at the floor and pressed a hand over the center of his chest as if he could ease the pain gathering there. When it only worsened, he hung his head and struggled to breathe. Higgins put a concerned hand on his shoulder, and James attempted to explain his behavior. "It was horrible." He didn't realize he was crying until he sniffled loudly. "She suffered so much." He groaned. "Oh, heaven help me."

"Are you all right?" Higgins asked as James bent over and pressed his hands over his thighs, lowering his head with the hope of keeping his equilibrium. He struggled to catch his breath. "I haven't seen you like this since—"

"Don't you say it!" he ordered without looking up. It wasn't Caroline's death that had once crushed him; it had been her betrayal.

"Eventually you're going to have to admit that it happened."

"I *have* admitted it," he growled unkindly.

"Only bits and pieces," Higgins said, unaffected. "One day you're going to have to accept it and talk about it, or you'll never be free of the pain."

"I've got all the pain I can handle right now. I just . . . don't know what to do with it." His voice became raw as it trembled. "I thought I was going to lose her, and now that I know she'll be all right, I wonder how I will ever . . . console her." His tears increased, and he cursed as he wiped his cheeks and stood up straight, turning away from Higgins.

"Your tears are nothing to be ashamed of. Such emotion is certainly understandable, given the circumstances. And especially considering how much you love her."

James looked at him abruptly, while his heart began to pound. He bit back the words on the tip of his tongue, knowing they would make him look like a fool. Still they echoed through his head. *What makes you think I love her?* Higgins's expression made it clear he'd expected such astonishment at the suggestion, but he'd always had a way of getting James to look at things he couldn't see—or chose not to acknowledge. But he could say nothing. He had no rebuttal.

Higgins smiled wanly and added, "There's something I need to say, James. And you need to hear it."

James met his tight gaze, knowing he was serious. He could only recall two other times this man had called him by his given name. They'd shared a close and trusting relationship for many years, but rarely did he step fully out of his role as an employee.

"It's time to forgive and let go, James."

James sighed. "I've worked very hard to forgive Caroline. As much as she hurt me, Frederick, I do not hold malice toward her. It's in the past."

"I'm not talking about Caroline," he said, and James was startled. He couldn't think of any other person he had cause to forgive for anything. "I'm talking about *you*, James. You need to forgive yourself."

"For what?" he asked with a breathlessness that indicated he recognized the truth in what he was hearing.

"For letting her deceive you. For giving her your heart and letting her break it. For giving your children a deplorable mother. For being vulnerable, human, blind."

James took a sharp breath and couldn't let it go. The pain and lightheadedness returned, and he hurried into the closest bedroom, which happened to be David's. Sitting on the edge of the bed, he lowered his head and pressed it into his hands. While he was still trying to digest what he'd just heard—and the way it made him feel—Frederick Higgins, his loyal friend and companion of many years sat next to him and put a hand on his shoulder.

"Until you forgive yourself, my friend, you will never be able to let go of the pain. But you need to understand that it's pride you've put in place to protect that pain. It's pride that keeps your heart from her." James snapped his head up to look at him. "It's not a crime to give her your heart, James. I think she's earned it." The words pierced James deeply and left him frightened. "You think about it," Frederick said and stood. "You know where to find me if you need to talk."

He moved toward the door until James said, "Frederick."

"Yes?"

"Thank you. And . . . now that we're in America, let's just . . . stick with given names. We're all as good as family."

Frederick smiled. "Whatever you say, sir."

He left James sitting alone, attempting to accept what he'd just learned. He was stunned to feel the truth in everything his friend had said. Was it possible? Had he really been so blind? And perhaps worse, had he been so oblivious to what his own heart was feeling? How could he think that what he felt for Eleanore was anything less than love? How could it be anything else? And if he *did* love her, then he had to face the rest of the truth. It *was* pride holding him back. Pride and fear. But what was the solution? He barely thought the question before the answer came. Frederick had hit the nail on the head. He needed to forgive. Until now he'd never considered the possibility that he was holding himself so brutally responsible for all that had happened.

While his mind roiled with a thousand thoughts and emotions that he knew would take time to sort out, James returned to the bedroom where Eleanore slept. He sat near the bed and watched her, letting the truth settle into him. And he knew it was truth. He just had to become accustomed to accepting it in spite of the fear induced by past events in his life that had nothing to do with her. While she slept, he prayed for understanding—and forgiveness, for his pride as well as his stubbornness in holding to his pain and self-blame. While he prayed, his mind wandered back through the relationship he'd shared with Eleanore. He thought of the night, prior to their marriage, when his heart had been heavy and burdened with the past. They'd both ended up in the library, likely by some divine intervention. And she'd smoothly spoken words that had calmed him and given him peace. What had she said? She'd quoted scripture. There was one line in particular that seemed pertinent to this moment. He struggled to remember and prayed for his memory to be magnified. And then he heard the words in his head, as clearly as if she were speaking them again. *And now if Christ had not come into the world, speaking of things to come as though they had already come, there could have been no redemption.* That was the answer! He felt the warmth of it burn through him. Christ had already paid the price for the burden he carried, and it was time to let it go. His prayers explored a different path as he pleaded for his infantile understanding of the Savior's Atonement to be expanded, that it might work its miracle in his own heart.

James felt his heart quicken when Eleanore began to stir. He scooted the chair closer to the bed and leaned his forearms on his thighs, watching her closely until she opened her eyes and turned toward him. He saw the sorrow and torment come into her eyes as she recalled what had happened. He gave her a sad smile and brushed her hair back from her face, wondering what he could possibly say.

"How are you?" he asked, certain it sounded trite.

He knew immediately that her physical discomfort meant nothing as huge tears rose in her eyes, then fell unimpeded. "Our baby . . ." she said. "Our baby . . . is gone."

James closed his eyes and pressed her hand to his lips, keeping his head down long enough to choke back his own emotion. When her crying increased, he moved to the edge of the bed and carefully eased her into his arms, holding her close while she wept, grateful that she couldn't see his face when he was unable to hold back tears of his own. "Everything is going to be all right," he murmured when he could manage to speak. "It's hard, but . . . we're going to move on. You will be all right and that's the only thing that really matters right now." She drew back to look into his eyes. He felt compelled to confess, "I thought I was going to lose you too." New tears came with his confession. She touched his face as if his tears were precious. Did she crave evidence that he loved her? The thought caused him pain. He pressed a kiss to her brow if only to avoid looking at her while he felt so troubled. He was relieved when Lizzie came in with something for her to eat. He left the women and went outside, deciding a long, brisk walk might help clear his head and help him find peace in his heart.

James then sought out the children and spent some time with them, encouraging them to talk about what had happened in their family and how they were going to move on. Their sorrow added to his own, but their simple faith was a strength to him. As young as they were, he found comfort in sharing their grief. They were family; they were in this together.

* * *

James found it difficult to sleep that night while he continued to wrestle with his heart. He was keenly conscious of Eleanore sleeping beside him, aided by something the doctor had given her for the pain. He heard her come awake, then realized she was crying. He held her close and wept with her until she slept again in his arms.

The following day he sat in a chair near the bed with the Bible open on his lap. Eleanore looked at him between bouts of medicine-induced sleep and said, "You don't need to sit with me. I'm certain you have better things to do."

"Nothing more important," he said. "Besides," he added lightly, "I have great reading."

She closed her eyes and asked, "Are you searching for peace and understanding?"

"Yes, actually."

"Then read to me," she muttered and shifted carefully.

While he read from Psalms he noted the subtle distress in her countenance.

"Are you in pain?" he asked.

"It's getting better. But I feel . . ."

"What?" he pressed when she hesitated.

"Empty," she admitted, her voice heavy. He set the book aside and eased onto the bed next to her, wrapping her in his arms. She held to him and cried, "I miss my baby."

"I know. So do I."

"It was a part of you . . . and a part of me . . . and it's gone."

"I know," he said and kissed her brow. He didn't know what else to say. So he just held her, amazed that it seemed to be enough.

Four days after the loss of the baby, Eleanore was doing much better physically, although the doctor had recommended she stay down for a while yet. James sensed her attempts to be brave and positive over the loss, but he knew she was hurting. He left her in Lizzie's care to go into town on some errands, wondering what he might buy for his wife to cheer her up. He found a couple of novels he knew she didn't own, and hoped she would enjoy them. Perhaps they would help pass the time and keep her mind away from her grief. Then he stopped at the post office and was handed a letter, addressed to his wife, from New York.

James struggled with a new level of trepidation as he rode home. If his wife made contact with this new religion that had such power over her, would it change the serenity of their life? She had told him that her family meant more to her than anything, and that she would never leave him. He believed her. But if she was struggling with unrest over such a matter, would it not affect the life they shared? Still, there was no option beyond honesty. While she'd not mentioned the letter for weeks, he knew she'd never given up hoping for some response. It had been slow in coming. He just hoped the timing would be positive and not otherwise. At the moment, any new difficulty seemed too much to face.

Back at the house, he found Eleanore sitting up in bed, reading from her favorite book. He'd seen her reading from it countless times. But he'd never asked about it, and she'd never generated any conversation over it beyond the time she'd admitted her reasons for wanting to come to America. His own opinion hovered near a reluctance to believe that any book beyond the Bible could truly be considered scripture. But he realized that what he felt or believed wasn't as important as respecting his wife's feelings and beliefs, whether he agreed with them or not.

"Hello, Eleanore Barrington," he said, hoping his light tone would brighten her mood.

She smiled at him. That was a good sign. "Hello," she said.

"I've brought you something." He moved toward the bed but kept his hands behind his back. "Your very favorite thing in all the world."

"Books?" she asked eagerly, and he laughed as he pulled them out then tossed them on the bed.

"How smart you are!" She picked them up to glance through them while she kept the other book open on her lap. "I don't know if they're any good, but they looked intriguing. I hope they'll be worth the read."

"They're wonderful. Thank you."

"Aren't you going to smell them?" he asked, and she did so with mock drama as if to humor him. But it did make him laugh.

James wondered if he should wait to show her what else he'd brought, but he knew he couldn't. Better to get it over with. If she found out he'd had the letter for any length of time without showing it to her, she would surely be unhappy with him. Perhaps the letter would cheer her up.

"There's something else I got in town," he said, and she looked at him expectantly. He pulled the letter out of his pocket. "From New York."

Eleanore's heart quickened, and excitement pumped through her veins. She couldn't believe it! All this time, and finally an answer! She'd almost given up hope of ever hearing back, and had begun to wonder what other avenue she might take to get information. She reached out a trembling hand and took the letter, touching the postmark almost reverently. She attempted to break the seal, but her fingers were shaking. Then she stopped to consider the impression that had just come abruptly into her mind. Almost instantly the impression solidified into words that formed as clearly as if they had been whispered in her ear. She quivered from the inside out and absorbed their meaning into her spirit. *Trust your husband. He will protect you. Trust in Me. I will guide you when the time is right.*

James watched the excitement in Eleanore's countenance fade into a dazed confusion. Her eyes became distant, as if her mind had suddenly been taken to another world. "Are you all right?" he asked, and she snapped her head toward him, startled.

"Yes, of course," she said and held the letter toward him. "You open it. I'm shaking."

James carefully tore open the letter, hating the dread he felt. He handed the letter back to her, and she added, "Read it to me . . . please. I can't."

James took a deep breath and unfolded the single page in his hand. The brief paragraph written there initially gave him relief, then the deeper meaning sank in, and he felt a little sick at the implication, especially considering his wife's convictions. He had to read it again to make certain he'd gotten it right.

The Mormons left this area years ago and we're glad to be rid of them. They're probably scattered and gone by now, what's left of them. With any luck you'll never find them. Postmaster, Palmyra, New York.

"What does it say?" Eleanore asked eagerly.

James felt an instinctive desire to protect her from the harshness of what he was reading. He prayed he was doing the right thing. "Um . . . it says they left the area years ago. He doesn't know where they went. That's all." He saw more concern than disappointment in her face, almost as if she'd expected such an answer. Honesty overruled, and he held the letter out toward her. "Do you want to read it?"

"No," she said, "thank you."

James needed no further permission to toss it into the fire while he wondered what might fuel such negative attitudes toward this religious affiliation.

"You're disappointed," he said, sitting in the chair near the bed.

"Yes, but . . . I'll find them . . . when the time is right."

That's what I'm afraid of, he thought, wondering why her finding these people equated with fear for him, now more than ever.

Her eyes grew distant again while her hands rested on the open Book of Mormon on her lap.

"Read to me," he said, and she looked surprised. But she closed the book without putting a marker where she'd been reading and handed it to him.

"My eyes hurt," she said. "Why don't *you* read to *me*."

"Where?" he asked, and she relaxed against the pillows, closing her eyes.

"Anything; anywhere. It doesn't matter."

James thumbed through the book a little and let it fall open. He found the beginning of a paragraph that stood out and started to read. "'Thou fool, that shall say: A Bible, we have got a Bible, and we need no more Bible. Have ye obtained a Bible save it were by the Jews?'" He stopped, feeling a little stunned. It was as if the book had read his mind, a theory that was absolutely ludicrous! Not wanting to draw attention to the way what he'd just read tied into his ongoing feelings about the book, he continued to read. "'Know ye not that there are more nations than one? Know ye not that I, the Lord your God, have created all men, and that I remember those who are upon the isles of the sea; and that I rule in the heavens above and in the earth beneath; and I bring forth my word unto the children of men, yea, even upon all the nations of the earth? Wherefore murmur ye, because that ye shall receive more of my word?'" He paused again, but this time he couldn't keep reading. His mind was too absorbed with attempting to understand the words before him.

"Is something wrong?" she asked, opening her eyes.

Committed to honesty, he had to say, "No. It just . . . makes sense."

"Yes, it does," she said and closed her eyes again.

James silently read the words again. Maybe the book *had* read his mind. Or more accurately, God had guided him to this passage, if only to give him some degree of understanding of his wife's conviction. With that settled in his mind, he continued to read aloud. And after she'd fallen asleep, he kept reading. He didn't know if the stories were true or fiction, but he couldn't deny that the principles of Christianity were powerful. Perhaps her search for the Mormons wasn't such a bad thing after all—in spite of what the postmaster in Palmyra might think.

* * *

A week later, Eleanore was up and about as if nothing had gone wrong. Soon after that, she returned to her usual duties around the house in spite of James's insistence that it wasn't necessary. She simply told him she needed something to occupy herself or she would go mad. While he wasn't surprised by her dignity in moving beyond her loss, he could see the sadness in her eyes. She had lost something of the tender innocence that had always been there. He had thought that she'd become a woman by becoming a wife. But he knew now that only in losing a part of herself had she crossed that line. He often inquired over her well-being, and she would always say that she was fine. But he sensed the truth, and he knew that at some level he shared her grief. Still, as difficult as the loss was for him, he knew he could never understand what it meant to a woman who had felt life torn from her womb. He had put it there, she had nurtured it, and fate had stolen it away.

Weeks beyond the loss, James could still see a hollow sadness in Eleanore's eyes, even though she did well at disguising it with a brave smile. He felt helpless while he wondered every day what he might do for her, or give to her that might ease her pain. Then it occurred to him. He *did* have something to give her. It wasn't likely to be easy. But she certainly deserved it.

Chapter Fifteen
H E A V E N

Eleanore sat curled up on one of the couches in the library, staring more at the wall than reading the novel on her lap. By habit, she attempted to counter hovering feelings of grief with the perspective of all she had to be grateful for. The list was very long. She was surrounded by people she loved who enriched her life and treated her well. Her every need was met, and even her every whim. She loved her home in this place, the community, the land that surrounded them. And in her heart she believed that with time she would be given the gift of a child of her own. She simply needed to be patient. She could feel God teaching her patience. Thus far her patience had taken her a long way in the life she lived, and the love she shared with her husband. And God had promised her that in time she would be guided to find His true Church. She had learned to trust in Him. He had guided her well in finding the path of her life. But there were moments when patience came with difficulty, and the tiny bits of her life that felt wrong blossomed and spread through her spirit, suffocating the gratitude for all that was good. This was one of those moments when the emptiness of her womb felt tangibly painful, and the possession of the Book of Mormon without finding its source left her feeling entirely alone.

Eleanore heard the door open and turned to see James enter the room. That worried crease on his brow was becoming familiar, but for all her efforts to be positive, she didn't know how to erase it. Still, his concern was touching. His awareness of her emotions couldn't help but warm her. And she couldn't deny that the grief they shared in this mutual loss had deepened the bond between them. She'd felt closer to him in spirit since that tragic day. She wasn't certain exactly why, but she considered it a gift that helped ease her grief.

"Hello," he said nonchalantly, but she sensed a purpose in his manner.

"Hello."

He sat beside her and asked what she was reading. They chatted over trivialities for several minutes before he said, "There's something I need to say." He stood and moved to the window, holding his hands behind his back.

"I'm listening." She remained sitting.

"I lied to you once," he said, taking her off guard. "I don't think I intended to. I believe it was just too difficult to admit." His sigh was deep and weighted. "You asked me if I'd loved her. I told you no. I had stopped loving her long before she died. But there had been a time when . . ." His hesitance hinted at an attempt to sustain his emotion. "I . . . I loved her very much. I loved her eagerly, with my whole heart. And I had no reservations about expressing my sentiments freely. She told me she loved me too. Every time I said it, she said it back. And then I discovered the truth. When I found out he was her lover, I felt my love for her turn to hate in an instant. Over time I realized the hate was just an angry mask for the love I couldn't bear to acknowledge. With time, hate smothered the love until I felt nothing at all. When the truth came out, I asked her . . . if she'd ever loved me, if she'd ever meant it. She told me no."

Eleanore found tears on her face, not only for his grief but also for the fact that he was speaking of it. She pressed one hand to her pounding heart while the other briefly covered her mouth to keep from audibly halting his confession. She was stunned by his admittance—and what it meant in relation to herself. She wasn't certain where this conversation was headed. It didn't matter. He was talking about the most difficult thing he'd ever endured. And she was more than willing to listen.

"She admitted to being fond of me," he went on, "of respecting me, of being grateful for the life I'd given her. But she'd never loved me. It had all been a lie. She'd loved him . . . from the start. Before we were married she told me they were friends. I had no reason for suspicion, so I believed her. As it turned out, she had loved him for years. But he was poor. Her family's estate had dwindled to practically nothing. Her parents had pressured her to marry well in order to preserve their standard of living. I fell in love with her, and she needed to marry a wealthy man. So it worked out very nicely."

He sighed again, and Eleanore fought to keep her tears silent as he continued. "She *was* innocent when I married her. I know I was the first. I should be grateful for that. But within a year, they became involved. The last I heard, he has never married. As you know, until *you* told me that the children bore a resemblance, I was never sure . . . if they were mine. I saw him at the funeral. At first I wanted to kill him. I wanted to tell him he had a lot of nerve showing his face. I wanted to shout in front of everybody that it had been his baby that had killed her. Then something changed in me, and I just felt sorry for him. He'd just lost the woman he loved. I'd lost her years earlier. I remember trying to imagine being him. He'd been born into poverty and was stuck there, living in a society that made it unacceptable for him to marry the woman he loved. But mostly I felt sorry for him because he'd been too stupid to let her go once she'd married another man. Maybe he could have found happiness elsewhere if he hadn't been so obsessed with stealing another man's wife. They committed adultery, and they were both ruined for it. But I was ruined too."

Silence fell while he remained with his back to her. She wondered if he was attempting to conceal his emotion, but she was grateful that he was unaware of hers.

"Going back," he added, "once I knew there was another man, I stopped going to her bed. We'd always kept separate rooms, but we usually slept in the same bed in one room or the other. I remember more than once feeling so sick with the realization of what had been going on that . . . well, I was just . . . sick. Physically sick. How could I ever reconcile with the fact that everything I'd been sharing with her, she had been sharing with someone else?" He shook his head and groaned. "All that was most wondrous, and personal, and sacred between us, she had been dividing between the man she loved and the man who bought her everything she wanted."

James allowed more silence in which to let the words settle. His own relief at having uttered them was a surprise. He should have confessed the full depth of his broken heart to her long ago. Curious over her reaction, he finally turned, surprised even more to find her face streaked with tears. "You cry for me?"

"Why would I not?"

"Or perhaps it is for yourself you cry," he said. "I should not be so presumptuous."

"What reason would I have to cry for myself when it is *your* heart that has been so cruelly broken?"

"But you have suffered for it." He leaned against the windowsill and folded his arms. "I made a conscious decision to keep my heart from you, Eleanore. I never thought it would matter. I believed I could make up for my lack of love in other ways."

"I have never suffered," she said. "I've struggled to understand, and I cannot deny that I've wished. But my life is full and richly blest, because you are the finest of husbands."

"A fine husband would give his heart, my dear, not keep it under lock and key." Eleanore wanted to tell him that he *had* given his heart—over and over. But she believed he needed to figure that out for himself. He surprised her by adding, "I have another confession." He sighed loudly. "I've been praying, Eleanore."

"Is this something new?"

He smiled subtly. "That wasn't the confession."

"Ah." She returned his smile.

"I've been praying for courage and strength, and I have no question that God hears such prayers—because they were given to me. I was finally able to do something I thought that I could never do."

When he didn't go on she said, "Will you keep me in suspense?"

"It's not easy to say, but . . . I'm learning that in some ways such thoughts are even harder to keep silent. I want you to know how grateful I am to have such a dear, sweet wife as you— who will not only listen to *anything* I have to say, but who never gives me cause to question whether she will safely keep my confessions."

He looked at the floor. Eleanore took in what his words meant. He trusted her with his deepest feelings, and considering his history, she knew such a level of trust had not come easily. Her expectancy heightened when he lifted his eyes. She saw courage there, and it was manifested further by the tightening of his lips, which indicated his anxiety. She wondered what he might have to confess that would cause such conflicting emotions. When he didn't speak, she asked, "And what is it that God gave you the strength and courage to do?"

He lifted his chin and exhaled loudly. "I turned the key. I opened those rusty, creaking gates around my broken heart and . . . I looked inside."

Eleanore's heart quickened just before she saw the subtlest glisten of moisture in his eyes.

"Once inside," he said, "I wondered what I'd been so afraid of. I had expected to see ugly remnants of betrayal . . . and pain . . . like some deserted battle ground. But they weren't there. No, what I found there was amazing and beautiful—a miracle. What I found there was the undeniable realization that . . . I am hopelessly, and irrevocably, . . . in love with my wife."

James held his breath while he watched and waited. Her eyes widened, then filled with fresh tears that fell immediately. Her lips curved into a vague smile, a smile of contentment. Her countenance became perfectly serene. Just absorbing her expression and what it meant gave him more fulfillment than anything in this life ever had. He felt compelled to add, "I've loved you all along, Eleanore. I was just . . . too blinded by my own fear of being hurt again to allow myself to see it."

Eleanore wondered what to say. No words could possibly express what his confession meant to her, especially because she knew it had come so deeply from his heart. Their commitment to being completely honest with each other left her with only one possible response. She fought the smothering emotion in her throat enough to say, "I know."

James felt his heart quicken. It took him a moment to be certain he'd heard her correctly. "You *know?*"

"How could I *not* know, James? The evidence of your love surrounds me every hour of every day. It has from the start. Such tenderness and caring as you have given me do not come from duty or obligation. How could a woman be kissed the way you kiss me," her breath heightened just to speak of it, "and not feel perfectly loved?"

While he was too stunned to speak, she stood and crossed the room. Placing her hands on his chest she looked up at him and said with tender conviction, "I love you, James."

He inhaled her words—and her love—into his spirit, feeling as if a tremendous weight had been lifted from his chest. He'd been carrying it for so long that he'd become oblivious to just how heavy it was. But now it was gone, and in its place he felt only peace and light. He took her face into his hands and spoke with the same conviction. "And I love you, Eleanore." His voice quivered. "More than I ever imagined it could be possible to love anyone. I thank God that he put you under my roof and kept you there until He gave me the good sense to make you mine. I will never question God's presence in my life, Eleanore, simply because you are there too."

And then he kissed her, holding her fully in his arms. Eleanore drew him impossibly closer, feeling his admittance of love filter into her spirit, healing her troubled heart. The grief of their mutual loss became suddenly more bearable. He loved her! She'd never imagined such joy.

James eased his lips from hers and smiled down at her. "You've made a hypocrite out of me, you know."

She laughed softly. "No, my dear, you did that all by yourself."

He laughed as well. "So I did." He kissed her again.

They sat together on the couch, talking for the better part of the afternoon, sharing their feelings for each other and the path they'd each taken to acknowledge them. The children interrupted a few times, but they talked on and on, holding hands and intermittently kissing.

When it was almost time for supper, he said, "I have a proposition for you."

"More exciting than 'Will you marry me and come to America?'"

"Not likely, but long overdue."

"And what might that be?" she asked.

"A honeymoon," he said. "I've heard of a quiet little city on the river. What do you say we just . . . go there and stay for a few days?"

"It sounds marvelous," she said and touched his bearded face. "When can we leave?"

"How about tomorrow?" he asked and kissed her again.

* * *

A hint of spring hovered in the air as they set out in the buggy, going east toward the Mississippi River. They took the journey slowly and stayed at a hotel halfway between home and the river. On the second day, they arrived and spent the next four days with no agenda beyond just being together. James made a point of instigating a long conversation about the loss of their baby. She cried long and hard, and he cried with her, and they were both able to admit that they could move forward. After that, she did seem more at peace over the loss, even though he knew it would take time for her to fully heal.

The day before they were scheduled to return home, they ambled slowly down the main street, enjoying the warmest temperature in many months, although it still felt more cool than warm. Eleanore had thoroughly enjoyed their vacation and the time they'd spent together without the distractions of everyday life. But she felt anxious to return home. She missed her lovely house and the people there. And she especially missed the children. They'd purchased souvenirs for everyone, and she had filled many journal pages with the joy she had in her heart. While they walked she kept her hand tucked over his arm and briefly rested her head against his shoulder, feeling perfectly content. Then her eye caught something oddly familiar and completely unexpected. She took a sharp breath and stopped walking, which forced her husband to do the same. She focused more closely on what she was seeing, certain her eyes had deceived her. But they hadn't!

There, sitting on a bench was a man, older than herself and younger than James. His clothing was humble. His countenance looked weary and dismayed. And he was reading from a book identical to the one she'd found lying in the road two years ago. She told herself it couldn't be true. Surely the book just looked similar; it must be something else entirely. Without bothering to offer her husband any explanation, she let go of his arm and approached the man.

"May I ask what you're reading?" she said, and he looked up abruptly, surprised and uncertain. He glanced at her, then at James, who was standing nearby. He stood and took her in with a searching gaze.

"Why do you ask?" he said, and his accent betrayed that he was British.

"Because it looks very much like a book I found in the road near my home in England. I've been searching ever since for . . ." She struggled to find the words.

"For the fullness of the gospel of Jesus Christ?" he asked, his countenance brightening.

"Yes," Eleanore said, her voice trembling. She felt James beside her, his hand on her back. She took the book from this man just to assure herself that it was the same, then she gave it back. She had to ask, "What are you doing here?"

He chuckled self-consciously. "Truthfully, I've been wondering that very thing. I felt like I needed to come to this place, to be here; that perhaps I might find someone who needed what I have to share. But I've run out of money. My traveling companion has returned home. And I've been wondering over the reasons why I felt compelled to be here. I was reading with the hope of finding some peace and understanding." His smile broadened. "And here you are!"

Eleanore turned to James as she said, "It's incredible!"

"Yes, it is." He held out a hand toward this man, who shook it firmly. "I'm James Barrington, and this is my wife, Eleanore. This book of yours is very precious to her. It would seem we have much to talk about. May we buy you some lunch, my good man?"

Eleanore thought he looked as if he might cry. But his eyes simply sparkled with an unmistakable joy as he said, "Oh, that would be very much appreciated, sir. Thank you."

"A pleasure," James said and took hold of Eleanore's hand. And the three of them walked together.

AUTHOR'S SUGGESTIONS FOR READERS GROUP DISCUSSION

In what way is James and Eleanore's relationship affected by their moving to America? How might James's relationship with Caroline have differed if they had been Americans?

What message can be found in James's willingness to love the children unconditionally in spite of believing they were not his own?

What aspect of Eleanore's attitude toward her husband most affected the softening of his heart? And what might have been the outcome if she had allowed herself to be defensive or angry over his withholding his love from her? What can we learn from Eleanore's attitude that might help us in dealing with a loved one who is difficult or inactive?

What does the story teach about love being an action, as opposed to merely an emotion?

What is it about James and Eleanore that makes them prime candidates to receive the gospel?

While age differences in marriage were more common historically than they are now, they certainly still occur. What were the advantages of James being so much older than his wife? What could be the advantages or disadvantages of drastic age differences in marriage in any time period? How could an individual's character traits eliminate or create challenges in such a relationship?

How does the course of James and Eleanore's relationship differ from the typical process of love and marriage? How does the reverse order of the physical relationship (with the kiss coming last of all) provoke a deeper comprehension of the stages of intimacy and the importance of understanding them in our own relationships, and in teaching our youth?

How does James's ability to communicate effectively, even when addressing sensitive issues, thwart the likelihood of problems between him and his wife? If he had brushed off her concerns on their wedding night or treated the topic differently, how might it have adversely affected their relationship?

How does the positive, intimate relationship between James and Eleanore strengthen the bond between them as they face challenges in life? How does their attitude about intimacy, as a God-given privilege within their marriage, coupled with respect and commitment, give them an ongoing peace and contentment in spite of other difficult issues?

What can we learn from James about pride and humility? How can a person who is humble and good still struggle with pride over a particular issue? How are pride and fear often interrelated? What created the insecurity that was at the root of his fear?

How might poor communication have been destructive in their marriage when James became suspicious of his wife's behavior?

How does the characters' ongoing resolve to be mindful of and grateful for their blessings contribute to the resolution of the issues between them?

ABOUT THE AUTHOR

Anita Stansfield, the LDS market's number-one best-selling romance novelist, is a prolific and imaginative writer. Her novels have captivated and moved hundreds of thousands of readers, and she is a popular speaker for women's groups and in literary circles. She and her husband Vince are the parents of five children and reside in Alpine, Utah.